CLEO BROWNE

Rhodie

Devil's Rose MC Book One

Contents

|

Trigger Warning

This book deals with a badass heroine, a badass hero, and a badass grandfather.
Please be aware that in order for these characters to be badass, this book contains content that some readers may find disturbing, such as graphic descriptions of violence and torture and R18 sex scenes.

Chapter 1

Tuesday

I've been camped out and pressed up against the building for a little under 30 minutes and I'm not sure how much longer I can do this. I know I have to be patient, but at this very moment I have a piece of rough wood that is touching a spot on my lower back where my hoodie has risen and all I can smell is wood, smoke, and hints of leather. This should not surprise me, seeing as I'm camped out on the far side of the local MC headquarters or whatever you want to call them. Hang out? Gang Pad? Who knows? All I know is that my target hasn't moved from where he is sitting. So as long as he's camped out, so am I.

Taking a deep breath I move an infinitesimal amount and my hoody drops back into position. Thank fuck. That means I can get back to my mission without all the extra sensations distracting me. Stalking my target until I can find the perfect time to pounce, tag him, bag him, and take him back to my shed for a little interrogation. Which reminds me, I'll have to call one of my brothers for help with this pickup, probably Tav. He's the one least likely to give me shit.

I bet if anyone was watching, they'd think I was an absolute bad bitch. Suppressing a snort, I know I'm far from that. I'm a chubby, accident-prone weirdo who just happens to be skilled at hacking, stalking, and interrogation. Although, only my brothers know what my hobby is. Thankfully, they don't seem to mind. Although it works out well for them too. Turns out that losing your parents to a home invasion as children helps you grow into the type of people who want to keep others safe. And, in my case, mete out justice.

Rustling breaks through the silence and I notice my mark has crept a little closer to the corner of the building he seems fixated on. I won't move just yet, to not give away my position this early in the game, and I can see him perfectly well from where I'm standing. I've been watching this guy for seven days now. Well, through my monitor anyway.

This is the first time I've come to be in the same location, and that was really because I had a feeling if I didn't move now I'd never catch him. He turns to look both ways before moving on again, the light of the moon reflecting across his face, highlighting him in just the right way to make him appear sinister. But he doesn't scare me. He should be the one who is afraid.

I've been stalking him for years. Since I was thirteen years old and my Grandpop came to live with us after his only son and daughter-in-law were murdered. I heard whispers of his name around town, a no-good thief, in and out of prison. The man who had stolen in, under the cover of darkness, to take items worth a lot less than the lives of my parents. But that's OK, we are here now and I plan on making him pay for every minor transgression he's ever committed against humanity, and thanks to my hacking skills, I know there are a lot.

He's on the move again, so I creep slowly forward, making my way to another outbuilding on the property. I have no idea why motorcycle people need so many garages, but they come in handy for hiding behind, so I won't begrudge them that. It leads me to wonder yet again what this guy is after. Doesn't he know these guys could kick his ass? Seriously. I mean, they're no 1% club, but they are all big and badass, so I wouldn't want to take my chances. However, I'm guessing I'm a hell of a lot smarter than this guy.

Fuck! I inhale sharply as I move into position after whacking my knee on something. If I could change anything about myself, it would be that. I have shit spatial awareness. I have a great brain, can learn almost anything, and thanks to my three older brothers, I can throw a mean punch. The downside is that I seem to have the spatial awareness of a Roomba so spend a lot of time bouncing off of things: doors, furniture, and buildings. Whatever.

I hunker down and continue to watch my prey, pondering why the hell he's here. I know the bad people that make up the seedy underbelly in Rose Grove, and the Devil's Rose MC isn't them. They've been around longer than I can remember and own a few shady businesses in town. However, they keep to themselves and keep everything legitimate (I know, I've looked into them), so I leave them to their business. If this guy is after drugs or girls, then he's stupider than I thought. Before I can even finish my musings, I hear a grunt and suddenly, my mark is gone. What the hell?

Instead of moving closer to get a better look, I take a deep breath and freeze. Where I could smell wood, smoke, and a hint of leather before, the leather smell has now become a lot stronger and I can smell something slightly spicy and rich, like smelling an unlit cigar. I can also smell the faint tang of body odor, which always smells like old cooked onions. I'm no longer out here on my own. Someone is here with me. Someone who isn't who I've been following.

I stay stock still, ready to move if need be. The only problem is that in terms of running, I've never been the fastest. I'm 5'1" on a good day and can only be described as curvy or solid. I'm fit as hell, just built for comfort rather than speed. I'll have to be clever to get out of this. I turn slowly to my left and walk directly into something hard. Damn spatial awareness. I feel two massive hands wrap around my biceps and my fight kicks in. I deliver two quick jabs to their hard stomach before kicking out their knee. Hearing a loud grunt a massive hand comes around me from behind, the large arm crossing over my chest, gripping the opposite shoulder. I let my legs drop from under me before scurrying backward through this guy's wide leg stance, then I kick him in the ass from below before heaving myself up and running as fast as these short stumpy legs can take me.

Of course, it's not long before I'm tackled to the ground with a large oof! Me on the bottom of the pack with one large guy on top of me. Thankfully, it appears to not be "Old Onions".

"Argh fine, OK? I give up. I promise I won't kick or hit you if you just get your massive ass off me!" I wheeze out as I struggle to tip the weight off my back.

Before I know it, the weight disappears abruptly and I'm yanked to standing. I'm marched into the glow of the security light that just flicked on. Fat load of good that was, it was about 20ft out of the range of both me and my target. I'm twisted around by my arm until I'm facing two massive guys. Someone yanks off my hood and my hair flies everywhere. I swear I had it in a bun or something, but giant No. 1 must have yanked my scrunchie off with my hood. I hope he gives it back.

"Shit brother," I hear "Old Onions" on the left mumble. I look over at him and read the name on his cut. His name is Rider. I give a little snort. Of course, that's his name. MC people are never called Josh or David.

"Listen, lady," the other giant rumbles out. His voice sounds like he's been chain-smoking since he was born. And the proper stuff, not cotton candy-flavored vapes. No, he's been smoking cigarettes, probably with all the bad stuff in them.

"Hey! I asked you a question! What the fuck do you think you're doing here?" His cut says his name is Rhodie. Which is weird because you would think you would spell that Roadie, but I have no idea what level of education these dudes have, so maybe they spell it that way. Either way, I realize that yet again he asked me something, and I ignored it thanks to my train of thought.

That's something that happens to me quite a lot. I have a busy brain and not the greatest people skills, which at this point are probably non-existent because I came here for a reason and that reason does not seem to be here anymore.

Turning to Rhodie, mainly because he seems to be the one calling the shots at the moment, I look up. And up and up until I settle on his face, about a foot above my head. I don't really enjoy looking people in the eye too much, mainly because I never know how much eye contact is too much, so I settle on looking at his nose instead.

"If you take me to your president, I'll explain everything. Then I'll take that guy I was here for and leave you to your business, OK?"

Rider and Rhodie share a look that basically screams "WTF?" before Rider snorts, whacks Rhodie on the shoulder, and strides off, chuckling.

Rhodie fixes me with a look that says I've just become his number one pain in the ass, but given that he's grabbed a hold of my arm again and we seem to be moving in the right direction, I'll let it go.

We stomp through what appears to be the main room, or hall, or whatever. It's a lot cleaner than I thought it would be. I don't really like playing into stereotypes, but I thought it would be dark and manky and smell like booze and vagina, but it's light and clean and smells of some type of citrusy air freshener. The type of place you'd want to hang out to catch up with friends. There are even pictures on the walls interspersed with some questionable art, but I guess that's par for the course in an MC Clubhouse. I'm taken through a side door and then pushed into an office.

"Whoa, it smells like Pops in here," I mutter to myself before taking in my surroundings. Rider was already there, his lean body relaxed on a couch at the side of the room. There's an absolutely massive man hunched behind an office desk, his enormous fists resting atop. Looking at him, I can see he shares similar features with Rhodie; I wonder if they're related. His cut says Marx with the words Prez underneath, so this is who I'm here for.

Before I can say anything, Rhodie cuts in. "This is the second one, the hunter. The prey is tucked away in the back shed waiting for us to–"

Rhodie

Before I can even get my sentence out, the fiery little stalker spins around at me

"Hey! That fucker is mine! I'm not sharing him with you. But in good faith, I swear I'll ask him why he's been staking you guys out for the last seven days."

My eyes shoot towards Prez and his eyes widen, looking at me before the scowl returns to his face. He's wondering, like the rest of us, what the fuck she's on about. According to Wire, our security guy, he's only been here the past two nights.

"If you could just let me call one of my brothers to come pick him up, I can take him back to my place and interrogate him, get my business all buttoned up, and then let you know what he says. I could even do a full written report and everything -"

"Enough!" Prez roars at this random woman who lets out a huff before planting her ass in the seat across from Prez.

"First off, what the fuck were you doing in my compound, little girl?" Prez sneers at her.

"Little girl? I am not a little girl. I'm fully grown and yeah, I might be short, but Jesus, not everyone can be giant-sized." She says, gesturing towards my brother's bulk with her hand. Rider lets out a snort and I see Prez quickly narrow his eyes at him, essentially shutting him up. For a split second, I see his lips twitch before resetting his face and glaring at her again. I know that even though he's being intimidating as hell, there is no way we would hurt this woman. It's just not in us. Whether or not she knows that, she's not letting on. But given that this is the most unusual woman I've ever come across, I'm not really too sure what I should be expecting. Wire spotted her about an hour ago on our cameras and that was only because he was following the guy we noticed last night. He called me and Prez in to watch along, and it wasn't long before we noticed something odd. Originally, we thought the dude had brought a partner to help him do whatever it is he was here to do. However, after about 10 minutes we realized our guest didn't know he had a tail.

We never thought it was a woman, just a small guy; but his stalking skills were pretty tight. His movements were not so much. At one point we wondered if he was high as he'd bumped into a few things along the way. But, the ability to stay hidden was still well done. Instead of coming across a "little ninja dude" as Rider described them, we've nabbed a slightly odd little woman who I swear muttered "Smells like Pops in here" when we walked in.

"Why the fuck are you here? I'm not asking again!" Prez roars out. He's now leaning over his desk, towering over her small body, glaring down at her and she seems to be staring at... his nose?

"I thought I told you why? I'm after the guy you guys nabbed about 10 minutes ago. Been watching him for the last seven days through your monitors and figured he was going to make a move tonight. If I was going to catch him, then I needed to grab him now. Simple really," She folds her hands in her lap, still staring at my brother and Prez, but not in the eye, still slightly off.

"No, not fucking simple! What do you mean you've been watching him through our monitors? How the hell did you get into the compound in the first place?"

"Ooohh compound! That's what it's called. I've been calling it headquarters." She shakes her head at herself, her long messy curls bouncing all around her. "Anyway, that stuff was easy. I just rigged the far side alarm to not go off, and I walked in through the back gate." she shrugs her shoulders, her dark hair bouncing as she does. I watch my brother run his massive paw down his face before flopping back in his chair.

"Fuck me. Take her to one of the guest rooms and make sure there's a lock on the outside of the door. Put her there while we go talk to Wire and figure out why the fuck he didn't pick up on any of this. Jesus Christ." He motions with his hand and I grab her soft arm and pull her to standing. Even though she's dressed in what looks to be tactical pants and a bulky hoodie, my entire hand almost wraps right around her bicep. She doesn't put up a fight, but she does look up at me.

"Right, so after you lock me up, you'll have a chat and then you'll let me out and give me the prisoner? Oh yeah, and you might not want to keep me too long, otherwise, my brothers will get all weird about it"

I stare down at her for a bit. I notice this time she's looking directly at me, with the most golden whiskey eyes I've ever seen. That added to her long, espresso-colored hair and her full lips, she looks like a slightly sexier version of the girl next door. Fuck, I really need to get laid if I'm using words like "espresso-colored" to describe her goddamn hair.

I let out a sigh. "Listen tiny, I don't know who your brothers are and I don't care. All I care about is my brothers and you've put them on edge and even maybe in danger." As soon as I say this her eyes go huge, even bigger than normal and she looks horrified.

"What? I would never put anyone in danger!" She slips out of my hold and shuffles away from me, heading further down the hall.

"Oh my god, disarming the alarm!" She suddenly spins and comes barrelling toward me again. I brace myself as she looks like she's not going to stop moving anytime soon.

"Shit, I'm so sorry! If you take me back out there, I'll get it going straight away, shit shit shit!" She continues mumbling the word shit as I guide her down the hall and into the room before her head snaps up, "Smells like green apples in here. I like it." What is it with this woman and smells? Anyway, it seems to have gotten her out of her thoughts for a quick minute.

"Listen, you wait here and we'll be back soon."

"OK, but promise to put the alarm back on to make everyone safe, OK?" I frown as I take her in, she really seems preoccupied with safety. I give her a quick nod before closing and locking the door and heading to Wire's room.

Prez turns to look at me. "You good man? Shit, she was a live one, wasn't she?" he chuckles away to himself. "I thought we were going to crack one part there. I can't tell if she's nuts or just eccentric "

"She's definitely not nuts," Wire breaks in. "She's right. He has been watching us for the past seven days. From all different points of the compound, both outside and inside the gates. I've been through all our tech and found where she got into the monitors as well. This is high-level work. We would never have detected it if she hadn't mentioned it. She's good, really good. Even getting through the alarm took fucking skill. She say why she was here or what her name is?"

Wire spins in his fancy as fuck ergonomic seat to look at us. All the brothers hate that chair, trying to assemble that fucker with seven brothers who refuse to read the instructions almost finished the MC before we even started.

"She's said loads of shit, but from what I can gather she's

been after him for a while, wants us to bag him up and send him with her for "interrogation" I use air quotes.

"Yeah, she seems pretty fucking adamant," Rider adds. Prez rubs his beard, which he does when he's thinking, and because it's a habit he picked up years ago when he was the only bastard who could grow facial hair.

"I say we let her sit and stew for a bit. See if she's a little more receptive to giving us some info. Also, it'll give us time to ask our other guest a few questions," he looks at me. Being the Enforcer, this falls into my category, and it's something I enjoy.

"Oh, I should probably warn you brother, she did say not to keep her too long, otherwise her brothers will worry," I let him know, then we all look at each other before laughing.

"She sounds like a loose unit. I can't wait to meet her," Wire chuckles whilst turning back to his monitors. We're just about to head out when Wire clears his throat. "Um guys, might wanna postpone that wee chat with our other guest. I'm guessing the woman's brothers have arrived."

Me and Prez turn to look at the monitors to see three dark-colored SUVs all pull up in a line outside the gates.

"Fuck," Prez mutters under his breath. "Tell the prospect to open the gate; Wire, Rhodie, and Rider, you're with me. Let's go meet the family."

By the time we make it out of the front door, three big fuckers are standing outside their vehicles. I have no idea how in the hell these guys could possibly be related to that tiny woman. If it wasn't for the dark hair and caramel-colored skin, I wouldn't think they were related at all because of the sheer size of them.

"Where the fuck is our sister?" asshole number one growls out. He must be the guy in charge, and at second glance I see a little grey at his temples, so he must be the eldest. Prez steps forward in front of the trio with me to his left and Rider to his right.

"We caught your sister trespassing on our land tonight. This was after hacking into our monitors and then disarming our alarms. We have women and children here. We can't have anyone putting them in danger," Prez grits out. Watching their expressions, I see a look pass quickly over their faces. Interesting. Much like their sister, they seem to not like the idea of people in danger or being hurt. The brother to the left of the main guy clears his throat.

"Look, we don't want anyone in danger. I'm Tav, these are my brothers August –" he indicates the oldest looking brother "–and Jules," his brother on the other side. I note this one, Tav, seems to be the most laid-back of the three.

"Do you mind if we come in to talk? And maybe check on our sister? We know Tuesday can be a bit of a handful–" one brother snorts and I hear the other mumble "Pain in the ass."

"– but she means well." He looks at me with eyes similar to his sister, but way, way less hot. I look toward my brother and Prez before giving a slight nod. Hell, they seem like OK guys and they're only here to check on their sister. Giving them a chin lift to follow me inside, I pull up a seat at one of the long tables we have in the main room. Prez sits to my left with Rider on the other side whilst they arrange themselves across from us. August is in the middle, and Tav and Jules are on either side.

"So, you can start by telling us why the hell your sister was in our compound in the first place," I watch the brothers all share a glance before August says,

"I'm guessing she's not the only person you caught on your

compound tonight?" I glance at Prez, who gives him a curt nod. They all curse under their breaths before August speaks again.

"Look, our sister is...special. Not in an 'all baby sisters are special way'. But in a 'special set of skills' type of way." He looks each of us in the eye for a moment.

I speak up. "Listen, man, you're not really telling us anything we couldn't figure out for ourselves." Tav nods before continuing, "Our baby sister is a hacker. Went to school for computer science and uses her powers during the day in our security company. During the night hours, though, her primary hobby for the past seventeen years has been hunting down people who hurt others and meting out her own form of justice, so to speak."

I whip my head towards Prez and Rider, each of us slightly baffled, before Prez snorts out. "Her own form of justice? By what? Talking them to death? Stop bullshitting."

Jules shares a look with his brothers before turning his cold eyes on us. Of the three, he seems the most reserved and the least trustworthy.

"Well, boys, looks like these fuckers don't believe us. Maybe they need a little show and tell." His brothers both nod in unison. "Let my sister interrogate your prisoner. She'll get all the info she needs as to why he was here at your compound and she gets what she's after. It's really a win-win situation for us. The only stipulation is that we are there with her the whole time and we clean up."

These guys look serious and judging by the looks on my brother's faces, they weren't exactly expecting that from them. Prez and I share a look and I just know he's going to go along with their plan.

He rubs his hand down his beard once more before nodding. "OK. Let's see what your wee sister can do then, huh? Rhodie, go get *Tuesday* and bring her and these boys to the shed. Let's see what everyone is about." He stands and stomps off with Rider, shoulder-tapping a couple of the other guys on the way out.

"Follow me then. Let's get this over with."

Chapter 2

Tuesday

I've been moving around the room cataloging things I can see, smell and hear. The room is tidy and not sex-pit-looking at all. The sheets smell like laundry detergent and even though the furniture is a little dated, I'm sure it serves its purpose. Hearing the deadbolt sliding on the other side of the door, I stand at the end of the bed and wait.

The door slowly opens, and I can see Rhodie's massive body blocking the light from the hall.

"Come on, Tiny. Looks like you get to interrogate your man." I do a bit of a wiggle to celebrate and when I look up, I see Rhodie's eyebrows are up by his hairline. He turns without a word and I follow his giant bulk down the hall until we come to a door. I'm guessing it leads to a staircase and a basement because that's where people always think about interrogating people. However, when Rhodie throws the door open, it leads outside. I have to trot after him as his legs are so much longer than mine. He's not saying anything and frankly, I'm not bothered. I'm vibrating with excitement that I finally get to come face to face with the man who took my parents.

I've been building up to this moment for years and pictured it in my mind for a long time, but now that it's here, there are just so many ways I can go about this. Rhodie stops in front of a shed and turns to me.

"You better be ready for this, little lady. It ain't for the faint of heart." Reaching up I slap my hand on his gigantic, hard shoulder, "No need to worry about me, buddy. You just worry about yourself."

Rhodie lets out a little snort and shakes his head before throwing the door open, gesturing me to walk in. Everyone in the room turns to look at me and I see my brothers all lined up, arms crossed in front of their chests.

"Dammit! You got here a lot faster than I expected. You can fuck right off if you think you're taking me home," I growl at them. August shakes his head at me while Tav smirks.

"Little sis, it looks like it's your lucky day. The President here has agreed that you can interrogate their prisoner," August says before Tav breaks in.

"Yeah Dayz, these boys don't seem to think you have what it takes." Turning, I look at all the men in the room. All are leaning along the walls, with expressions that I guess probably show skepticism. I'm not sure, that was never one of the emotions on the flashcards my mom used to teach me. Either way, they seem to be smirking at me or just plain shaking their heads. I square my shoulders before turning to my brothers. "What was the deal?"

"You interrogate him. We clean up." Nodding at August I remember, "Shit, I don't have my things!"

"No worries, Dayz, I've got your backup kit right here" Jules throws my bright floral duffel on the ground at my feet and once again I do a little wiggle dance. What can I say? It's an involuntary thing like a dog's tail wag, I guess. Clapping my hands a couple of times, I pick up my bag and head toward a stainless steel bench table that is handily pushed up against the wall.

This whole time I haven't looked once at the man who killed my parents, but that doesn't mean that I'm not totally aware of him. He smells like old cigarettes and the inside of a taxi - musty and a little pukey. I take a peek at him from the corner of my eye and I can see he has a trickle of blood running from his nose, but other than that, he looks perfectly healthy. Which is good for me. More time for me to play with him. I pull the items out of my bag and lay them on the table one by one.

"Holy fuck, is that a mini saw?" A rough voice breathes out. I smile to myself as I can hear the murmurs of the MC crew. They are starting to sound intrigued. I turn and clap my hands. "Right, let's get this shit started!" Turning back I walk directly toward the captive. He's tied to a chair that is situated over the top of a grate. I nod to myself. This will come in handy. Gesturing, one of my brothers brings me a chair. I'm not sure who does it, but one materializes behind me, so I take a seat. I stare at him for what feels like an eternity. Taking in every aspect of his face, from the greasy hair down to the pockmarks on his face. It doesn't take long before he sneers at me.

"What the fuck do you want, bitch?" I look around the room before turning back to him.

"Oh, were you talking to me? I don't answer to bitch. My name is Tuesday, and I'd like you to use it. I know that sometimes it's hard to remember new names and all that, but I have a few ways to help you remember. "

Before he can open his mouth to spout more shit, I take the

scalpel that I had hidden in my hand and slice down his jeans, starting from the top of his thigh. His eyes go wide as he looks at the trail of blood I've left down his leg, so mesmerized that he doesn't seem to notice that I've ripped the jeans wide apart. I carve into his thigh, ignoring his grunts and growls. Once my name is done, I look back at him. "There, now you won't forget my name, will you?"

"Argh fuck! You dumb bitch! You've just left evidence of who you are. How stupid can you be?" He grits out a laugh, which stops abruptly when someone from behind me steps forward. I take a glance and see it's Marx. Instead of addressing me, he speaks to my brothers. "Look, maybe this isn't the best idea?"

August raises his hand and then nods toward me to continue. The MC guys are looking none too impressed. I mean to them I've just signed my guilty plea. I turn back to the douchebag.

"Hmm, you're right, that probably wasn't very smart, was it? Oh well, better fix that." I give him my sweetest smile before leaning forward and cutting a perfect rectangle around my carved name. Then, digging deeper and cutting through the skin and the top of his muscle until I've cut a lovely flap of skin off the top of his thigh, all with my name attached. Quickly walking over to the table in the corner I grab a hammer and one of the small tacking nails I like to use when I reupholster things.

"I don't really enjoy having to look people in the eye too much. It's so unnerving. And because you can't seem to remember my name I think if I just stick this right here -" I take the small nail and tack the skin flap with my name on it to his forehead

"- I can kill two birds with one stone. You can remember my name and I don't have to make eye contact. Oh, and afterward

I can burn this and no one knows it was me. Perfect!"

I've ignored his screams and grunts this whole time, so I'm quite surprised when I realize that there is no other sound anywhere in the room. I turn to look behind me and I see the looks on the faces of the guys from the MC have changed. They look impressed. Rhodie gives me a small smile and a quick nod and I remember where I am. I turn back to my prey and give him a little shake. He must have passed out from being a pussy or something. I know that he's got a lot of life left in him because I've tried these methods before. I give him a quick kick to the shin and he jerks awake.

"Welcome back! Right, I need you to tell me why you have been here the past seven nights. What are you looking for?"

He shakes his head from side to side and the skin I've nailed to his forehead flaps around a little, making a sound like someone being slapped with a tortilla.

"Listen, buddy, we can do this the easy way, where I won't have to use any more tools on you or the hard way. Where I work my way through my tool kit. The choice is yours." I shrug, but it's not like he can see much around my name.

"OK, time's up. Let's try something else, huh?" Wandering back to my tools I pick up my small wire cutters. I open and close them a couple of times before I look up at Tav.

"Please don't leave too many small pieces Dayz, I get sick of having to pick them all up afterward," he whines at me.

"No worries Tav, I have an idea" Smiling back at him he gives me a wink. I love how my brothers understand why I need to do what I do. It's not just because I'm their baby sister and they'd do anything for me. It's more than that. I think they all know that out of the four of us, I'm the only one that can. I don't process emotions in quite the same way. Everything in my world is black and white, good or bad. I love it or I hate it. There is no in-between. I feel no remorse for putting the world back to rights and ridding it of bad people. It helps me sleep at night knowing that I have saved someone the same fate as my family or worse.

I turn back to my plaything, snapping my wire cutters along the way."Ok, let's start off with something easy. What's your name?" He sits stoically, still shaking that damn skin flap about.

"Times up, say bye bye pinky finger." I cut the top of his pinky off at the first knuckle

"Little girl, you don't want to do the whole finger?" I hear Marx say over douchebag's screams.

"Nah, this way I can cut this finger off in pieces, at least three pieces per finger. So instead of ten questions, I get thirty before starting on other body parts."

"Holy shit, that's fucking genius. Rhodie, why didn't you think of that?" I hear someone say, I think it's Rider.

"I will now, fuck that's the best idea I've seen in a while," Rhodie says back.

I turn back to my work. "Now, my brother kindly asked that I not leave too much of a mess, so you're going to clean this up," I tell the man in front of me. When he goes to open his mouth to say something, I quickly pop the end of his finger in there, then clamp his mouth and nose shut with my hands. I hold on until I feel him swallow.

There are a few gasps from the men behind me before I hear one grunt out, "Shit, this shouldn't be making me hard, should it?"

A slap sounds out, so I'm guessing one of my brothers has hit him. I ignore it for the time being, as I have more work to do.

"I'm going to ask again, what's your name?"

"It's A-Alan,"

"A-Alan is a shit name for a murderer. Now, why the hell were you staking out the MC?" He hesitates for a moment, not too long but long enough for me to swoop in and cut off his pinky finger at the second and then third knuckle, a twofer. The little bitch screams again, which was very convenient for me to pop a part of his finger into his mouth. Before I can get my hands on his jaw and nose, two large hands appear and do the job for me. Looking up, I see Rhodie smiling down at me. I gaze at his entire face, something I haven't done until now, and a jolt of electricity hits me. I make a mental note to come back to that thought, but at the moment, I'm on a roll. I can do this all night, and by the looks of it, I have someone to give me a hand.

Rhodie

Grabbing dickhead Alan's nose and jaw I hold them closed until Tuesday is ready to drop his next finger segment in. She looks up at me in surprise, her odd gaze holding mine before her eyes roll down to the now open, waiting mouth. She smirks before dropping the other segment of the finger in and I go to work holding Alan's thrashing body until the fucker swallows again.

"Alan, Alan, Alan, how many times do we have to do this before you learn? I ask a question, you answer it, and keep all your body parts. I bet you were a slow learner, huh? Right, so one more time, why were you staking out the MC?" Tuesday smooths her clothes before sitting back down in front of him, waiting for his answer.

No part of her body is moving other than her eyes, which seem to dart all over our prisoner, seeming to take stock of his breathing, demeanor, everything. I'm standing directly behind Alan. I can feel his shuddering breaths. I should probably take a step back, but standing right here I get a front-row seat to Tuesday's interrogation techniques, and they're good. Really fucking good.

Devils Rose MC may not be a 1% club, however, that doesn't mean we don't have to get our hands dirty now and then. The bulk of us are ex-military, the type of guys who got cut loose after one too many shit deployments but still looking for brotherhood and the honor with which we served. Because of this, DRMC runs the usual type of businesses you'd find any MC running; strip clubs, wreckers, mechanics, that sort of thing, but we also like to keep our small part of the world safe. If that means ridding the streets of scum drug dealers, abusers, rapists, and murderers, then so be it. In that respect, I'm thinking Tuesday and her brothers may not be that different from us. I'm so caught up in my thoughts that I haven't noticed that Tuesday has gone on a bit of a snipping spree.

Looking down, I see he now has three fewer fingers than he did before. I do my job of prying his jaw open and watch in awe as she pops them into his mouth one by one. Clamping his jaw shut I wait patiently while he thrashes and heaves in my arms. By the time I feel him swallow, my hands are covered in snot and tears. I release him roughly and watch him dry retch a few times before he pitifully whines.

"OK, OK, I'll tell you. Shit," My eyes drop down and watch dipshit taking a shuddering breath. "Fuck, he's going to kill me."

Tuesday leans forward and puts a comforting hand on his knee. In a soothing voice, she coos, "Alan, *I* am going to kill you. Before whoever he is can even get to you. At this very point in time, *I* am the biggest threat to your life. Now, why were you staking out the MC?"

"I wasn't watching the whole MC. I was sent here to watch one guy, Rhodes Paxon. My spine stiffens and I whip my head up towards my Prez and brothers.

"Why the fuck were you sent here to watch him?" my Prez growls out.

"I, I don't know, man. All I had to do was watch him and report back. The guy I work for never said why. Just that he'd pay me $10k to watch this guy for as long as he asks me to. I don't even know which one of you is Rhodes Paxon!" Alan is panicking now, he's trying to appeal to the Prez, but because of that fucking bit of skin that Tuesday nailed to his forehead he's flying blind here, so all he's doing is swinging his head back and forth trying to follow the Prez's voice.

If this was any other day, the scene would be hilarious, but it's not. It's a weird fucking day, with a certifiably insane but cute as hell tiny woman, her giant brothers, and some motherfucker that thinks he can come up in here and watch the hell outta my MC and me. Not fucking happening.

"What have you told him so far, Alan?" Tuesday asks, and I have to admit it's a good fucking question. Because of the tension in the room, all of us men hadn't thought to continue the interrogation, more so stuck in our heads.

"I've told him 'round about how many of you seem to be here, overall movements in and out, n-nothing of real importance. Like I said, I don't even know which one of these guys is the one I'm looking for. I was hoping to find that out tonight, but then all this happened," he bites back a sob. Stupid pussy. Prez steps forward but before he can get a word out Tuesday softly tuts, shaking her head.

"Alan, don't you see? You've already said too much, I'm afraid. There are women and children here, good innocent people whose security you've put at risk with your little secrets. It really, really sucks to be you right now." She stands up and walks back to the table in the corner, where her things are laid out methodically. She runs her fingers over a few of the tools, looking like she's in a world of her own. I can vaguely hear her murmuring to herself, but I can't make out what she's saying. I stride over to my brothers, thinking up the best plan to keep everyone safe.

"Prez, I don't know who the fuck this guy is or what he wants with me, but either way, if this fucker has reported back our movements, I'm not feeling fucking down with that. Do we want to lock down or send all the brothers with families off-site?" I can see my brother's eyes working, and I thank fuck I've known him all my life. Marx is five years older than I am, same father, different mother, and I've always thought he was the biggest, baddest bastard around. The day he earned the President patch was the day I knew I would live to serve him as best I could.

"No, Rhodie, let's just see how this plays out. No full lockdown yet, but we'll put a hold on parties with townies and we'll put a couple of prospects on the women and children for now. Let's see what else Tiny can get out of him" he lifts his chin in Tuesday's direction. She's still looking at her tools, with no expression on her face. Her body is very still. To anyone watching, she looks as if this is just a normal day for her. Hell, maybe it is. I know nothing about this woman, but something in me wants to know it all. I want to know what makes her tick. I want to know what makes her smile and laugh, how she tastes. I want to see her when she wakes up in the morning, and the look on her face when I slide my thick cock inside her. I have never been intrigued by a woman as much as I'm intrigued by her.

"Alan, you are going to die. But there are a couple of things I need to know. First off, I need to know the name of the man you work for. You also need to tell me why, seventeen years ago, you broke into 1172 Mercury Close and killed the occupants all for some shitty jewelry." I hear the intake of breath from a couple of my brothers. I feel my gut clench and think back. Seventeen years ago, I was stationed in some sandbox somewhere. I enlisted straight out of high school. However, a home invasion where the occupants were murdered isn't something that happens in Rose Grove all that often. I think I can vaguely remember a story like that, but nothing that I can grasp hold of.

"W-what? You want to know about that? Fuck. That was years ago. Why would you want to know about that?" He clears his throat and sniffs a little.

"You know what? Fuck it, it's not like I'm getting out of here alive. That was the first job I ever took. I was desperate. All I had to do was go to the house and get rid of the couple. The guy I work for gave me the file and told me all I had to do. That was it! I swear! I'm so, so sorry. I'm so sorry," Alan has now totally lost it, sniveling and snotting everywhere, but I can't pay attention to him.

As soon as Alan revealed it was a hit, I saw Tuesday's brothers stiffen, all their gazes locked on their sister. Tuesday has the same look on her face as her brothers. However, she seems eerily still. Apart from the fingers on her right hand. I watch as she taps her pinky to her thumb, then her ring finger, middle, and pointer all tap her thumb before starting over again. Something is definitely not right. I look toward my Prez, who is also watching her with a frown on his face. Suddenly Tuesday shakes her head, pulls her shoulders back, and in a cheery voice announces,

"Well, I'm parched. I'm going to pop out and get a little refreshment. Alan, I'd love to offer you something, but, well, there's no real point. You're going to die and anything I put in you is going to come back out. Be rude of me to make the cleanup an even bigger job. You wait right here and we'll be back in a minute. Oh, and before you get any ideas of escape," her words drift off as she pulls out the longest fucking screws I've ever seen in my life and proceeds to screw his thighs to the chair with a fucking DeWalt cordless drill. My brothers hiss out a couple of breaths as his screams stop abruptly as he passes out.

"Right, now that he's out and not going anywhere, I need to think this shit through." Tuesday says to her brothers before walking out the door and leaving all of us standing in the room without her.

"Well boys, your sister is something else," Marx says to them as we go to follow her out.

"You don't know the half of it," August states on our way back into the clubhouse. Tuesday is pacing and mumbling to herself again, walking the length of one of the main tables and back.

"Dayz, what's going on?" Tav asks his sister gently, throwing his arm over her shoulder and squeezing her to him. She settles immediately and I feel something akin to jealousy which is fucked up, given that this is her brother and it's not right for me, a fucking stranger, to want to comfort her.

"Did you hear what he said? It was a hit, Tav! What the actual fuck? Why the fuck would anyone put a hit out on Mom and Dad?" Wait, what? I look over at her brothers and they look a mix of spitting mad and fucking devastated. They share a look before August takes control.

"Tav, take Tuesday to get an ice cream. You know she thinks better with a scoop" Marx swings his head in their direction. I swear if he did that any faster, his head would have rolled off. I don't blame him. That is so fucking out of left field, I have no idea what is going on. Tav gently leads his sister away and August gestures at us to sit.

"A fucking ice cream? Really? She's just fucking maimed a dude in there for information and now she's what, going to skip off into the sunset to eat a fucking cone?" I can tell Marx is getting more and more worked up over the absolute ridiculousness of this situation, but before I can tell him to settle, Jules speaks.

"Look asshole, as you said yourself, our sister is something else. She's fucking damaged in a way that even her autism diagnosis can't explain," Jules grits out. Before he can carry on, August interrupts.

"She's the baby of the family. I'm eight years older than her. Jules is seven years and Tav is the closest to her at three years older. Our parents were killed seventeen years ago, and she was the only kid at home that night. The police report states it was a B&E that went wrong. Mom and Dad were both shot in what looked like a robbery, but Tuesday never thought so. She has never spoken about what she saw or heard that night, no matter how many detectives and child psychiatrists she had to speak to."

"Who raised her after that?" I don't know why, but I need to know more about her story. I need to know how she can torture a man and then head off for an ice cream. This shit just isn't computing right.

"Our Grandpop moved in to raise her and Tav, with us two moving home to help." August takes a breath before speaking again. "I know for a fucking fact that she knows something, and that's what's been driving her all this time. She graduated high school at fifteen, and then went straight into college. She's one of the best hackers around and the most stubborn person you'll ever fucking meet. I'm guessing if she's tracked this Alan here and gotten wrapped up in this, then she has a plan, and that now includes you guys. Whether or not you want it, she's going to figure out what the fuck is going on."

Chapter 3

Tav

I lead Dayz out to my SUV, help her in, and curse yet again that none of us put running boards on our SUVs so our sister can get in without help.

"OK Dayz. How do you feel about stopping at Dairy Queen and picking up a cone through the drive-through? That good enough? I also have a gift for you, I'll give it to you after you eat." I gaze over at my baby sister and see that she's doing her thinking stim - squishing her bottom lip between her thumb and pointer finger.

To people outside of our family, you'd think it was weird, but since Dayz was little, we all knew there was something a little different about her. Not in a bad way, not at all. In some ways, she's completely normal. Super girly when she's not in her "hunting outfit", goofy, and a little weird. I guess you'd refer to her as one of those manic pixie girls that were big in the 90s. But she's also a fucking genius.

The downside is that for her to use that genius, she has funny little rules and rituals that she needs to work at full capacity.

She stops squishing her lip and turns to me with a massive smile.

"Dairy Queen sounds perfect! I may as well get a burger, too. I'm starving! Totally forgot to eat in the run-up to this wee adventure," she snorts to herself. A psychologist she saw as a kid explained to us that her brain is so focused on what she's doing that those normal things to us, like eating and using the bathroom, take a backseat for Dayz. It's not until she's out of focus that things like remembering to eat come back online.

"You need to put that food reminder back on your watch, Dayz. Remember the last time you got caught up in a case and lost all that weight? Jules basically kept you prisoner and force-fed you. You don't want to go through that again," I warn her. Yeah, it was drastic, however, it was necessary. And Jules is the type of bastard to lose his mind if we're not looking after ourselves properly.

"That was overkill and you know it! Jules is a bossy bastard," she huffs back at me. He is, but he idolizes our sister. In a way, I think we all do.

Nodding my head I guide us to the drive-thru to place our order. I sit happily in silence because I can tell judging by the frown on her face she's working through something big.

"I need to talk to Gus and Jules. They're older than us. They might remember stuff about Mom and Dad that I don't. I was a kid and let's face it, I spent most of my time in my room practicing magic. I'm certain I would have missed a lot of things about Mom and Dad's lives." I smile when I remember those magic days. Dayz was completely obsessed with the sleight of hand magic, and completely and utterly shit at it. I remember sitting through the terrible magic shows she put on for us. She turns to me with her large eyes.

"Do you think maybe they weren't good people? Do you think that maybe someone sent shitty Alan to kill them for a reason?" Before I can answer her, the car behind us blares its horn, signaling us to get a move on.

"I really have no idea Dayz, I was sixteen, and I was more interested in trying to have sex with hot girls than what Mom and Dad were up to. Hopefully, it's something Alan can shed some light on."

I see her bob her head from the corner of my eye as I navigate our way back to the Devil's Rose MC compound. It doesn't really matter what I think, anyway. Dayz will figure it out, she always does.

Rhodie

I check the clock on the wall again and see that only 10 minutes have passed since Tav took Tuesday for ice cream, and yet it feels as if she's been gone for hours. I signal the prospect to bring over some beers for us while we wait. Popping the top off mine I take a long gulp whilst eyeing up August and Jules. In terms of personality, August has a similar way about him as Marx. He's calm and collected, and yet you can feel the weight that rests on his shoulders. Jules, I find somewhat unnerving. He has a similar way about him as Tuesday, slightly detached, but his eyes are more calculating. Where Tuesday is warm and goofy, Jules is cold. The only time he seems to warm up is in the presence of his sister.

The door bangs open, pulling me from my observations, and Tuesday comes stumbling in with Tav, grabbing her arm to keep her from falling over. He shakes his head and smiles down at her. It's clear these guys adore her.

She has her ice cream gripped in her hand and, for some reason, it looks as though she has ketchup on her top. I glance over at Marx and my poor Prez looks like he's going to have a coronary. Never in one night have I seen his face in so many baffled expressions. She flops down in the seat next to mine and I watch her as her little pink tongue darts out to lick up the ice cream that's dripped on her hand. Jesus Christ, is it hot in here?

"Right, lemme finish this and then I'll get back to work. I think we can agree that he has no more info on why he was watching you, dude" she says as she uses her ice cream hand to gesture my way. "But once we get a name for the guy he works for, I'll be able to get a little more info, I'm sure. So rest easy, sweetheart. We'll sort this out." I choke on my spit when she calls me sweetheart and I can hear Marx's chuckle and Rider's pain in the ass high-pitched laugh.

She goes back to licking her ice cream in the most fucking erotic way I have ever seen, and I discreetly have to move myself to stop my zipper digging into my hardening cock. As I rearrange myself, I look up and catch Jules looking at me with his dead eyes. His eyes flick from my face to my crotch, then to his sister, and back to my face before he slowly raises his eyebrow at me. I smirk back, then a full-blown grin, when I see his nostrils flare. That's right, fucker, you can't intimidate me.

"Holy shit! You're Tuesday Tombs! Fuck Prez, you never said that our trespasser was from Tombs Security!" The excitement in Wire's voice as he comes into the common room has us all looking at him, baffled.

"What the fuck are you on about, Wire? You know these people?" Marx barks out.

"I didn't recognize her over the camera footage, but yeah. That's Tuesday Tombs, youngest person to be put on the FBI Black Hat hackers list and then taken off the FBI Black Hat hackers list. Owns Tombs Security with her brothers, which I'm guessing is you guys," Wire turns to look at Tuesday's brothers while Tav throws him a chin raise, "and the hacker that helped behind the scenes with that whole shit that went down with Demon Spawn MC. Her brothers were also the ones who gave us that list of out-of-state safe houses to keep the girls in until things blew over."

Wire rushes towards the table we're all sitting at. "You guys are fucking legends!" Tuesday giggles over Wire's pathetic fangirling. However, the whole family has gone up in my estimation. I look over at Marx and I see the same thing in his eyes.

Recently, we got called in to help find a truckload of girls that the Demon Spawn MC had been transporting. It was such a massive job that Wire couldn't handle all the surveillance and hacking on his own, so he reached out to a friend he knew who then put us into contact with a family of hackers and security experts willing to help, which I'm guessing now was the Tombs family. We never met them, all contact had taken place online or on burner phones. With their help, we got all the girls back to their families.

"Wait, that was you guys?" I ask no one, in particular, looking at the siblings. Tuesday shrugs her shoulders as she pops the last of her cone in her mouth and August tips his head in confirmation.

"Shit, that was some good work. Without your help we would

never have found them," Marx states. Wire nodding his head behind him. August waves off the compliment.

"It's what we do. Right Dayz, are you ready?"

Tuesday slaps her tiny hand on the table before standing up. "Let's do this shit, brothers! Biological AND MC" she says with a snort giggle and for some goddamn reason, all us big imposing bastards follow the little woman like she's the fucking Pied Piper.

Wire rushes ahead to open the shed door like a goddamn butler and I have no idea why that pisses me off. I shove him with my shoulder a little as I walk past. I know it's an asshole move, but I don't really care at this point. I just want to get back to watching Tuesday work her magic.

"Wire? Do you think you could bring a laptop in here and maybe do some research on the name that I'm gonna get out of our guest here?" Tuesday asks sweetly as she turns to look at Wire. Dude looks like he's going to come in his pants at this request, and I can't help but growl a little. What the fuck is wrong with me? I catch Marx's eye as he raises his eyebrows at me before I turn to look at the wall and pull myself the fuck together.

"Hell yeah, Tuesday. I'll be right back." Wire slams the door wide open in his haste to collect up all his geek shit and get back to the show. I watch as Tuesday pulls something out of her oversized hoodie pocket and grins at her brothers.

"Aw, shit Tav, did you bring that shit? You know I hate when she uses that fucking thing!" Jules grits out, disgust written all over his face.

"Fuck's sake, Tav! We spoke about this!" August joins in while Tuesday looks ecstatic and Tav laughs his ass off.

"OK fuckers, what the fuck is in the jar? Enlighten us because this has been a fucking circus so far and I need to get a handle on whatever the hell is going on here before I lose my goddamn mind," Marx barks out.

"This" Tuesday gestures as she holds up a glass jar with water and some stuff floating in it "Is my friend the Candiru fish. This sneaky little thing usually lives in the Amazon, but I've replicated its usual environment in a tank at home so I can breed them. Anyway, this little guy likes to swim up the urethra of unsuspecting gentlemen bathers." I feel a little queasy and as I look around the room, I can see matching looks of horror on my brother's faces, mixed in with the disgusted looks on the Tombs brothers' faces. Well, all except Tav.

"Hold up, so that fish swims into dudes' pee holes?" Rider says, looking a little green.

"Yup," Tuesday says, popping the "p". "Given that most of my job requires me to interrogate penis owners, I've found that this little guy is the best incentive. Dudes really don't like things crawling up their dicks, you know?" She cocks her head looking at us and I'm not sure if I should look at her in admiration or fear. Marx runs his massive paw of a hand over his face and then gestures at her to carry on. I think he's given up. I look over and see Jules give Tav the evil eye, whilst mumbling, "Smart ass fucker knows I hate that thing". Tuesday walks over to Alan, who is still completely out to it. She runs a hand gently through his hair whilst cooing at him.

"Oh, Alan, wakey wakey, my friend. We still have a way to go in this little chat." Alan rouses himself, tensing a little before sniveling again. Tuesday claps her hands together.

"OK buddy. Right, so first off, the man that gave you the hit on 1172 Mercury, was that the same guy you work for now?" Tuesday takes a seat and waits patiently.

"N-no, that guy was different. The same company, though. Or business or whatever."

"Whatever do you mean, Alan? Are you saying that there is a small business out there hiring lowlifes like you to murder and watch innocent people?" Alan shrugs his shoulders, then starts to cry again. "The guy who asked me to watch this Rhodes guy, he's the boss. The guy who first contacted me about the hit was a lower street guy, looking to recruit new members. I swear I don't know anything else about how this all works! Please, just stop!" He's really blubbering now and Tuesday is just looking at her nails like she has all the time in the world. She lets out a big sigh and leans forward, gripping one of Alan's thighs and squeezing so hard I can see blood bubble up through the hole where she screwed him to the chair. He squeaks and stops crying.

"I need a name, Alan. Who is the man you've been working for?"

Alan clears his throat, "H-his name is Nado, N-nado Kraykowski. He's going to kill me, he's going to fucking kill me!" I can hear typing in the background and turn to see Wire doing his thing. I was so mesmerized by Tuesday that I didn't even notice his return.

"Nado Kraykowski, an orphan, grew up on the streets of Poland before emigrating here under what looks to be dodgy circumstances. Self-made man owns a series of strip joints in and around Texas. His business seems to be growing. Apparently has a penchant for underaged girls and is said to be mixed up in trafficking, but nothing ever sticks. Why the fuck is he looking into your ass, Rhodie?" Wire looks up completely baffled, but I can't answer that.

"I have no fucking clue who this guy is. I've never heard of him. Do you think this has something to do with Demon Spawn and that shipment of girls we stopped?" I look toward my Prez.

"Nah, that was all of us. Why watch my enforcer rather than me? None of this makes any fucking sense," Marx grunts out. Tuesday is staring off into space, a little frown on her face. "Alan, have you always worked for the same company, so to speak?"

"Yeah, they recruited me. That hit was my first job to prove my loyalty. I've only ever worked for them. Please, I've told you everything I know. If you let me live, I'll promise to disappear. You'll never see me ever again. Please, just let me go!" he pleads with her.

"Nope," Tuesday answers back and before we can do any-thing, she pulls a small handgun out of her hoody pocket and pops one in Alan, straight between the eyes. Or where his eyes would be if they weren't still covered with a piece of his thigh. "Ah dammit! Didn't get to use my fish! Ah well, maybe next time." She shrugs, and like a well-oiled machine, her brothers work on cleanup.

Chapter 4

Tuesday

I sit in my chair across from Alan, watching as my big brothers take care of my mess. Yet again. They're like a well-oiled machine. As soon as I had dispatched Alan, they grabbed their duffle bags and roller case I hadn't even noticed they had with them, and put on their full body cleaning suits. I watch Jules unscrew Alan's legs from the wooden chair whilst Tav unrolls the electric blanket from the wheeled suitcase behind him. August has the massive bottle of bleach out and has attached the hose sprayer, spraying Alan in a fine mist of the stuff.

"What's with the sprayer and electric blanket?" Rider asks the room. None of my brothers answer, so I take the lead. "August is spraying bleach all over Alan, essentially getting rid of any DNA evidence any of us may have left on the body." Jules pulls the flap of skin off Alan's face and tosses it onto the floor. "The electric blanket is to keep the body warm. We'll wrap him in that, and then attach him to this cool setup Tav invented. It's basically a rotisserie turner. We'll slowly let him turn for a bit. That way, there will be no blood pooling in the body. So when we finally dump him in Nado Kraykowsi's territory, any forensics that are done on the body will place the time of death well after the actual time his heart stopped. Giving us all alibis should we need them." I turn to look at the MC brothers. Marx, Rider, Wire, and Rhodie are the only ones I kinda know. The others are sort of room meat, filling it up but with no real purpose at this stage.

"Holy fuck, that is really, really badass. How many people have you killed if this is the type of slick operation you lot have concocted?" Wire breathes out.

I smile to myself. If only he knew. Instead, I just shrug my shoulders. I catch Marx's eye as he studies me. He has the look that I've seen many times before. Almost like admiration mixed with wariness. He's a tough man, reminding me a lot of my brother, August. He's the oldest, the natural leader, however, the weight on his shoulders because of what we do, what I do, I think it gets to him sometimes. Unlike August, Marx is much harder for me to read. Mysterious bastard. I hope I can be like that when I grow up.

"So I'm loving this little show, but we have shit we need to sort out. So far, independent of what you lot have got going on, all we know is that Nado Kraykowski wants info on you, Rhodie. Why? Wire, look into this shit. Rider, hit up your contacts in the streets, someone must know something." Marx hands out his orders whilst looking around at his men.

I have no idea why this guy wants Rhodie, but whatever it seems to overlap somehow with my parents. Nothing is ever a coincidence. Everything connects. I spin around to look in Rhodie's direction.

"Rhodie, I need to know everything about you. Your family,

where you went to school, what you do for work, who you've fucked -" his eyebrows hit his hairline, but I ignore that. "I need to know everything about you. This guy wants you for a reason. I need to know why."

"Whoa, hold your horses, little girl." I hate when Marx calls me that. Makes me want to go stabby on a dude. He's stalking closer to me and I don't want him to have the upper hand by towering over my sitting form. So I do what any self-respecting short woman would do and I stand on the chair. Yes, that's right, it's me looking down on you, ha! I cheer a little to myself in my head. Slick move Tuesday, slick move. Marx pulls up short before tipping his head a little to look into my eyes. He studies me for a moment before letting out a sigh.

"Look Tuesday, we really enjoyed the show, learned some new shit too-"

I smile before interrupting him, "Every day is a learning day, Marx." Rider bursts into laughter in the background and I'm pretty certain Rhodie let out a snort "Anyway we gave you your time, but now I think it's time to leave and let us take care of the rest of this business."

I size him up. He's a big guy, protective of his men. I respect that. I also get that it's probably been a long, weird night for him, so I'm willing to let him be, for the time being. I'll let him think he's won, but I know that this whole thing is going to buzz around my head until I have an answer, so I'll just let him think I've backed off.

I mean, I can find out all the info I need on Rhodie online anyway. I just thought it would be nice to talk to the guy. There's something about him I like, and I don't like many people. In fact, there's something I like about being here, at Devil's Rose MC. Shaking off my thoughts I stare down at Marx, slapping my hand on his very large, hard as-granite shoulder. I may even give it a little squeeze.

"OK hulk, I'll back off for the meantime. It's been a long and eventful night. How about we get outta your hair, yeah?"

He raises an eyebrow before giving me a subtle nod. I quickly survey the scene and see that my brothers have finished. Everything including a snug as a bug in a rug, Alan, is ready to go.

"Right, Dayz, you riding with us or you got your own wheels?" Tav asks me while swiping me off the chair with his arm around my waist, and then setting me down on the floor.

"Nah, I'm good. Got my own wheels. I wanna go for a wee ride anyway, clear my head. See you guys tomorrow in the office, yeah?"

They all nod, then one by one they all kiss me on the top of the head as they walk past. They even get friendly fist bumps from the MC members. How very macho.

"OK then. Well, pleasure doing business with you all." I smile and do a little bow, because I'm back to my awkward as hell self, but as I turn to leave Rhodie calls out to me,

"Let me see you out. You got all this, Prez?" Marx gives him a chin lift and Rhodie opens the door for me. We walk in silence for a bit, and I notice that he's slowed his walk down, so he's striding at my pace, which is very polite. I like it. Rhodie clears his throat, so I look up at him.

"So, ah, how did you learn to do all that? I'm the enforcer so it's my job to get information out of people, but I've never seen those techniques before."

I smile up at him. "I think a lot."

He grunts as we continue walking. "So, you were thirteen when your parents died? That must have sucked. Your brothers said that your Pops moved in to look after you."

I look back up at him again. The moonlight is casting a glow onto his face, and my stomach flutters a little. This man is definitely attractive and my body is reacting in kind. I may be a little odd when it comes to people-ing, but I'm no virgin and I know what I like.

"Is there a question in there? You can just ask straight out. I don't mind."

He takes a deep breath before answering. "Fuck, I don't know Tuesday. I want to know things about you. You intrigue me, and you can bet your sweet ass I'm going to be using some of your interrogation techniques." He smiles at me and I can feel those flutters again. It makes me happy that a fellow "interrogationist" likes what I do.

"Well, I'm thirty. My parents were killed when I was thirteen, and my Pops came to take care of me. He was a bit eccentric thanks to being in Nam but he told me cool stories and we researched medieval torture techniques for fun. Pops and Tav helped me make all sorts of gadgets and stuff. He's Alfred to my Bruce Wayne. But my parents were not rich enough for me to be Batman. Not that I would. Dude is basically a rich bully." I hear Rhodie's rich chuckle at my statement.

"Aw I dunno, you would make a cute Batman." He grins down at me. Flirty bastard. "Can I ask another question?"

"Shoot, big man." I hear him snort. I'm on a roll with my comedy gold tonight.

"Tuesday is a kinda unusual name. There a story there?" Rhodie asks.

"My parents weren't really all that imaginative, I don't think. August is the eldest. Guess which month he was born?" We're still walking alongside each other, so I tip my head sideways a little to look over at him. I see the smile on his lips.

"Then Jules was next. When do you think he was born?" his smile broadened before I see the slight frown on his face.

"You're thinking 'But Tav isn't a month' right? Tav's full name is Octavius, a nod to October."

"So how come you didn't get a month?" A smile plays on my lips. My birthday is one of the best things I like about myself. "I share a birthday with August. He always says I was his very favorite present. Anyway, the option they had for my name if they went with the tried and true would have been Augusta, and nobody's got time for that. Instead, they named me Tuesday. Although my family calls me Dayzy, or Dayz. I like it."

Looking back up at him I see he still has a small frown, and he's slowed his walk to a stop. I see his shoulders raise before he lets out a breath and drops them.

"My name is Rhodes Paxon. I'm thirty five years old. My dad's name is Max Paxon or Mad Dog. He was the Prez before he retired and my brother took over. That's Marx. He's five years older than me. My mom's name was Annie. She died when we were kids. Marx is my half-brother, same dad, but my mom raised him. I retired from the army almost eight years ago and I work as a mechanic in one of the garages the MC owns. And I haven't fucked anyone in about five months. Does that answer all the stuff you wanted to know about me?"

Rhodie

She's looking up at me wide-eyed and I can't say I blame her. What the hell was that? For some goddamn reason, I'm blurting shit out like I'm thirteen and trying to get my crush to like me. I don't know why, but I feel the need to share things with her, things I would never tell anyone on the first night that I met them. After getting to know her a little, I figured the least I could do was answer the questions that she had asked me earlier, before Marx told her we had everything taken care of. Cock blocking bastard. I see a funny little smile cross her face before she gives me a brief nod.

"Yup, thanks for that. If I need to know anything else, I'll just ask" She starts walking again and I finally take in our surroundings. We've wandered out the back to a covered corner of the compound. She comes to a stop along the fence line before looking back up at me.

"Right, well, this is me. Thanks for walking me out and all that." She waves a hand at me and before I can comprehend what the hell she's doing, I'm watching her climb up the chain-link fence. I want to grab her or yell at her or do something, but I'm pretty much frozen in place by watching her cargo pants pull tight across her ass as she climbs. Before I've pulled myself together, she is up and over the top and has plopped down onto the other side of the fence.

"What the fuck was that? Why didn't you just walk out the front gate?" Even I can hear the bewilderment in my voice. She looks up, hair all around her face.

"Huh? Why would I do that? I parked over here. Walking the long way makes no sense." I look around her and I cannot see a vehicle at all. She bends over in the bushes and when she straightens up, she's pulling on elbow pads one at a time. I peer over the bush and see she has already pulled on a couple of knee pads as well.

"What the fuck are you doing?" She looks over at me with a look that screams, 'What the hell do you think I'm doing?' before perkily saying, "Safety first," and smiling big. She pushes her hair back and pulls a bright yellow helmet onto her head, pressing a button on the front that has the thing lit up like a Christmas tree.

"Hold up, what the hell is happening? Why are you dressed like that? Where is your car?"

"That's a lot of questions buddy, but, well, I'm getting suited up. It's for my safety and I don't have a car." She shrugs like that all makes fucking sense.

"If you don't have a car, how the hell did you get here, then?" She heaves something out of the bush and my eyes almost bug out of my head.

"A fucking scooter? You came out to the compound on a fucking scooter?" This woman is going to give me a heart attack. I'm not sure why, but since I met her, all my instincts want me to protect her. I know that's terribly chauvinistic of me, especially since I saw her torture and kill a man, but sue me.

"Yeah, isn't she a real beauty? Full electric, can go up to 25 miles per hour. She's a dream to ride. I even got special decals made for her, made her look real custom." She wiggles her eyebrows at me and I'm lost. I have absolutely no words.

"Anyway, man, this has been real. Thanks for tonight. I'll contact you during the week or something. Get this stuff all sorted out." She smiles big and waves at me, and before I can even get my words out, she rides off in the dark on her fucking electric scooter, helmet glowing and flashing like a disco ball. I open my mouth and laugh harder than I have in a long time.

Chapter 5

"How you getting on, Dayz?" I break my concentration to look up and find Tav standing in the doorway to my office. If I wasn't so focused, I probably would have smelt him there. He must have come from a meeting with a hot mom client because he has on his favorite Tom Ford cologne. Apparently, it gets all the moms' panties wet.

"Tav, my strong-smelling MILF hunting brother. Thus far, this investigation is really busting my lady balls. Which sucks. So far, I cannot find any reason why Mom or Dad would have been targeted by Nado Kraykowski. Even if he's just a link in the chain to some higher-up, I still can't find anything that links our parents to any kind of criminal activity."

"Well, how far back have you gone? You know sometimes when we're investigating, we have to go back decades before we find anything."

"Birth, Tav. I've gone all the way back to birth. I'm thinking of starting on their parents next, but to what end? Why the hell would someone put a hit out on them and then nothing?

Surely if they were Big Bad's, someone would have hit one of us up for something. I mean, my brain is brilliant and you know it's bad when I'm too dumb to figure this out." I let out a deep sigh. This puzzle is really grating on my nerves. I don't like unanswered questions. "What about you? What have you found on Rhodie?"

He wanders further into my office and then flops down onto my big, fluffy armchair that my brothers gave me shit about, but will fight over who is sitting in it when they come to visit.

"Nothing too much on Rhodie. Normal childhood, if you call growing up in an MC normal. Half brothers with Marx the Prez, father was the Prez before stepping down to retire. Mother died when Rhodie was eighteen, just before he enlisted. Marine for ten years before being honorably discharged. Voted as Enforcer for Devils' Rose MC and has been for the past seven years. I think you should probably speak to him for more information you may want to know."

"What more would I want to know? And why would I need to speak to him? Do you think he can't read?"

"Why the fuck would I think he couldn't read Dayz?" Tav looks at me confused.

"Because you said I should speak with him. Usually, I just email people." He looks at me like I've grown another head before snorting, "Dayz, sometimes you scare me with your sheer brilliance. Other days, you scare me with how stupid you can be."

He athletically jumps up from my fluffy throne then he knocks twice on my door jamb before walking off. He never answered my question either, the big bastard. I heave out another sigh and lean back in my chair, staring at the ceiling and spinning a little. Sometimes movement gets my juices flowing. Thinking back to my childhood, everything seemed normal, apart from me. I was always something separate from everyone else. Don't get me wrong, I love my family and was loved, but I was always something a little extra. And at this point, that something extra is not helping me.

We lived on a large section with a big house. It could almost be classed as a small farm because the house was surrounded by land. All the surrounding houses were. When Mom and Dad died, no one wanted to live in the house, so we - me, Tav, and Pops - moved into a trailer on site while we built a new home. When August and Jules moved back they built their own cabins on the land, and then in time so did Tav and I. So now Pops lives in the big house and the rest of us Tombs kids live in a small neighborhood of our own making on the land that we grew up on. To outsiders, we probably look weird, but I don't care. I feel safe being surrounded by the men in my family, even though I am by far the most dangerous of us all.

Whilst spinning, my musings take on the neighborhood when I was a kid. I remember Tav and Jules being friendly with the neighbor kids, especially the ones to the left of our house. They even cut a hole in the fence so they could go back and forth between houses. The house on the other side never had children living there, but I remember a beautiful lady living there with her husband. They were foreign and had thick accents, but they were always really nice to me. All the men in my family had built me a treehouse that sat on the fence line between our house and theirs, and I remember when I needed to decompress, I'd sit in that little treehouse and watch them go about their lives. In a totally innocent, non-creepy way, of course.

I think back to a time I remember seeing them have what

looked to be some type of disagreement. I remember this vividly because at twelve years old my mom had been helping me learn to read faces, and I'd finally mastered the angry face. They both had angry faces, the husband more than the wife. They moved around the rooms on my treehouse side of their house, and I watched their argument play out disjointedly as they paced and stopped in front of different windows. Sort of like a peep show, where you only get tantalizing snippets of what you really want to know. I never saw what happened in the end because I got called in for dinner. I never thought much of it with my 12-year-old brain, but now, maybe there's something there.

I kick my shoes off, surprised they're even still on, bring my legs up, and cross them criss-cross applesauce on my office chair before yelling

"GUS, TAV, JULES!" at the top of my lungs. Within moments, I can hear a stampede of giant brothers barrelling down the hallway. Gus and Tav reach my doorway first, both of them elbowing each other before Gus makes a break for it and dives into my fluffy chair from the doorway. Tav kicks him in the leg on the way past to then lean against my window whilst Jules walks in, giving them both the stink eye and resting his ass on my desk.

"You bellowed, dear delicate sister?" August says with a smirk.

"Yeah, what can you remember about the foreign couple that lived next door when we were kids?"

I watch all my brother's eyebrows furrow. That's the great thing about being family, everyone has the same facial expressions.

"I remember mowing their lawn one summer. They paid me

like, $20 once every couple of weeks, to do it while they were overseas. Was an awesome gig," Tav says.

"Why do you want to know, Dayz?"

"I've been looking into everything about Mom and Dad and nothing. Figured I'd start up on the neighbors. The Parkers are still next door and pretty boring. The other couple, though, were intriguing. Can you remember their names, Gus? Jules?"

"The Voronov's. Kaz and Kaya. Kaya was really hot for an older woman. I remember seeing her a few times when I was back from college," August adds.

I spin in my seat a little to get the thinking juices flowing. Which is not as easy as you think, given my legs are crossed up under me, so I'm not very elegantly gripping my desk to help with the swing. I look up and my brothers are smirking. Bastards.

"What are the chances that the Voronovs know any Kraykowskis? Or is that me being prejudiced?" I continue spinning, catching glimpses of my brother's faces as I make my pass.

Tav has been looking out of the window and I see him turn to me with a frown on his face,

"I remember they left suddenly. Like immediately after Mom and Dad died. I remember because I was staying at Brandon's house that night of the party, and it was his mom who woke me up to tell me I needed to go home. She dropped me off at about 8 am. She left me down the road because of the police cordons, but they were letting people out of the street to go to work and the stuff. I remember the police had stopped the Voronovs, and they were saying they really had to get going, they had a flight to catch, and that they never saw or heard anything, but if they thought of anything they'd call. I never saw them again after that."

I stop spinning and stroke my imaginary beard. "Hmmm, veeeery interesting. Looks like I have a bit of a lead, boys. Lemme see where this line of investigation gets me. What are you all working on?"

"The MC has hired us to tighten up some of their security. It's not bad, Wire did a good job, however, we can beef it up a little more. Oh, yeah, by the way, I told Wire I'd send you over when you have time. He wants to bounce some ideas off you for tightening up their cyber security," August says as he stands and heads for the door.

"Can't he just email me?"

"Nope."

"Argh fine! Can I catch a ride with one of you? It's raining and you KNOW Delilah doesn't like the rain."

"Dayz, you know we love you, but you really need to learn how to drive and get rid of that damned scooter. It's not safe!" Jules growls at me.

"You hush your mouth, Jules! Delilah is VERY safe, thank you very much. She just doesn't like to get wet. And another thing, I can totally drive. I just choose not to." I flip him the bird and he rolls his eyes as he walks out the door.

"Keep telling yourself that, kid, and one day we might all believe it," Tav says as he walks past my desk and moves all my shit around before leaving. I need new brothers. These ones suck.

Rhodie

It's been a week since a tiny whirlwind maimed and murdered a guy in my back shed and I can't stop thinking about her. It's starting to piss me off. I'm in an MC, for fuck's sake. We have bunnies ripe for the picking. All I have to do is give them the eye, and the next thing you know, my cock is down their throat.

I gave up fucking them when I realized I didn't want to keep sticking my dick where my brothers had been, although blow jobs from the bunnies are fine if I can't find the time to head off-site to pick up a little strange. I didn't lie when I told Tuesday that I hadn't fucked anyone in five months. Thanks to the success of the garage, I haven't had time to pick up any women. Maybe that's why my brain is stuck on Tuesday? It hasn't had dick-in-pussy action for a while, so it's latched on to the first woman I've had contact with. It's the only explanation.

What makes it worse is that other than her giant whiskey eyes that only look at you sometimes, and her masses of dark curls, I can't actually recall what she looks like other than remember she was pretty in a girl next door type of way. Which, when you compare her to the blonde hair and tits and ass here on the compound, is pretty average. I think my dick wants average. This has never happened before.

It must be because of all this Kraykowski bullshit. For a whole ass week, my brothers and I have been dredging up everything and anything we can think of to figure out a link between me and him, and nothing. It's starting to set me on edge, which is not what I need my mind on if I want to keep my brothers and the MC safe.

Still feeling jittery and unsettled, I get up off my bed, deciding a workout is probably what I need. Maybe someone might want to hop in the ring with me and go a few rounds. Rider is usually up for that kind of shit. If I blow off some steam, my brain might come back online. Yeah, that's a great idea. It's probably just stress. I head down the hall and find Rider at the pool table, chatting up a new bunny. She's tall, blonde, has pasties on her nipples, and it's only lunchtime.

"Yo, Rider! Wanna go a few rounds? I want to blow off some steam and punching you seems like a good idea." He swings his shaggy dark head towards me before giving me a chin lift. He turns back to the bunny, who now has a full-on pout on her lips, but once he whispers something in her ear, she perks up and runs a tongue along her very large and very shiny lips. I wonder where we find these girls? I shrug to myself and head on back to the gym.

The compound used to just comprise of the main building, but as the MC has grown over the years, other buildings have popped up such as the gym which is out the back door and sits alongside the shed where we take unwanted guests. As basic as it looks from the outside, inside it's a gym bro's wet dream. All the equipment you could ever want, weight benches, weight rigs, cardio machines, the lot, and in the middle of the room is the ring where we all like to throw a few punches or practice our moves. Some brothers are trained in Jiu-Jitsu and have given us all a few lessons. They're great skills to have. Rider's feet stomping through the space let me know his lazy ass has finally turned up, and I offer him a little smirk before we plow into each other in a flurry of fists and feet.

Stepping out of the shower I feel so much better, apart from the slightly swollen jaw where Rider got the jump on me one part there. Now I feel it's time for beer and maybe I'll find one of the girls to give me a blowy. Locking up my room I make my way to the common room. As I pass by Wire's "headquarters," as he calls it, I hear a feminine giggle that ends in a snort, and then a full-on belly laugh. I smile to myself before giving his door an obligatory knock and pushing it open to see who the owner of the less than melodic laugh is. I come up short and feel as though I've been hit in the gut when my eyes land on none other than Tuesday.

Instead of the cargo pants and oversized hoodie I last saw her in, she's wearing what I'm guessing are her office work clothes, but with a bit of an edge. She has on a tight black dress that comes down past her knees with a split up the side, a baggy black and white cardigan, and platform Doc Marten boots. It's classy and professional and yet somehow not. Just like Tuesday. I take another moment to run my eyes over her from top to bottom and back up again. The dress leaves nothing to the imagination. Who knew that under those baggy clothes, Tuesday was hiding a large round ass and a magnificent pair of tits? My eyes land on her face once more, and I realize that my memory of her is wrong. Tuesday isn't Girl Next Door pretty or average. She is, in fact, breathtakingly beautiful.

"Yo, big man, you get eyes for Christmas or something?" I register what she says and I take in the smirk on her face.

"Tuesday, what gives us the pleasure of your visit?" I'm trying to play it cool but I can't shake the feeling that if she's here in Wire's room maybe it's him she wants, which is not sitting well with me at all.

"Wire had some stuff he wanted to run by me, so we're colabbing on a project. The usual work stuff. How's it hanging, anyway?" At her question I see her eyes run down my body, then linger on my cock for a moment before I hear her snort indelicately "Looks like it's to the left, big man." Wire chuckles next to her and I get the overwhelming urge to hit him.

I ignore his ass instead and ask, "How's your side of the investigation going? Find anything out that would be of any help?"

She lets out a big sigh before looking all around Wire's room. I've noticed that even though she seems slightly better at making eye contact, her eyes still seem to flit about while thinking or talking.

"So far, nothing of any substance. The only lead I have that I'm chasing down is our old neighbors. Our old neighbors got outta Dodge the morning after my parents were murdered. The Voronovs. I figure surely the surname alone may mean they could have some type of connection to Kraykowski."

My brow furrows. "Did you just say Voronov?" Her eyes dart directly to my face. "Yeah, Kaz and Kaya Voronov. They lived next door to us when I was a kid. Not long before this whole thing went down, I remember seeing them argue. What do you know?"

"Not them as such, but there was a girl at school that I dated a few times, Katya Voronov. Wasn't ever serious enough to meet her parents or anything, so not sure if there's a link there or not." By the time I finish speaking, I notice Tuesday has commandeered one side of Wire's desk and is tapping away at a keyboard. I take a second to study her, the way she's sitting at the desk, face in a frown as she concentrates, her citrus scent wraps itself around me and I breathe her in.

"I don't ever remember there being another person living in the house with them, I only ever remember them, BUT there is no way that with all this-" she waves her hand in a circle above her head, before accidentally hitting it on Wires desk light. "Dammit! Ugh, as I was saying, there is no way that this is all some hinky coincidence. There's no way."

She continues typing for a bit and I look to Wire for help. He seems mesmerized by what she's doing and seeing as neither of these geeks wants to explain anything, I figure I'll sit down and wait them out. It's not like I've never seen Wire like this before, it's just funny that this type of weird ass behavior is apparently par for the course if you're a computer person. Before I can settle into the chair too much, Tuesday triumphantly hits a button and a large yearbook picture of Katya comes up on the big screen behind her.

"This her?" I take in the blonde girl on the screen and her shy smile. I remember the first time I saw her; she turned up at the start of the school year and was incredibly quiet. We got paired up in some biology class and I found her to be sweet, if a little quiet. I immediately liked her, not to mention I thought she was hot as hell. We went out on a couple of dates, and I noticed then that she didn't have many friends or anything. She never really fit in. So I took to eating lunch with her.

"Yeah, that's her. Sweet girl, we went out a couple of times and spent a lot of time together throughout the school year. Even went to prom with each other."

"Oh re-he-heeeeeeallly? Tell me more, big man." I see Wire grinning like the Cheshire cat bastard he is while Tuesday is sitting with her legs up on the desk, wiggling her eyebrows at me.

Fuck, I didn't want to have to tell anyone this, mainly because it's private, but then again I'm in an MC and have seen almost all of my brothers fucking at least once.

"Fine, we lost our virginity together, happy?" I scowl at both of them, Tuesday clapping excitedly and Wire still sitting there with a gleam in his eye. I clear my throat. "Anyway, you dicks, she left town not long after and I shipped off. Never saw or heard from her again."

Tuesday is still sitting with her feet up, but now she's stroking her chin, like an imaginary beard. She's such a weird little chick and yet she's been all I could think about this week. I can see something working behind her eyes. Whatever it is, she's not ready to share just yet.

"Ok, so let's assume that the link between Tuesday's parents and Kraykowski, and you and Kraykowski, is the Voronovs. First, we need to establish how Katya Voronov is related to Kaz and Kaya. I mean, they could be no relation at all, however it seems pretty fucking unlikely." Wire taps away at his keyboard. "Ok, so by the looks of it Katya came to the US with her Aunt and Uncle, wait for it, Kaz and Kaya."

I look at Tuesday and instead of looking jubilant, she's as white as a ghost, which is surprising given her tanned skin. She's sitting stock still. Nothing is moving on her, which from the few interactions I've had with her, seems unusual.

"Yo, Tuesday, are you all good?" Wire reaches out to lay a hand on her and she doesn't take any notice whatsoever. "Fuck, I don't know what's happening, dude. She looks catatonic. Her brother brought her here. He's in with Prez. Better go get him," Wire barks out.

I really don't want to leave, yet again I'm drawn to protecting her, but I don't know what the fuck is happening, so I hustle my ass to the common room where I see August leaning in talking to Marx. "August! Something's going on with Tuesday."

His head whips up, and he is running toward me full steam ahead. Fucker is fast for a big man. We barge into Wire's room and Tuesday is still there, unchanged.

"Fuck! She had a shutdown. She hasn't done this since after Mom and Dad died. What was happening in the room before this?" While he's talking, I watch and he bundles her up off the chair and squeezes her tightly in his arms. He stands there holding her, looking around the room, for what I'm not sure.

I reach out and place my hand firmly on his shoulder, waiting until his eyes meet mine. "What do you need?"

He takes a deep breath, "She does this if she's become either sensory or emotionally overwhelmed. She's like a gaming console that overheats. Her brain just shuts down, and she needs time to reboot. We need a small space, closet, cupboard, anywhere small and cozy, doesn't matter if it's dark or not."

Before I can think, Wire is up across the room pulling shit out of the bottom of his closet. August nods at him before squatting down and gently placing Tuesday's curled-up form on the floor.

"She likes weight on her, do you have something I can place on her?" He looks up at me, and even though this man often has the air of total control about him, when it comes to his sister I can see that she is his heart. I look down and realize the heavy leather of my cut might work, so I take it off my shoulders and gently lay it over her. I hear her take a deep breath and I see her fingers start to tap against each other. August gently kisses her head before standing and looking at me and Wire.

"Um, thanks, man. I'm sorry about that. She hasn't done that in a long time. Fuck. Something must have set her off. What was going on before she shut down?"

I want to answer him, I do, but I have to admit I'm still a little shaken. I look at Wire, but he seems the same. This is our second interaction with her and she's hard not to like. I take a deep breath and then I feel a hand land on my shoulder. I turn and see my brother, Marx. He gives me a tight smile and a nod.

"Right. Wire had just found out the connection between all of us. I dated a girl called Katya Voronov at school. Kaz and Katya were her aunt and uncle, and your neighbors. "

August breathes out. "Shit, that's the connection, I thought–"

"Alan wasn't the only one there that night."

Chapter 6

Tuesday

"Alan wasn't the only one there that night" I watch as all the giant-sized men swing their heads towards me. I figure I must have had a bit of a shutdown, because the last thing I remember is sitting in Wire's spare chair only to then find myself breathing in the scent of Rhodie, leather, spicy and clean.

I take in my surroundings and see I'm on the floor of a nice closet. I'll have to remember this place. Love a good closet when I'm overwhelmed. August must have put me in here. I should feel ashamed that as an independent woman my big brother had to come and help me out, but there's little I can do when my brain decides it has had too much. The best I can do is shut off my emotions and think rationally about what's going on. I move to get up and Rhodie's big hand reaches out towards me. Taking it, I look up at him, expecting to see pity, but it just looks like he was worried about me. That makes my tummy feel a way. Not sure what.

"Thanks Rhodie." I hand him back his cut and I see Marx

raise an eyebrow behind him. "Right, sorry about that. Freaking out and freezing up isn't very tattooed bad bitch of me." I huff out a laugh to settle the alpha men in the room, but no one laughs at my joke. Dammmnnn, tough crowd. I take my seat back where I was before.

"Dayz, what did you mean when you said Alan wasn't alone? I thought you couldn't remember anything that happened that night?" I see the concern on August's face.

"Usually I remember nothing other than the ambulance people cleaning blood off me. But something must have triggered in the ole dome. Brains are weird like that." I shrug my shoulders and get my thoughts into some semblance of order. "I remember there being another voice in the house, not just Alan's. It was a man, thick accent, and he kept saying over and over 'Where is your niece?'." I look around at the men in the room before landing on my brother

"I don't think Mom and Dad were the targets. I think the Voronovs were and, for whatever reason, the intel was bad." I watch as Marx comes further into the room, a frown on his face and his enormous arms crossed over his chest as he leans his weight against the far wall.

"So, we can surmise that Kraykowski, or whoever he works for, may have wanted Katya, your old girlfriend-" he tips his head towards Rhodie.

"I wouldn't call her my girlfriend as such. We were kinda friendly, hung out, went on a few dates."

"Sounds a lot like a girlfriend," I hear Wire mumble before I see Rhodie try to kick out at Wire's leg. Wire just smirks and flips him the bird.

"Well, whatever you want to call it, little brother. So they want Katya, decide to go rough up her aunt and uncle who brought her here with them. Instead, end up at the wrong address and get the Tombs. That tracking about, right?" Marx lifts his brow towards my brother and me.

"Sounds about right to me. I guess we need to find out why the hell he wanted Katya. If even Rhodie wasn't overly sure about his relationship status with this girl, why is Kraykowski now interested, almost eighteen years later?" August speaks into the room. This conundrum is really conundruming. Which sucks harder than a $2 hooker on a Sunday and my brain is too fried to even think properly at this stage.

"Argh! My brain isn't working up to full speed yet, guys. But once I get her up and running like the fine tuned machine she is, I'm sure I'll be able to figure this all out. God, it must suck to be walking around with stupid normal people's brains," I say this mainly to myself, but I notice that when I look up there are a few amused looks aimed my way.

"Mr. President, do you mind if I borrow your kitchen for a bit?"

Marx's eyebrows hit his hairline before he lets out a long sigh "I know for a fact I don't want to know what you're up to, but sure, be my guest. Rhodie and Wire? You're on Tuesday duty. August, if you would like to follow me, we can continue on with our business, if you're comfortable with your sister being left with my men?"

August looks at me before letting out a snort. "Marx, she'll be fine. It's them I worry about." He pats me on the head before following Marx out the door. I look up to see two sets of eyes looking back at me.

"To the kitchen, fellas! I've got to fuel this brain and nothing helps me think better than baking."

"Baking? Like you can do that? Make cookies and shit? We

haven't had fresh-baked cookies since your mom, Rhodie! Fuck Tuesday, lead the way, girl!" Wire jumps up and waits for me to exit first, Rhodie bringing up the rear with an inquisitive look on his face.

"Come on, Big Man. Tell me your favorite cookies and I'll see what I can do. "

"Chocolate chip. I like them simple." The faraway look in his eyes makes him look like a little kid. This is something I can give him as a thank you for lending me his cut so I could regroup. Thanks to Wire as well. I've never really had a lot of friends growing up, because of weirdness, I guess.

Don't get me wrong, my brothers love me, but non-related company is a little sparse. I've never really had girlfriends or guy friends, but here at the MC, they just seem to accept me. And maybe even like me. At the very least, they seem to not be bothered by my quirks, and I like that.

I ask Wire and Rhodie to pull out all the ingredients I need, as I'm not sure where they all live and we all get settled at the long stainless steel workbench. Even though I'm in an MC kitchen, it looks nothing like I would have pictured. I figured the place would look more like a gross frat house, but this thing is top of the range, complete with two double ovens and all the equipment you'd expect in a commercial kitchen.

I bark orders to the guys and before long we are in the swing of things, measuring, mixing, getting baking sheets ready, and the first batches go into the ovens, timer set. My head jerks up when an incredibly pungent smell heads my way.

"Jesus hell, what is that smell?" I pull the sides of my cardi together and button it up in front of my nose to block the sickly sweet, cloying smell of perfume. By the time my makeshift mask is complete, I look up to find two women, one bleach blonde and one fire engine red with very little clothing on and very tall hair.

"Who the hell are you?" The blonde one who looks exactly like a praying mantis hisses out at me.

"Oh hey, I'm Tuesday."

"So? Who the hell are you, and why are you here?"

"Um, I'm pretty certain I answered that when I said 'Oh hey, I'm Tuesday'."

I hear manly sniggering behind me before Rhodie says, "Stop being a bitch, Whitney. If you don't need anything, head back on out to the common room and find someone else to annoy."

The so-called Whitney narrows her eyes at me and glares for a moment before turning giant, fake, innocent eyes to Rhodie. "Aw, but baby, I was looking for you. I thought you might want to spend some time with me and Monica. It's been months since you last fucked us." She blinks up at him and I can't help but snort inside my cardi.

Her over-mascaraed lashes are flapping about like she has some type of hairy caterpillar stuck in them fighting for his life. She whirls around and jabs a finger in my direction.

"What the fuck are you laughing at, bitch?" she screeches in my direction and I can't help but jump a little at the sheer volume and pitch this woman reaches.

"Umm, I was just mesmerized by your lashes. Flapping about like that. It's really rather hypnotizing. I can see why the guys would be into them. Did you know it's actually referred to as aggressive mimicry? In the animal kingdom, predators use this type of ploy to lure their prey, usually promising sex. Of course, it never works out well for the prey and the predator sucks the life out of them, but it really is fascinating to see such aggressive mimicry at work in an MC clubhouse." Before

I can stop myself, I leave the room and head out to see Marx, interrupting business between him and my brother.

"Hey Marx, quick question. This place is an absolute hotbed of sexual and animal behaviors. Do you mind if I hang out here now and then to observe the inner workings?" He just stares at me through squinty eyes and mumbles, "What the fuck?" before looking at my brother.

August is no help because he too also looks a little confused. Before I can open my mouth to argue my case, we all hear raised voices coming from the kitchen.

The three of us head that way in time to hear Rhodie saying, "Tuesday is not a bitch. She's a fucking genius and in a completely different class to you whores."

Walking through the door behind Marx and my giant brother, they come to a stop side by side, blocking my view so I have to bend a little and peer through a gap between my brother's arm and his side. Thank god he never skips arm day and his arms sit a little way out from his body.

Wire wraps his hands around both Whitney and Monica's upper arms before manhandling them out of the kitchen. "Tuesday is 100x the woman either of you are. Find someone else to fuck, because me and Rhodie aren't putting up with your shit tonight. "

I shove through the wall of man to apologize. "Aw shit guys, I'm sorry! I didn't mean to rub them up the wrong way or anything. Don't deny your dicks for me! I'm all good. I should have kept my science facts to myself. Sorry." I hang my head because these people are becoming my friends.

I feel kinda like I have a chicken flapping about in my tummy when I think of them sticking up for me. No one outside of my family has ever done that before. But at the same time, I don't want them to ruin their sex lives over me. They have to live here, not me. I'm only wanting to visit to people watch. Wire comes back into the room to hear the end of my monologue and throws a meaty arm over my shoulder, leading me back to the island.

"It's all good girl, no one talks about my buddy like that.",

Rhodie frowns at Wire's arm but nods in agreement. "Damn straight. You and your family have business with us, and frankly, we like you, even if you are a little 'eccentric' some-times," Marx growls out.

I don't think I've ever heard this man not growl. The timer beeps in the background and I get my ass into gear to take the cookies out of the oven. The delicious smell wafts out and by the time I've placed them on the bench to cool and look up, I see instead of the five of us, there is now half the MC gathered in the kitchen.

"Holy fuck, are those cookies?" I look over and see Rider looking hungrily at them. Before he can reach for one, Wire lunges across the room and slaps his hand.

"Hands off fucker! They're ours. Chewy made them for us!"

"Well, I mean, I made them to get my brain working, but yeah, sure. Wait, did you just call me Chewy?"

"Sure did. Tuesday is just too long, and you needed a nickname. So Chewy it is. Get it? Like Chewsday?"

"Um, you know that has the same number of syllables, right?" I squint up at him and Rhodie, who are both wearing big smiles.

"Yeah, we know. But we both agreed it was a cute name, and we can't call you Dayz. That's what your brothers call you. So Chewy it is," Rhodie shrugs his shoulders and then slaps a cookie out of Rider's hand . "Back off fucker!" he growls out.

"Hey guys, with the amount of dough we measured out, we have enough for about 120 cookies. Maybe we can share?" I look around at them and a smile splits Wire's face.

"Well, shit. Better get onto the next batch then Chewy," I smile up at my new friends. I've never had anyone give me a friend's nickname before. Don't get me wrong, I've been called all sorts of things, but no one outside of my family has called me something like an endearment. I'm finding I'm really liking it here. I smile to myself and set about working on the next batch with my friends. I'll sort out the Kraykowski mystery later.

August

Watching Tuesday navigate these men is amusing. She has never been anything other than herself. It was important to our parents, hell important to me and my brothers, that she never felt different or small because of the way she is. Is she a pain in the ass? Of course she fucking is.

There have been times in the past where no matter how much we have tried to prepare her for situations or drilled manners into her, she's made things infinitely worse because of her lack of filter or her inquisitiveness. The only reason she hasn't been sent to prison is because of our protection. My little sister is absolutely brilliant, if not a little psychotic.

Marx and I grab a couple of cookies and head back out into the main room. We settle into the corner table where we have been unsuccessfully trying to come up with a plan to protect not only his brother Rhodie and the MC but also my sister. Because I know her, and she is already wrapped up in whatever the fuck is going on here, and she won't stop until it's done.

"Right, so with the extra security you and your brothers have put in, we should be a lot safer than we have been. I've got more men rotating on the perimeter and Wire's looking into anything he can find online. Now that we know that Kraykowski's men found Alan's body, it won't take long for him to figure out what happened to him."

I nod my head at him before adding, "You've also got Tuesday and her skill set as well. With this whole Katya thing, I'm sure she'll be like a dog with a bone. I just can't figure out why anyone would want to look into Rhodie now."

"Rhodie was in the military when your parents were murdered, and I'd say whatever he had with Katya was well over by then. But yeah, seems like a weird fucking coincidence."

"Tuesday would say there is no such thing as a coincidence. If worse comes to worst, I have another contact who can work cyber magic, but unlike Tuesday who prefers to stay a white hat, my contact is happy to dabble on the dark web if needed."

Marx frowns for a bit. "I didn't know there was a difference when it comes to hacking?"

"There isn't usually. I mean, it's still hacking. Tuesday doesn't really like the dark web, said it's full of the worst of humanity and far too many people for her to kill without getting caught, so she stays away. If she has to go there, she will, like when she helped Wire with the sex trafficking cases."

Marx nods his head. "We appreciated the help on that one." He signals the Prospect to bring us both a beer.

His face is giving away his worry, and if I'm being honest, there isn't really much I can do to ease that. I'm worried as fuck about my little sister because even though she isn't great with people, when she attaches herself to something or someone, she is fierce in her protection. The way she already seems friendly with Rhodie and Wire is giving me some concern. Enough to have texted Jules and Tav to let them know what's been happening here. They weren't happy when I told them to stand down. The last thing Tuesday needs is all three of us breathing down her neck. That'll just piss her off. I open my beer and take a long swig before wiping my mouth with the back of my hand.

"Look Marx, if I can speak freely, I'm fucking worried about my sister. The fact that tonight is the first time in seventeen, almost eighteen, years that she's actually remembered shit from that night worries me. What else does she know? What else hasn't been unlocked?"

He studies my face for a while. "Can't you just ask her? Perhaps maybe get her some therapy?"

"If it was that easy, we wouldn't be in this position. She saw no less than nine therapists as a kid and no one could get anything out of her. Her psychologist said that someone on the spectrum like Tuesday can compartmentalize everything. So she put it all in a box and moved on with her life. But now..." I let out a sigh. Tav and Jules have been blowing up my phone since I told them about her shutdown and new memory and I feel bad not talking to them about it, but I have a feeling that Marx knows what it's like to worry about his family, his men. He understands the need to protect and plan and put his needs last. He rubs his hand down his beard for a moment.

"Tuesday is basically a genius, right?" I nod. "I imagine she knows more about science and shit than the average person. So maybe those therapists weren't clever enough. Or maybe they were too sterile. I'm guessing she's seen loads of doctors and shit in her time? If you combine that with her 'special abilities', you're looking at someone that is a fuck of a lot different from the usual therapy client."

I nod my head. "Go on."

"What about someone who has seen the worst of humanity? Someone who has also tortured for the greater good?"

"I'm not sure if Rhodie would be a suitable candidate, not with their fledgling friendship or whatever is going on there."

I see Marx tilt his head at me, understanding in his eyes. I think we both can see the interest our siblings have in each other. Well, Rhodie definitely, Tuesday won't know until one of us spells it out to her.

"Not Rhodie. My ole man, Mad Dog. Was military, then enforcer before he was the Prez. Has had to make a lot of hard calls and put down a lot of scum. He's good at lending an ear and a lot of the guys with PTSD have all sat with him at different times to sort through their shit. Tuesday seems to be comfortable around men. Might be a good fit."

I let his words run through my mind and I have to admit, the idea sounds like a good one. "Shit man, that might just work. You think your dad will be down for that?"

Marx looks up from where he's been texting. "Done. He'll be here tomorrow around 4pm if you want to bring her in then."

I nod my appreciation and he tips his chin up as we both understand what we each would do to take care of our family. I get up to stand and hold my hand out to shake.

"Right, Prez, thanks for all your help. I better get my pain in the ass little sister, and hit the road. After a shutdown and the adrenaline that follows it, she'll be getting tired soon. Will probably sleep for 12 hours or so, so I should get her home."

Heading into the kitchen I find Tuesday waning. She's slumped over on the bar stool, taking really long blinks but still trying to keep up the banter with Rhodie, Wire, and now Rider.

"Come on sleepy head, I better get you home to bed." She looks up at me, lets out a sigh, and heaves herself up off the stool. I was right. She's exhausted.

"Don't worry, little one, you can come back anytime you like." Rider smiles down at her. Wire comes up to hug her and I don't miss the growl that comes out of Rhodie. Rider and Wire both smirk in his direction, but he ignores them as he stands and gives her a gentle kiss on the top of her head. She stares up at him with squinty eyes before shrugging and huffing out a breath and shaking herself more awake.

"Don't worry, Dayz, you're coming back tomorrow. Mad Dog, the old Prez, wants to have a chat with you, so I'll bring you back then." She doesn't say anything, just nods and lifts my arm, snuggling into my side as I walk her out to the car. I help her in and yet again curse why the fuck none of us got running boards put onto our SUVs so she could get in and out. Shutting the door behind her, I wave out to the men who have followed us out, Rhodie, Wire, Rider, and Marx. I throw up my chin as I get in the car and head home.

I look over at my sister, her messy bun flopping around as her head bobs in the moving vehicle. Her eyes are closed and I can tell by her breathing that she isn't quite asleep just yet.

"Do you want to talk about what happened back there?"

"Which part? Me remembering stuff or me being weird and ruining the guys' sexy times for tonight?"

"Whichever part bothers you the most?" I could tell that something had upset her. She's so good at wearing a mask with people, but when you know her and know her insecurities, she's easy to read.

"Sometimes I don't wanna be different, or special, you know? Sometimes I just want to be a normal lady with a normal brain that probably doesn't store random facts and stuff."

"Yeah, but if you were a normal lady, then you wouldn't be able to help all the people that you have helped, Dayz. The kids and women that you've kept safe. You've been able to do that because you're you."

She smiles up at me with her crooked grin before snorting. "That's right. I'm a mother fucking boss!"

I chuckle as I drive toward her little house on the back of our property, nestled between mine and Tav's place. "Yeah, a total badass bitch that lives in a cartoon house." I see her glare from the corner of my eye.

"Whatever dick bag," she says, unbuckling herself as I pull to a stop in front of her impressive collection of Marvel Super Hero gnomes. She jumps out of the SUV and turns to look at me. "I love you, Gussy. Thank you for always looking after me."

"Love you too, Dayzy" I watch her walk up onto her porch and unlock her bright yellow door, turn on her lights, and wave to me through her front window before I drive to my house a few hundred feet away. My mind echoed the last words Marx said to me before we left. "Take care of that sister of yours. I feel like she's going to be someone important to all of us". I couldn't agree more.

Chapter 7

Rhodie

I quickly check the time on the wall and yell out to Rider that it's time to pack it in. Walking over to the washbasin, I try to scrub the grease off my hands. I'm thankful that when I got home, after getting out of the military, and had no idea what I was going to do with my life, my brother had the foresight to purchase an old, run-down mechanic shop. Yeah, it took a while and a lot of hard fucking work to get it up and running, but now it's a big money-maker for the club. A lot of the town are loyal customers, coming to get their cars worked on, and it means that we always have space to tune up our bikes and whatever other vehicles we have at the club.

To say today has dragged would be an understatement. I think we are all a little on edge over the current state of things, and even though we now know the link between me and Chewy's family, there are still a shit ton of questions left unanswered. I snicker a little, thinking of the nickname Wire and I gave her.

I'm so eager to get back to the compound that I leave Rider

to lock up; that'll teach him to be a slow bastard. It's almost 4 pm and I'm eager to see Tuesday. Marx let me know that he's called in Dad's help. Maybe he can help unlock some of the shit in her head. I get that she's wired differently, but the thing about PTSD is it doesn't give a shit who you are. Chances are she has some trauma from when she was a kid, and that is some shit we need to wade through to hopefully get answers.

But it's more than just wanting to know what she knows. I want to be there with her when she talks to my old man. I don't know what it is about her, but I have a fucked up feeling inside my chest like it gets tight just thinking about her. I didn't think I'd ever want a woman to settle down with and have kids, but there's something about Chewy that intrigues me. But I'm not thinking too deeply about it just yet.

Pulling into the yard, I see two SUVs with the Tombs Security logo on them and a beat-up pickup truck that I've never seen before. Walking into the common room, I can hear Marx barking at someone and a rough voice barking right back.

"Listen here you fucker, I don't care who you're the President of. That's my grandbaby and I will be wherever the fuck I want to be where she is concerned."

Walking into the room I see a short, stocky older man with a deep tan and white hair combed military style standing toe to toe with Marx even though Marx stands about a foot taller. I take in the rest of the men in the room and note that none of the Tombs brothers seem to be overly worried.

Tav has a grin on his face, August is smirking, and as per usual Jules is blank-faced with a raised eyebrow. I swing my gaze around to find Chewy and when I do, I notice she is also unbothered by the goings-on. She's wearing what looks to be spray-on jeans and I can't wait to catch a glimpse of the back of her. She also has on a t-shirt with Willie Nelson on the front and her look is topped off with a pair of platform Chucks. Shit, she's cute. She's perched her little ass on a bar stool, swinging her legs back and forth drinking some girly looking drink that the prospect must have made her.

"Listen, old man, I get that you're concerned for Tuesday's wellbeing. But I'm telling you, Mad Dog knows what the fuck he is doing, and she will be safe with us-"

"You better watch it, Skid Marx, otherwise I'll light your ass up!"

"Are you threatening me, old man?" Marx growls out.

I'm getting a little concerned but before I can do anything I hear a hearty "AHHHHHH what a refreshing beverage. Come on, Pops, settle down before you hurt yourself. Marx, thank you for thinking of my feelings, but I'm fine for anyone to hear all this stuff we're gonna talk about," Tuesday announces.

Everyone swings their eyes towards her. August finally clears his throat. "Are you sure, Dayz? I mean, you might talk to Mad Dog about private stuff or you might remember something upsetting."

She waves her hand dismissively at her brother. "It's fine, Gus. I mean, shit, half the time I don't have private thoughts because I have no inner monologue anyways. Besides, whatever is locked up inside me is something that will impact most everyone here. So we may as well just do this whole thing right where we are." I see her look toward Marx, who gives her a raised eyebrow.

I've noticed even though he hasn't said as much, he seems to have a soft spot for her, just like the rest of the brothers. He looks at me and I give him a nod. She seems calm enough, and she doesn't strike me as the type of woman to be self-conscious or nervous about much. Before I can even open my mouth to state my views, the little older man Chewy called Pops is up in my face, gnarled finger jabbing me in the chest.

"So you're Rhodie? I hear you have a hard-on for my grandbaby. Better think again, motherfucker, cuz I ain't letting any old shitstain near her until they prove themselves. Got me?" He mean mugs me for a moment before stomping back towards Chewy and throwing an arm over her shoulder.

What the hell? I look towards her three brothers and all three fuckers are smirking back at me. I'll get them back, smug bastards. Before anyone else can say anything to upset Chewy's Pops, I see my dad, Mad Dog, walk through the kitchen door. I walk over to give him a hug, and so does Marx, before we look to the room.

"Ok Mad Dog, this here is the Tombs family from Tombs Security. Left to right, we have August, Tav, and Jules." All of them nod at Mad Dog after sizing him up, and I see my father doing the same back to each one of them, too.

"Hi! I'm Tuesday. Although a lot of the guys here call me Chewy now. I don't mind." Chewy gives my dad a blindingly big smile and there goes that fucking feeling in my chest again. She waves enthusiastically, but that seems to throw her off balance a little as she's still swinging her legs and she starts to topple sideways. Without thinking, I'm by her side and I scoop her up before she can fall. I place her back on her stool and look up in time to see her Pops' squinty-eyed look before giving me a head tip.

"And that old grumpy bastard is our Pops," Tav speaks up, and then laughs when Pops growls in his direction.

"Well, OK then. It's nice to meet you, love. Are you happy to have a chat with me? Maybe talk about what's going on and we can get to know each other a little?"

"Yup, sure thing. We're just gonna do it here, I don't mind anyone hearing,"

Mad Dog looks around the room to decide the best place to sit. "Let's go sit on the couch, girl, get nice and comfy, yeah?"

Chewy gives him a huge smile and I feel the need to let him know to keep his hands off. Not that he would try it on. He's old enough to be her father, but it pisses me off that even at his age he's still got the touch when it comes to the ladies. Even ladies as unusual as Chewy.

As if my thoughts have come to life, I watch her curtsy in front of Mad Dog before sitting. I see his eyebrows hit his hairline before he grins big, looking over at me and giving me a little head shake while he chuckles. We spend the next while bringing him up to speed on the goings on and I can see he's already pissed off. Although he did ask that next time Chewy tortures someone, he has front row seats. I see her Pops also looking fucking proud as punch over his granddaughter's methods and now I'm wondering if he has had a hand in any of her schemes.

"OK, Tuesday, so you said you had a flashback. Something you had never remembered before. Trauma, especially when young, can be a mind fuck. Have memories ever been triggered before by words, smells, that sort of thing?"

Tuesday thinks for a moment before nodding. "I guess. Smells more often than not remind me of things. Sometimes by the way something feels or a sound. I'm pretty sensitive to that type of stuff anyway," she shrugs.

"You're autistic, yeah? Forgive me, but I know little about it. Would you mind telling me about it?" He leans back and lets Tuesday organize her thoughts. I notice a lot of the brothers have come in and they're all invested in what's happening. Her brothers and Pops seem pretty calm, so that makes me feel a little better. I look back at Chewy and I'm surprised to see that she looks a little uncomfortable.

"It's not really anything too special. I'm not like Rainman or Sheldon from Big Bang Theory. I'm fairly average. There are some things I still struggle with, but I'm not super robotic or unfeeling or anything. I can empathize now and I can read people to an extent. I'm not super emotional and I can compartmentalize very well. Hence, I never remembered anything. I just put that stuff away and moved on." I can see she looks uneasy, and it's the first time I've ever noticed her look self-conscious.

I have a feeling that maybe she's not as comfortable with her abilities and the way she's wired as we think she is. Shit, I can't imagine growing up with that monkey on your back would've been easy and kids can be really cruel. I bet she was teased, and it's probably why her brothers are so fucking protective of her.

"I read it can be a bit of a superpower. Is that what you think?" Mad Dog leans towards her, and I hear her scoff.

"Well, if being good at computers and killing people is a superpower, then yeah."

"Girl, I'm not judging you on something that you think is a shortcoming. Hell, the opposite, really. I find you fucking remarkable in your abilities to not only compartmentalize what happened to you but in your ability to thrive in the aftermath. The problem is that after a while, shit gets out of the nice tidy boxes that you put them in. Like remembering the other man there that night. Once shit sneaks out, there's no way to put it all back, and there's no way to control what comes out and when. I can tell you love your work, but you don't want to be halfway through hanging a bastard and have a flashback or a shutdown either. That's why we have to sort out your PTSD. Get out what you don't need to keep inside and get rid of it." As Mad Dog is saying all this, I watch Chewy's expressions. Sometimes she can sit incredibly blank like Jules, but now and then, when you watch closely enough, you can see every little thing she is feeling. She blanches a little.

"Wait, you mean I could start feeling bad about killing people? Or I might get squeamish and not be able to do my job properly? Oh no, fuck that. Fix me, Mad Dog!" The look on her face is one of pure horror, and I can't help the bubble of laughter that comes out of me. Before long, I see half the club and her brothers are also laughing along, and poor Chewy has no fucking clue why.

My dad pats her on the knee and she grabs his hand and holds on tight. She looks up at him and looks so panicked at that moment that it almost breaks my heart. Mad Dog leans over and pulls her in for a hug and I'm thankful once again that this man is my dad. He knows how to make everything better.

"She fucking loves old people." I swing around and see Jules standing beside me.

"Huh?"

"Tuesday, she loves old people. I think it's because she hates babies. But you better watch him. Next thing you know, he'll be wrapped around her finger just like Pops and any other random old man she picks up on her travels." With that, he slaps me on the shoulder, and I watch as he leaves. Before I can ask where he's off to, Marx answers my question.

"He's going to canvas a few contacts he has. There have been whispers out on the street about Kraykowski, but our usual intel doesn't seem to know much. Apparently, Jules has friends in all sorts of places, so he's going to check it out," I nod my understanding. Jules has friends? I have a feeling I'll never be able to figure this family out.

Tuesday

Holy shitballs Mad Dog gives the best hugs. But I'm not going to say that out loud. It might upset Pops, who also gives stellar hugs. But Mad Dog's are like Rhodie's, all-encompassing and warm. I can hear the very slow, steady thud of his heartbeat before I feel large hands on my shoulders, pulling me back and out of Mad Dog's reach. I know it's Rhodie, I can smell his spicy leather.

"Hey! What are you doing? I was fine with Mad Dog. His hugs are like a mother kangaroo's warm pouch and I'm his baby, all snuggly and warm." I let out a sigh while Rhodie lets out a growl.

"You need a hug, Chewy, you come to me," he grits out.

He's frowning at me, so I shrug and look back at Mad Dog, whose eyes are flicking between the two of us.

He has a smirk on his face, but he just clears his throat to get us all back on track. "OK Tuesday, how about you get comfortable, close your eyes, and talk me through what you remember of that day?"

Rhodie has sat his large ass behind me. I can feel the heat of him along my back, as I'm sat with my legs crisscrossed, facing his dad on the couch. I don't mind though; I feel safe with both of these large men, so I lean into Rhodie a little and close my eyes. Usually, I'm disturbed by smells and sounds, but everything is incredibly quiet. It's like everyone is too scared to make a noise in case it distracts me. It's very thoughtful of them.

"I remember I had school that day. Nicola Marchetti dumped applesauce on me at lunch because she said I was staring at her jock boyfriend, but I wasn't." More than a couple of grumbles and growls go around the room at this recollection. "I remember going to my locker to grab my spare t-shirt. I always had a backup because of my clumsiness. That one said 'Geeks have bigger hard drives'. It used to crack me up."

I hear a few snickers in the room and Wire says, "Damn right, we do!" before the sound of someone slapping him.

School was a real ball-ache because of the bullying, but it made me appreciate what I had at home even more. I never rebelled against my parents or caused any teenage drama because I knew how good I had it. Home was my safe space.

"After school, Mom made me a snack and then I remember going up into my treehouse to chill out. My windows over-looked the Voronovs. I remember watching them argue not long before that day, and since then I'd been a little more pervy than usual. That day they seemed fairly settled, but I saw them bustling around the house. They looked like they were packing suitcases and getting ready to go somewhere."

"That tracks, Dayz. I saw them leaving the police cordon early the next day. They told the police they had a work trip to make, but we never saw them again. I kinda thought maybe after what happened to Mom and Dad that was them getting outta Dodge, but maybe they were always going away?" Tav adds in. I keep my eyes shut but nod at him, or where I think he may be standing.

"Hmm, maybe they knew someone was after them?" I let

my question hang in the air because at this point we are all in the dark.

"Good girl Tuesday, you're doing good, love. What about that evening? Can you tell me what you did after dinner?"

"Hmm, I ate with Mom and Dad. Tav had already left to go to his party, and he was sleeping over at his friend's house. After that I went to my room; I spent loads of time in there. I read, then did my usual nighttime routine before getting into bed and reading again." I take a few breaths and fall into the image in my head. I was reading "Catcher in the Rye," because I hadn't read it in school yet and I liked the idea that Holden Caulfield hated phoneys, as did I. "It was late, I had heard Mom and Dad head off to bed, and they called good night to me. I was meant to be asleep, but I was like five chapters away from the end of the book, so I figured I'd keep going."

"Good girl, keep picturing that night in your mind. Describe to us what's going on,"

"I heard a sound. I didn't know what it was, and I didn't want to move out of bed either. I heard Dad walking past my room, and then not long after, I heard Mom's footsteps. Hers were always a lot lighter and for the life of her she always stood on the slightly squeaky part of the floor by the bathroom."

"She always did. No matter how many times Dad told her to avoid it," I hear August's deep voice murmur. I smile to myself. That's a good memory.

"I could hear voices coming up from downstairs. I tried to ignore them, but they were seriously interrupting my reading. I figured I'd tell them to keep it down. There's no yelling or anything, so I figure it must be one of my dumb older brothers." I crack a smirk and one of my eyes opens to see August and Tav roll their eyes.

"The voices were coming from the kitchen area. I couldn't recognize the other voices, but Mom sounded scared. She kept saying, 'We don't know who you're talking about! We don't have a niece! Please, just leave and we won't tell anyone'. I could hear Dad trying to keep Mom calm. I remember hearing a noise like someone dropped a slab of steak on the floor, and then a grunt and Mom crying harder. By this stage, I was standing in the dining room. I couldn't see into the kitchen but I could hear better. I heard shuffling coming my way, so I hid under the table." My breathing is getting faster and even though I'm telling my brain that I'm fine, there's no danger, my body isn't listening. A large, calloused hand wraps over mine. I like the feeling of it, it helps me feel grounded. I feel a kiss on the top of my head before I hear Rhodie's deep voice in my ear.

"It's ok, Chewy, you're safe. You're doing a great job, babe. If you need to stop, just say so." I snuggle back into him, his warm, strong presence helping me to relax. I take another deep breath before getting back into the moment.

"My breathing sounded so loud in my ears. A man was talking loudly, telling Dad not to pull any shit or he would shoot him. That must have been Alan. Although in all my years stalking the person who killed my parents, he never once looked or sounded familiar to me."

"That's fairly normal, sweetheart. Your 13-year-old brain has been trying to protect you. It put everything away really tight, never to be thought of again until something recently triggered a memory."

I nod, taking onboard what he's saying.

"So, I'm guessing the man yelling at Dad was Alan because he didn't have an accent. The accent guy just kept asking questions about their niece, and Mom was crying hard because they didn't have a niece. I crawled out from under the table and moved beside the huge buffet we had in the dining room. From this angle, I could see into the kitchen. Mom and Dad were on the floor. Dad was lying with his head on Mom's lap and he had blood on his face. Alan kicked him and Mom lay over him to protect him." I shake my head to clear the images. There's a tight pain in my chest and it feels like I can't breathe. "Alan then says 'Nado, they don't have any information. Do you want me to make them talk?'"

"Nado Kraykowski. We have an ID. Good girl, Dayz," I hear Gus murmur and I feel him gently touch my hand.

"No, I hear the accent guy say, Get rid of them. Make it look like a robbery or something'. I could hear Mom getting really upset and then... nothing."

Rhodie

I want to wrap my arms around Chewy and pull her into my lap. She's done so well. I can tell this is hard on her. She has tears streaking down her cheeks, and she's shaking slightly, but I don't want to distract her as she still seems to be deep in her memory. I whisper in her ear that I've got her, that she's doing so well, that she can stop anytime she wants, but she squares her shoulders and carries on.

"Alan must have used a silencer because I never heard a bang, but I did smell burning and then the smell of blood. I couldn't move, I couldn't look away. I stood looking into the kitchen and I saw Nado walk past the doorway opening. He was on the phone. He was speaking English but I could kind of hear the person on the other side. It was a man. He also had an accent, but not the same as Nado's. Nado was saying, 'Couldn't get anything out of them. They denied they had a niece.' Then I remember vaguely hearing the other voice say, 'Find my daughter! They stole her from me and I want her back!'"

I look around and see my dad and brother both have matching frowns on their faces. The Tombs brothers look similar. We have an ID on Nado Kraykowski being there that night, but now we need to know who he was working for. Kraykowski is Polish, so his boss being Polish is slim given that they spoke English to each other. This whole thing is pissing me off. As soon as we get one answer, another question appears. Suddenly, Chewy goes quiet and still. Her voice is low when she speaks.

"I watched Alan mess up the kitchen. He was moving stuff around and told Nado he was going to head upstairs and look for jewelry. I turned to hide back under the table, but I ran into someone. It was Nado. I don't know how he got past me or how long he'd even been there. I never even heard him finish his call. He grabbed me by the arm and shook me, asking me where my cousin was. We don't have any cousins, both of my parents are only children. I told him that. He stopped shaking me, pushing me up against the wall. He told me I was a pretty girl and he could make a lot of money out of me. But first, he wanted to see what I could do. "

Oh fuck no, please don't tell me that fucker Nado touched her. Please no. My gut is churning at the thought of it. Looking around the room every man in here is vibrating with nerves and anger. Her brothers and Pops look like they could kill, as do my brothers and dad.

"Tuesday, it's okay love, it's okay if you want to stop," Mad Dog's voice soothes.

She shakes her head no, her eyes tightly closed. "He touched my cheek and then his hand went to the buttons on his trousers.

I knew what was going to happen because we learned all about stranger danger in school. He was going to make me touch his penis, and I remembered that penises were very sensitive, and if a stranger was going to molest us we had to attack. The chant was 'nose, throat, balls'. I was too short to reach his nose and throat but I could reach his balls, so I waited for my moment." I can see everyone in the room holding their breath.

"I thought he was just going to show it to me, but instead, he touched my mouth with it. It smelled weird, like rubber and fish. He grabbed my chin hard and told me to open wide, so I did."

"Motherfucker!" is yelled out. Looking over I see that Pops is seething.

"I opened my mouth, and when I felt it touch me I bit down hard. He screamed and screamed and there was blood. I let go of it because I didn't want bitten off dick in my mouth and when he bent over, I scratched his eyes and punched him in the throat. By that time Alan had come back and he seemed to panic. He slapped me hard. I remember my head bouncing off the wall, he grabbed Nado and they left. I'm not sure how long I lay on the ground or even if I was the one who called 911. I woke up after they arrived and that's when you got there, Pops," She opens up her eyes and looks toward her grandfather, who looks as if his heart has been broken. Poor bastard didn't need to hear about his only son and daughter-in-law being murdered and his granddaughter sexually assaulted, but he came to support his grandbaby, and that tells you what type of man he is and how close his family is.

He shakes his head before striding over to Chewy and wrapping her up in his arms.

"Did good, baby girl. You did so well. You were so brave. You got that motherfucker then, and when we get hands on him, you'll get him again. And this time you'll end him for good, you hear me?" I see Chewy pull back from her Pops and give him a nod.

She frowns for a moment and then she wipes her hands along her cheeks. She looks confused as to why her hands and cheeks are wet and she looks over to Gus and Tav before whispering, "I'm crying? I never cry."

Gus clears his throat before he says to his sister, "It's all good to cry, Dayz, but only this once, yeah?" He gives her a thin-lipped smile as she rolls her eyes and nods at him. When her Pops moves back, both Gus and Tav come over to sweep her up in their arms.

Rubbing my hands down my face I look up to see my dad squatting down, face to face with me.

"You alright, son? That was pretty intense" He raises his eyebrow and I know there's no point in bullshitting him. He can always tell when I'm lying.

"Yeah Dad, I'm okay. That was just hard to hear. Chewy is...." I cut off and heave a sigh because I don't exactly know what she is just yet. All I know is that she feels like mine. His big hand comes down onto my shoulder, giving me a small squeeze before jiggling me. "Yeah, son, I know what she is."

He stands and wanders off. The brothers are all chatting with each other in groups. Some have wandered off, probably to hit something. None of us like men using or abusing women, and the fact that Chewy is not only fucking tiny as a full-grown person, but at thirteen years old she would have been a hell of a lot smaller and legitimately a fucking child. I want to go out there right now and hunt this Nado fucker down. But even if I caught him, his punishment isn't up to me. That's up to

Chewy. Godammit I need a drink. I stand to head to the bar, and that's when shots ring out.

"GET DOWN!" Marx's voice booms out as everyone dives behind tables, couches, behind walls, anywhere to dodge what sounds like semi-automatic gunfire. There is a pause in shots and I look around, trying to find Chewy and make sure she's tucked away somewhere safe. Instead, my heart skips a beat when I see her dive over a table and duck walk closer to the door, gun drawn. Her brothers are flanking her whilst Pops is positioned behind them with a rifle. I do a double take. What the fuck? Where the hell did he get that? We don't own a rifle in the clubhouse.

I shoot a confused look to Marx, who mouths, "What the fuck?" back at me. Good to see neither of us knows what the hell this family is up to. The Tombs are positioned by the door, looking like a military unit. My brothers and I are all fanned out in pretty much the same positions, just around the common room. Things have gotten very quiet outside, but none of us are letting our guard down because that's when people get killed. I look back over to the Tombs and the front door in time to see them all look down at their watches, then in sync, they all stand and put away their weapons.

"Stand down. Jules has neutralized the shooter," Gus shouts. Chewy waves Tav to look through the peephole and he nods and steps back, allowing Jules to enter, AR15 semi-automatic over his shoulder, dragging some guy wearing blackout clothes behind him by the foot. He dumps this douche in the middle of the common room before dusting off his hands and handing the assault rifle over to Marx.

"A present for you. May I suggest we take him to the shed for a little show and tell?" He raises an eyebrow at Marx before our Pres gives the guy a swift kick in the ribs.

"Prospect! Get this piece of shit in the shed. Rhodie, this one is yours. Want him strung up or sitting down?" My gaze catches with Chewy's and she gives me a big grin. I smile back at her.

"Strung up Pres, I'm going to show Chewy what we can do."

She claps her hands and bounces on her toes. Her brothers shrug and follow me and my MC brothers out to the shed. Pops somehow has gotten rid of the rifle, and I can hear him chatting away to Chewy.

"I'm looking forward to seeing what this shitstain can do. Might learn some new tricks, hey?"

I smile to myself. It's showtime.

Chapter 8

Tuesday

It seems like it was a lot longer than two weeks ago that I was last in this shed, slicing and dicing my ole buddy Alan. It's weird how so much has changed in two weeks. Two weeks ago it was just me, my brothers, and Pops, and now it feels like I have all these new friends and I'm a different person. Don't get me wrong, I'm happy with my small circle of people, and I've always enjoyed my own company. But looking around at these men, I feel as if for the first time, I'm on the verge of having friends, proper friends. It's so very new and exciting and even though I'm still awkward as fuck, no one has run screaming for the hills so I'm taking that as a win.

I feel Pops' bony elbow prod me. "Dayz, do you see how they have that piece of shit on a pulley system? We should take note of that. You're tiny and I'm old, so we need to work smarter, not harder."

I look up and see that Pops is right. DRMC has this guy hanging from a block and tackle pulley system, like you'd see at a mechanic shop to help remove engines from cars. I look back at Pops with my eyebrows raised. I mean, why the hell have neither of us thought of this before? I shake my head, disgusted with myself. Before I can berate myself too much, I hear the first of three quick punches and the air whooshing out of our guest. The chains rattle from where his body is now swinging. Looking at Rhodie I find his brutal beauty almost breathtaking. He has a feral gleam in his eye and yet his face remains passive.

"Who the fuck sent you?" Rhodie growls out.

Our guest spits a mouthful of blood on the floor before sneering, "I'm not telling you shit!"

Rhodie looks at me and I give a slight chin tilt. I heard it too, the hint of an accent. Rhodie shrugs his shoulders and goes back to working this guy over methodically. I can tell by the punches he's throwing that he's hitting strategic places, places that will hurt like hell but will keep this guy fully conscious. By the time Rhodie has finished, Gun Guy is down a few teeth, his nose is so flat in his face he looks like Voldemort, and both eyes have swollen shut. I have no idea what the rest of his body looks like, but I bet he's feeling like shit. Gun Guy is showing that he's tougher than the last guest we had here. But Rhodie doesn't seem the slightest bit fazed as he wanders over to the table in the corner. I take a peek and see his tools are a lot different from mine. His are a lot larger and less pretty. Mine are very aesthetically pleasing if I do say so myself, but his? His are very manly. He picks up a small car battery and I straighten a little. I know I'm bouncing on the balls of my feet in excitement, but electric shock 'therapy' is something that Pops and I have dabbled with, and I'm keen to pick up some new tips.

Rhodie nods towards Rider, who presses the controller that

lowers our guest towards the floor. I note that someone has put two buckets of water below his feet, and Rider lowers him enough until he's standing in the water. Interesting. Rhodie then steps forward and using a knife that he took from his boot slices down the front of the guy's combat jacket and the t-shirt beneath, not being careful at all and slicing a nice red line down this dude's navel.

"Not sorry about that, motherfucker. Right, once more, who the fuck sent you?" Not a word is said, so Rhodie then attaches the clamps to Gun Guy's nipples, and then attaches the other ends of the clamps to the car battery. The guy jolts and grunts, his head thrown back, body arching and I can see all the tendons in his neck. Rhodie takes the clamps off and the man slumps, eyes closed, drool dripping down his chin. Before he can fully come to, Rhodie has cut a hole in the front of his combat pants and underwear and is busy attaching the clamps to his cock and balls. This is the shit I wanted to see! I look towards Rhodie, taking in the back of him whilst he gets busy, noting how broad and big he is. He is wearing his cut over a black band t-shirt and the tattoos on his arms dance as he gets to work. His hands are large with thick fingers but not ungainly as he not so gently gets his clamps into place. I glance over toward Pops and he, too, is entranced. He catches my eye and waggles his eyebrows at me. Gus is standing to the side of Pops, slowly shaking his head at us. I just smirk back at him before I hear a gurgle.

"Fuck stop! No, please no, leave my cock alone!"

"I don't think I will, fucker" Rhodie lights him up again, the guy screaming and writhing, swinging back and forth. I almost feel sorry for him. Not. The screaming stops and I can see how laboured his breathing has become.

"Kraykowski sent me. He's pissed that Alan is dead. I'm a

nobody. I just wanted to show Kraykowski that I could cut it with the big boys and take over Alan's workload now that he's gone. He paid me $5k to shoot up your clubhouse. That's all!"

Rhodie grabs his face, bringing him nose-to-nose. "Why is Kraykowski fucking with us?"

The guy splutters a little, he's heaving and I'm sure I would be too if someone electrocuted my flaps. "I can only tell you what I overheard. Kraykowski is looking for a woman. The guy he works for, he wants her. That's all I know, that's all I heard."

Rhodie looks back at Marx and they have some type of manly conversation that doesn't require any words. Rhodie gives Rider a chin lift and the pulley system raises Electro-Dick, the douche formerly known as Gun Guy.

"Ah, what? That's it? What type of pussy show was that? Jesus, they don't make bad guys like they used to. Gets his dick lit up once, and that's all she wrote? I reckon there's more in there. Wanna leave him with me for a bit?" Pops whines and then offers into the room. He looks around and I can see that both Rider and Rhodie want to laugh whilst Marx is looking unusually tense.

"Pops, I think it's probably time for your TV dinner and a nap," Tav says with a big grin, although after Pops reaches out and cuffs him around the head, that disappears fast.

"Don't get worried just yet, Pops. We ain't done with him." Rhodie grins wide at Electro-Dick while he whimpers back, "I told you everything I know!"

"Nah, I have more uses for you yet." Rhodie, quick as lightning hits him with his massive fist, knocking him out completely.

Pops lets out a snort, then turns towards the door.

"I'm thirsty. Where's that bar, Prospect?"

All my brothers and the MC brothers chuckle and follow Pops back into the bar area of the common room. We right whatever furniture was knocked over and considering not one hour ago this place got shot up, it is looking pretty good. Rider and Wire wave me over to their table and I see my brothers are now sitting with Marx at his table and Pops is having an animated conversation with the bartending Prospect. I take my seat and look up when Rhodie comes to sit down.

"I had to go wash that guy's dick off my hands," he tells me with a shudder. I don't want to think too hard about what type of dick germs that guy could have, so I move on, cocking my eyebrow.

"So, boys, what are we drinking?"

Rhodie

I haven't been able to take my eyes off the little temptress sitting across the table from me the whole time we've been out here after that shed session. I'm painfully hard and have been since I saw her vibrating with excitement watching me work on the dickhead that shot up the joint. Bouncing on her toes, I could clearly see her luscious tits jiggling away underneath her t-shirt. It was so hard not to just throw her over my shoulder and storm outta there, but I had work to do and Marx would kick my ass if I did that. But I seriously considered it and that thought shocks me.

I've never really thought about taking on a woman. I figured no one would want me with my background. PTSD from one too many tours, killed too many people, and it's not like I've stopped since I've been out either. I mean, we are a completely above board MC, but living this lifestyle sometimes you have to do some more than shady shit, and sometimes that involves taking someone out. We're good guys who sometimes do bad things, and most women wouldn't understand that.

Not Chewy. She has her own brand of darkness that, if I'm being honest, is much darker than mine. However, alongside that, she is sweet and bubbly and such a ray of sunshine. It shouldn't work and yet it totally does. She's so fucking adorable and badass all rolled into one. Wire, Rider, and her are currently in a heated debate about who they think would win in a fight between Batman and Elon Musk. According to Chewy, they are basically the same guy. Before I can get a word in, a hand rubs across my shoulder, down over my chest. Gripping the wrist attached to the hand I turn to look up and see that Whitney is smiling down at me, her red lips glossy in the light.

"Rhodie, it's been such a long time since I last felt your cock inside me. Why don't you come and fill me up?"

I can't believe I ever fucked this girl. Everything on her is plastic, and her eyebrows don't move. It's kinda creepy. I throw her hand off me, offended that she'd even touch me in Chewy's presence.

"Whitney, take off. Find another brother to fuck you."

"Aw, but baby, me and Monica miss you. Why don't you come with us and let both of us take care of that big cock of yours?"

Before I can tell her to fuck off, Monica materializes out of nowhere, gripping Whitney's boob before giving her a sloppy kiss. While this is happening, I feel Whitney run her hand down over my abs. Before she can get any further, I stand up, throwing my chair back.

"I've already told you bitches I'm not interested. If I have to tell you again, I'll make sure you never come back here. No one wants club whores that don't fucking listen," I growl out. I see both their eyes widen before they look down and scuttle off. I'm fucking embarrassed that Chewy had to witness that, but when I look across the table at her, I see her frowning at me.

"You know, you could have gone with them. I wouldn't mind. I mean, if I had two guys behaving like that and gagging to fuck me, I wouldn't be sitting here with you." Rider whispers, "Oh shit!" and I see Wire pull his lips in between his teeth.

"What do you mean, you wouldn't be here with me, Chewy?" I ask her in a low voice, heart thudding. Have I gotten the wrong picture here?

"Well, why would I give up a hot threesome to hang out with my friends all night? That seems like poor decision-making," she shrugs, her giant eyes holding mine for a moment before flitting away.

"Is that what we are, Chewy? Friends?"

Her eyes snap back to mine, and they're as big as saucers. "Um, did I get that wrong? Aren't we friends?" She looks around at Rider and Wire for confirmation. "Shit! Maybe I assumed that, but really, we're just work acquaintances?" She tilts her head at me with a frown, desperate for answers.

I let out a sigh, righting the chair I knocked down and taking a seat. I can see her brothers along with my own brother, looking over with interest. Glancing over to the bar Pops has a hunting knife in his hand that he points my way before drawing it across his throat slowly to show me exactly what he will do to me if I fuck this up. I have no idea what the fuck I'm doing. I'm never like this. Taking a deep breath, I decide to spell it out for her. She's clearly not picking up what I've been putting down.

"Chewy, Rider and Wire and Marx and all the other brothers are your friends. But, um, I would like to be a bit more than friends."

She tilts her head once more. "You mean, like best friends?"

I hear Wire snort before Rider says, "Maybe a bit more than that, Chewy, like with touching and less clothes."

Her eyes light up as she realizes what we're alluding to. "Oh, like fuck buddies, you mean? Why didn't you just say that from the start?"

She looks up at me like I'm an idiot. Wire and Rider can't keep their sniggering to themselves, so I give them each a kick under the table. I rub my hand across my face. Jesus, this is taking all the patience I have to explain what this is, which is a fucking nightmare because I'm not overly sure what this is either. All I know is that no matter how much time I spend with her, it's never enough. And I'm sick of having to use Rosey and the Palmer sisters every morning and night in the shower to get off.

"Ok, Chewy, stick with me. Yes, I would like to fuck you and all that good stuff, but I also want to take you on a date. Would that be ok with you?"

Suddenly, she looks very vulnerable. "I've never been asked on a date before," she whispers out.

I see her look down at her fingers. She's tapping again, which I know she does when she's thinking. I continue to hold my breath and I'm sure Rider and Wire are, too, as they seem to be as invested in this as I am. Gossipy fuckers.

She looks up at me and smiles wide. "Ok. I'm not sure I won't be awkward or anything, but I would like to go on a date with you, Rhodie. Will we fuck after that, or do you want to wait?" She looks up at me with a very serious look on her face and out of the corner of my eye I see Rider and Wire wearing matching shit-eating grins, leaning forward to hear my answer.

"Chewy, we'll just take it slow and see what happens, ok?"

She bobs her head in agreement. "Okidokes. Sounds good. Thanks, Rhodie." She gives me a shy smile then turns back to my ex-best friends and gets straight back into her original conversation. I scrub my hand down my face. It's been a long night. I'm stuck having feelings I've never had before and I'm certain this woman is going to be the death of me.

Chapter 9

Pops

As much as I don't want to like Shitstain, I mean Rhodie, I can't help but notice how he looks at my baby girl. I saw her light up when he asked her out. This will be her first date, so I'll have to give him a little bit of a scare so he knows to treat her like the princess she is. Might have to break out the knives to threaten him with. He's a big bastard and can clearly take me, but I'm a wily old sonofabitch, so I'll find a way around that. I take a quick look around the bar room here at the MC and I have to admit that I kind of like it here. There's a camaraderie that I probably would have liked to have when I came back from 'Nam. Ah well, I had my wife and my boy and life was good. Until it wasn't.

I down the last of my drink, and using the big ass knife I found on the bar scratch behind my ear. I know Tuesday also heard the accent that little fuckwit in the shed had. By the looks of it, no one seems to be in a rush to find out, and I'm not getting any younger, so I may as well go have a little looksee at our guest and see what comes up. I take a quick look around and no one is paying attention to an old man like me, so I get up off my stool and head on out the back.

Opening the door I see Fuck Knuckle still hanging where we left him. I take a look at Rhodie's table and scoff. Of course, everything is oversized. Compensating much? I pick up the smallest knife he has and the blowtorch. The kid hasn't woken up yet, but nothing like a stab and burn to get things moving. I get started cutting off his clothes first because as a man there is nothing worse than having to defend yourself stark naked.

This is something I learned when I was a fresh-faced corn-fed All-American boy shipped off to fight for my country. I sometimes think that Vietnam is what broke me, but I think I was always a little this way. There's no reason a young man like me could make it back from the atrocities I saw and slip back into everyday life without a nightmare or flashback. But then I look at my Tuesday and realize that she is built the same. The things we do together, when we are looking for people to pay the piper as it were, those things should cause us discomfort at the very least. And yet, we find nothing but peace.

So as I look up at the young man hanging naked from the hook in the ceiling, his body beaten and bruised, I feel nothing but the need to find out who he is and why he's fucking with my family and their friends. I have a good look at the kid and figure I'd start by slicing the webbing between his fingers. Using the small knife, I gently and very slowly make my first incision. He comes around with a start and a grunt. Before he can move his hand, I have the blowtorch on him, cauterizing the cut. The kid lets out a whimper, but I don't care for his discomfort one bit.

"Right kid, you made a hell of a mistake when you came around here on the word of Kraykowsi. But you're not just some punk wanting turf, are ya? What's your name, kid?"

I tilt my head a little to hear him, as his voice is so low. The kid is sweating. Good. I need him in this state.

"Bartosz" he whimpers.

"Imma call you Bart. So Bart, what's your surname? I'm guessing with that accent, you're Polish?" When he doesn't say a word, I take the knife and slowly reopen the cut I made. I watch the blood run a little before I seal it up with the blow torch again.

"Listen, Bart, I can do this all night. You got 10 fingers and toes. How long do you think you can last before I'll have you singing like a wee little birdy? May as well tweet now, kid, before I get bored and start using you as entertainment." And just like that, Bart sings like Aretha Franklin.

Rhodie

Chewy is still sitting there with a blush on her face and I like how my chest feels knowing that I put it there. I think I might be turning into a pussy.

"Hey, where'd Pops go? He mentioned he had an idea for booby traps and I wanted to shoot the shit with him," Rider says, looking around the room. As Sergeant at Arms, Rider is big into security. Hell, as Enforcer, I am too. It's unusual for a club to have both. However, given both Rider and I have a military background and protective streaks at least a mile wide, Pres said it seemed fitting. I'm not sure I'm down with any type of crazy ass booby traps Pops would want to set, but it could be fun to see what the old coot comes up with.

Chewy looks toward the bar where Pops was last seen before turning to look at her brothers, who are already standing and making their way to the back door.

"For fuck's sake" Marx slams down his drink and marches past the Tombs brothers, the rest of us hot on his heels on our way to the back shed. Marx swings the door open and without turning around, clear as day we all hear, "Ah shit, they busted me!" Pops spins around with a big grin on his face before beckoning Chewy to look at something.

"Explain!" Marx barks out, but as per usual, the Tombs family seems to not notice his tone. Chewy and Pops are peering at something on our guest's hands, whispering back and forth.

"You get one more chance before I throw you out, old man. What the fuck were you doing out here?!" Marx is doing a good job at not completely losing his shit. It's close though. I can see the vein in his temple throbbing to an EDM-like beat.

"Shit, keep your hair on, kid! I'm showing Dayzy Chain this new technique I've discovered. Anyway, you fuck knuckles were taking too long to interrogate this guy and I'm not getting any younger. I could die before y'all any answers."

I pull my lips in between my teeth and I see August and Jules roll their eyes at each other while Tav just shakes his head slowly with a smirk. My long-suffering brother heaves a sigh before waving his arm toward the guy currently still hanging.

"And did you find anything out with this new technique you're so excited about?" A big grin splits Pops' face before he gestures in a game show host-like fashion.

"DRMC, meet Bart, Kraykowski's soon-to-be late nephew." There is an audible intake of breath. Marx catches my eye and I nod at him, flicking my eyes toward Pops. I know he's asking me if I want to continue with the interrogation, but seeing how this is the happiest I've ever seen Pops, and I'm intrigued how he and Chewy work together, I decide to cede control here.

"Well Pops, let's see what else you can get out of the kid." Marx waves at him to continue, leaning his bulk up against the wall.

Pops and Chewy share a giddy look before putting their heads together. I'm guessing to come up with a game plan. Chewy turns to look at August and gives him the nod, and then he and his brothers leave the shed. Within a couple of minutes, they're back with Chewy's bag and an old army-issue duffle. Jesus Christ.

We all watch in silence as they don goggles. I should think that they look ridiculous. Chewy's eyes and nose seem to be smooshed against the plastic goggles, and yet she still takes my breath away with how beautiful she is. My brothers and I all share a look, but I notice Chewy's brothers look bored as hell, so I take that as a sign that this isn't anything too out of the ordinary.

About 10 minutes after that thought, I change my mind. Chewy and Pops give off a weird fucking energy while going about their work. There's banter, giggling, and clapping when something they try works out well, grumbling when something doesn't.

It's hard to hear what's going on between the crying and groaning, Chewy and Pops never raising their voices to inter-rogate and the hostage himself whispering back as I'm sure his voice is almost gone. In between peppering our hostage with questions and torture, they stopped to do a quick two-step like they were on a dance floor, the only music was the Johnny Cash that Pops was whistling, and I swear the tune was *God's Gonna*

Cut You Down.

All this obvious crazy should scare me away from Chewy, and yet it doesn't. It compels me to know more about her. How can she be so comfortable inflicting pain on someone, and yet find joy and wonder in everyday humdrum things? She just finished blow-torching this guy and yet I know that on Wednesdays she volunteers at an animal shelter. I feel like a lifetime would never be enough time to find out all her secrets, but I'm going to try.

A wet slop to my right snaps me out of my thoughts and I notice that Chewy and Pops are taking off their goggles. The Tombs brothers have already started tidying up, with Marx agreeing that we'll dump this one the same as Alan, so Kraykowski can find him.

"I'm just gonna clean up a little and then Pops and I will let you know what we found. Rendezvous in the bar, yeah?" Chewy tilts her head towards Marx, not maintaining eye contact as usual.

Marx grunts and nods and we all head back in. I hope they found something useful because I want this shit sorted and fast so I can move forward with my plans to get to know Chewy better and the last thing I want is her out there, too busy maiming people to go out with me. It's official, I'm a pussy.

Tuesday

It's been too long since me and Pops had fun like that. Not to mention we also got to come up with a couple of new techniques. The slow cutting and cauterizing we've used before, but never on finger webbing and it seems that it really loosens the tongue. Not so much the pain of it, more the psychological torture of watching someone cut you over and over.

I quickly wash my hands and face before drying off and heading into the bar. All the MC brothers are waiting eagerly to hear what we found out. Marx is brooding in the corner and I have to hand it to him. It must be chaos having my family here, especially me and Pops, and yet he is handling it quite well. I sometimes think that the gruff bossy exterior is a bit of an act, a way to shut down conversations and questions before they start and before Marx is ready to reveal his plan. There is a lot more going on there than we all think. He reminds me so much of August, just with a much bigger family to look after.

"Right, so Tuesday, Pops. What do we know?" Marx starts the ball rolling. I take a deep breath, getting my thoughts into order.

"Bart has been working for his uncle for a long time, started off selling drugs in high school, that sort of thing. He was telling the truth that after Alan's death, he decided he wanted to step up and take a larger role in the family," I start off.

"Because he's family, Kraykowski lets him into the inner circle a little more than he should. Fucker learned his lesson because that boy squealed like a piggy," Pops snorts out.

"Yup. He squealed good. So we all know Kraykowski is like, a bad guy. However, he isn't the top man. He's funded in part by some rich Russian oligarch. Apparently, he had a daughter that was smuggled out of Russia by her mother's sister and her husband." I look towards Rhodie.

"Katya?"

"Bingo Sunshine, you're not as dumb as you look."

Rhodie raises his eyebrow at Pops' comment, whilst Pops

grins and flips the bird back. I swear that man is still young at heart and a total menace.

"Turns out that not long after Katya left Russia, her mother died under mysterious circumstances."

Marx snorts. "Of course she did. What do they want with Rhodie? It's been nearly, what, eighteen years since you saw her last?" Marx looks toward his brother. Rhodie shrugs and looks at me.

"He give you any insight into that?" I hold Rhodie's eye contact, unsure how to word this next part. Fortunately, or maybe not, Pops answers instead.

"Yeah, seems after Katya went missing the second time, not long after her graduation, she had a kid. A daughter. Congratulations Rhodie, you are the father!" Pops calls out like he's on a talk show and the DNA results just came in. I hear Marx inhale at the same time Rhodie bursts into laughter.

"What the fuck?! I do not have a fucking kid. Don't be stupid."

Marx stands there with a thoughtful look on his face before interrupting his brother.

"Dude, Rhodie, are you SURE you don't have a kid? Is there in any way, a slight chance, that you could have knocked this girl up? Like any chance at all? Think about it. You and her spent time together, you slept together, then you both went on your way. No one knew what happened to her and then suddenly guys start turning up stalking you? Even if the kid isn't yours, they seem to think it is."

Rhodie looks shocked. I know that emotion; I've practiced it a lot because it was one of the emotion flashcards that used to confuse me as a kid. Seeing it up close on a live person, it's almost like I can feel the turmoil. I want to make him feel better, but I'm not sure how. I'm not the biggest hugger. I mean, I like it when certain people do it, like Pops and now Rhodie, but I'm not sure that it's the right time for me to approach him for a hug. Instead, I settle for walking closer and patting him on the shoulder. He turns his head slowly toward me before giving me a thin-lipped smile and pulling me in for a proper hug. This feels good, and it feels like I might be helping. I give myself a mental pat on the back. I read the situation, and I didn't fuck it up! Yusss!

Rhodie slowly drops his arms and clears his throat, "OK brother, I can't be 100% sure that I didn't knock this girl up, but Jesus, if I did, that kid would be close to eighteen years old. They're barking up the wrong tree thinking I know anything about a kid, let alone someone who is pretty much a legal adult by now."

Gus finally steps forward. "Well, then we need to find this kid. Dayz, I know you're not a fan of the dark web, so if you don't want to go there I can reach out to my contact"

"Socks?" I ask. I like Socks. We get on well online, have similar interests and I'm pretty sure they're a woman. I mean, a lot of the time with hackers you never know their true identities, but once you get to know them, you get a feel for them, and this is something my gut tells me.

"Hmmm, maybe let me look into all the white hat hacking I can and if I hit a dead end we'll call Socks, yeah?"

I overhear Rider whisper to Wire, "What the fuck type of name is that?"

I see Wire smirk out of the corner of my eye. "Dude, hackers use all sorts of weird ass names. Chewy's is Tombstone,"

"Yeah, but mine makes sense." Some of the MC brothers nod in agreement with me. I won't tell them Wire's online name though. I bet they all think it's Wire. But it's not. It's St Margarita. I have no idea why, but it did make me laugh when I finally met the big man.

"OK, let's call it a night. Officers, I'll see you in church. Tombs family, feel free to hang around as long as you like, and I'll be in touch. Tuesday, if you could look into anything that might lead up to Rhodie's maybe kid, that would be much appreciated. We'll set surveillance on Kraykowski once we dump his nephew's body and see what we can find out from our contacts, in case there's more info out there. Right, be safe." With that, the Prez walks off into the place where they hold church and my family decides to drain our drinks and head out.

It's been a hell of a day and I'm really keen to get onto my new task. Before I reach the door, I feel a large hand softly wrap around my arm.

"Hey, leaving without saying goodbye?" Rhodie smirks down at me.

"Oh, I thought everything was wrapped up. I didn't know I had to personally tell you I was leaving." I frown up at him.

He lets go of my arm and rubs the back of his neck. "I just wanted to talk to you and we have to set up a time for our date. How about tomorrow? I'll pick you up after work. Wear jeans and boots, we'll take my bike. That work for you?"

Holy shit, this is happening fast and I haven't even had time to Google dating etiquette. Shit. Oh well, I'll just have to wing it.

"Um, I have a lot of work on, but I'll be done at 5ish? Maybe you could pick me up from my house around six. I'll text you the directions." I look up at him, unsure what to do next, but off to the side, I see Rider and Wire smiling at me.

They mime hugging, then hug each other. They're telling me what to do next! My belly feels funny as I watch these big badass men hugging each other to help me out. Well, that's before I burst into laughter because I see Marx come up behind them with a scowl and cuff both of them in the back of the head. Rhodie quickly turns around to see what's going on behind him at the same time I launch forward for a hug and end up whacking my face right on his elbow.

"Ow! Shit!"

"Fuck, are you OK?" we both yell at the same time. My three brothers are pissing themselves laughing whilst Pops is just shaking his head in disappointment.

"Say goodbye to Rhodie, Baby Girl, before you injure yourself or anyone else more than you already have." I watch the men in my family leave before turning back to Rhodie's worried face.

"I'm OK. Would you believe this shit happens all the time?"

He rolls his eyes at me before he wraps me up in his arms. "Bye Chewy, I'll see you tomorrow, 6 pm."

I smile up at him and give a little wave before bouncing out the door, feeling light as air. It is weird when you think I tortured and maimed a man tonight, but oh well. Isn't life funny?

Chapter 10

Rhodie

It's 3 pm and I have no idea what the fuck I'm going to do on this date. I mean, the last time I dated was the few times I took Katya out, eighteen years ago. I was in high school, so the extent of those dates was going to the movies and then the diner for a bite to eat before walking her home. God Katya, isn't that an absolute mind fuck? The girl I dated in high school ends up having some criminals after her and I may or may not be the father of her kid. I bet it was some other guy. Has to be, we used condoms the couple of times we did it, so I'm pretty sure Kraykowski has his wires crossed.

I look at the clock and it seems I've been stuck in my head for half an hour already and still have no ideas. Fuck it, I'll go ask my brother. Knocking on his office door I walk straight in and drop into the chair across from him. He doesn't even look up, just grunts at me to say what I gotta say.

"I have that date with Chewy today. But I have no idea what the fuck I'm doing. Do you have any date night ideas?"

I watch my brother slowly raise his head until he's looking

directly at me. "Where the fuck do you think you are? You're in an MC clubhouse. I'm the Prez. What the fuck do you think I know about dates? We don't date. We fuck. How the hell should I know what you should do with your little crush? Jesus!" he grits out.

"Well, shit, you don't have to be an asshole about it," I grumble back at him. I mean, I could have asked one of the other brothers, but this is my big brother. I thought he'd at least know something. He lets out a long sigh while I continue to panic.

"Shit! You're right. I don't know anything about dating or treating a girl real nice. Fuck! I should never have asked her out, dammit! What the hell is wrong with me? I've turned into a pussy!"

Marx puts his pen down and gives me a thoughtful look. He opens his mouth, then closes it before squinting at me and then opening his mouth again.

"I don't think you're a pussy. What I think this is, is something bigger than a date. This is your version of Mom."

"What the fuck, man? I don't think she's Mom!"

"No! Shit, that's not what I'm saying. I'm saying she's like what Mom was to Dad. My own shitty mother doesn't count. I mean, that bitch cut out before I could even remember her, but Mom? Your Mom, she was meant for Dad. His soul mate. I think that's what Chewy is to you. The one meant for you."

I sit there staring at him. Surely it's not that serious, is it? I want to shrug off his words, but I know there is some level of truth there. Chewy is different from any other woman, hell, person I've ever met. No matter how long I spend with her, it never seems like enough. She is someone I not only want but need in my life. I let out a breath.

"Yeah. I think you're right. She's...different. Special. She doesn't make me feel like I'm dirty or full of darkness. After everything I've done, both in the military and for the MC, I thought no one would want a man like me. But Chewy, she sees who I am and likes it." Marx nods his head before pulling two short glasses out of his desk drawer and pouring us both a whiskey.

"Right. So it's serious. Figured as much. In that case, you need to take her somewhere she'd like and then take her out to eat. She's kinda different from other chicks, so I'm going to suggest perhaps that axe-throwing place out on Highway 1. That seems like something she'd like."

He shrugs his shoulders and I can feel a smile splitting my face. "You-" I point at him "are the best big brother in the world. Chewy is going to fucking love that! I'll take her there and then to the diner. She doesn't strike me as a fancy food type of woman."

Marx nods in agreement. I down the rest of my whiskey before standing and leaning over to drop my hand on my brother's shoulder. "Thanks man, I needed that. We'll name our firstborn after you." I run out when I see him pick up his stapler, ready to throw it at me. Makes sense. His real name is shit.

Right at 5:55 pm, I'm pulling into the drive at the address Chewy gave me. There's a nice house standing in the front part of the section, almost like a small version of a farmhouse. I followed her directions, which was to continue down the gravel drive past the main house and around the back, where there are four smaller cabins.

I'm about to take the path to the one with the yellow front door when I hear a gunshot ping off the back of my bike. Fuck!

Kraykowski's men must have been staking this place out! I brake fast, putting my bike down and sliding on the gravel driveway, pulling my gun from under my cut. Before I can do anything else, I look up to see Pops on the back porch with a fucking shotgun aimed in my direction. There are pounding footsteps coming my way and I hear Gus yelling, "Fuck, Pops! You just shot at Rhodie. What the hell?"

Wait, what? Pops shot at me? I get my leg out from under my bike, jumping up before I turn to the old bastard.

"What the hell, Pops? Did you just fire at me?"

Pops doesn't answer straight away, but he does mean mug me as he walks down the porch steps in my direction.

I hear Gus let out a sigh. "Pops, why the hell would you fire a shot at Rhodie? Explain. Now!"

Pops rolls his eyes at Gus and I almost want to hit an old man. "Stop whining. I made sure not to hit him on purpose. Look, this is the first date my grandbaby has ever been on. I'm giving him the terms and conditions," he answers Gus and his brothers with a smartass grin on his face.

"Jesus Christ, Pops! You could have killed him! Ugh, just give him the Ts&Cs and let them get on with it," Tav bites out.

"Fine! If you fuckover my grandbaby, if you hurt her feelings or lead her along, I will non-lethally shoot you. Then Imma take your bike-"

"Yeah yeah, I get it. You'll non-lethally shoot me, then stick my bike up my ass."

"No. I'm going to non-lethally shoot you, then I'll take your bike, ride over to the diner, and take Rosie for a ride. Then I'll fuck Rosie on your bike." I can hear Chewy's brothers all groan "I'll fuck Rosie on your bike and leave our juices all over that fine leather seat. Then Imma wipe down that seat and ride over to the clubhouse where you'll be laid up in bed, with your medic brother looking out for ya. Then Imma look after you real good. I'll hold that sippy cup up to that lying mouth of yours, and when you dribble, I'm going to use that cum towel to clean your face off. That's what I'll do if you fuck over my grandbaby."

With that, the crazy old bastard storms off. My mouth is still open in shock and I'm pretty sure I hear Tav grumble, "Why the fuck does he have to bring Rosie into this? She's a nice lady." In shock, I turn to look at all three of Chewy's brothers.

"Shit, are you OK man?" Tav asks with concern. I shake my head before I break into laughter. Holy fuck, if that isn't the best "don't hurt my daughter" speech in the history of speeches, I don't know what is.

"Yeah man, I'm fine. No damage done to me or the bike, so we're all good." I dust off a little more before I hear Chewy's voice.

"What the hell is going on out here? Did I hear a gunshot?" We all turn to look at her, before looking at each other and bursting into laughter.

Tuesday

I'm not entirely too sure what I missed, but I'm certain I heard a gunshot.

"Yeah, Pops just shot at Rhodie and gave him the 'Don't hurt my grandbaby' speech."

"What!? He shot at you? What the hell, Pops!" I look over at my Pops, who is rocking in his chair on his back porch waving a gun in Rhodie's direction. Looking back at my brothers they all have big grins on their faces, too. Rhodie, on the other hand, is busy staring at me.

"You look beautiful, Chewy," his gravelly voice whispers to me. I smile up at him and try to maintain eye contact, but it's a little too intense, so I look away at the last moment, but I'm still proud that I did it for longer than usual.

I take him in. He's in tidy dark jeans. These don't seem to have any grease stains like all the other jeans I've seen him in, although there is a mark where I'm guessing he scuffed them when Pops shot at him. He's wearing a dark long-sleeved shirt with the top couple of buttons undone and I can see his chest hair peeking out. He has his cut over the top and his dark hair is windblown and curls around his ears. By the time I look back at his face, I see a smirk on his lips, and his right eyebrow is raised.

"You looked your fill, or do you need a little more time?"

"Oh, um, you look good too, Rhodie. I like your shirt." He offers me a crooked smile before I hear all three of my brothers groan.

"Good god this is painful to watch," I hear Jules mutter.

"It's like watching two teenagers on their first date," Tav whispers to Gus, who has a smile on his face but elbows him to shut up. I give them all the hairy eyeball. Maybe if I'm lucky, they'll all head back to their own homes. Instead, they all stand there smiling creepily at us.

I clear my throat. "So, um, do you like, wanna go? And get away from these weirdos?" Rhodie gives me a grin, and bends to pick up his bike, standing it upright, with help from my brothers. Well, I think they're helping. They mainly look like they're getting in the way.

"Your chariot awaits."

Rhodie gets on, lends me his hand, and helps hold me steady. I stand on the foot peg and throw my other leg over the bike seat. I've been practicing getting on and off Tav's bike for the last few hours, as I knew deep down inside this is not something I could master with my shittily low level of coordination and grace.

Hooking his hands in my knee pits to pull me closer to him, my front molding to his broad back. I'm hit with his comforting smell and lean my cheek on his back and take in his scent, in a totally non-creepy way. I don't need this hot dude to know I'm sniffing him.

I feel his broad back rise and fall on a deep sigh before he pulls my hands around his waist to rest on his hard stomach. He pats my hands before firing up his bike, and the feeling of the engine vibrating runs right through me. Yes, it's obscenely loud. However, the rumble beneath me lulls me into a relaxed state. Which is what I so desperately need at the moment.

This is a first for me. Yes, I've had crushes on men I find attractive in my life. However, not once have I ever been on a date with them. In the past, men have approached me and because I've not been overly great at reading the situation or what their intentions may be, I've found myself in some not so savoury positions. Add in the fact that I was only sixteen when I first went to college. There are a bunch of added layers to my lack of healthy relationships with men I'm not related to.

But Rhodie is different. He's a safe person. He makes me feel like my quirks aren't something I have to hide. I like that. I would also very much like to fuck him and this bike vibrating my bits is not helping. Rhodie slows and I look up and see that we are pulling into the axe-throwing place.

"Holy crap, I've been wanting to come here for ages and no one would come with me!" I squeal probably a little too close to the poor guy's ear, but this is an epic date idea. I wait until he's fully parked before I throw myself off the bike in a not-so-graceful dismount.

Rhodie's hand wraps around my arm and yanks me upright before I completely face plant. "Thanks for the save, Big Man. Now come on, let's get in there!"

I grab his arm in both of my hands, definitely noticing how big this man's biceps are, but I choose to ignore the clenching in my stomach. As I drag him into the building, Rhodie is shaking his head and chuckling down at me.

"Bit excited there, huh, Chewy?"

"You bet your pretty ass! Now book us a lane while I feel up all these axes to find my perfect little throwing number."

I ignore him and the man behind the counter while I pick up a few axes to feel their weight. I've never done this before nor have I ever really been trusted to throw sharp objects given my accident prone-ness and the fact that I am not sporty AT ALL, but that won't be holding me back. No siree Bob! I feel Rhodie at my back as he peers over my shoulder.

"Found something you like?"

I excitedly nod my head, holding up the axe I've selected, stroking her gently. "I'm going to name her Monica. She's a pretty little thing, curvy in all the right places and she is going to kick your massive ass tonight, buddy!"

I wave Monica in his face while he laughs at my antics, and it's so nice to see him let loose.

He leads me to our lane with his hands on my shoulders, before putting me into place with my feet on the white line on the ground, indicating where I throw from. Looking up I give him what I think is a saucy wink before I line up the shot and throw with all my might.

I watch in horror as the axe handle bounces off the target and makes its way back towards me at what can only be described as the speed of light. Before I can do anything, Rhodie grabs me from behind and spins us away from my well-thrown projectile and into the wall beside us, my axe landing with a clank almost right where I threw it from.

"Holy fuck, Chewy! You could have been maimed! Jesus! I've never seen anyone throw something that hard before!"

I take in Rhodie's wide eyes and general confusion over what in the actual fuck just happened, and I burst into laughter. Before long, he joins in and by the time the guy running this place finds us to see how we're getting on, we are both in fits of laughter leaning on each other.

We each have a couple more throws before we decide to call it a night and head over to the diner for something to eat. I burrow into Rhodie's body on the back of his bike and breathe him in again. He's quickly becoming the best friend I ever had, and I can't help but want more.

Chapter 11

Rhodie

Note to self: Never let Chewy anywhere near an axe. Also, second note to self: When riding with Chewy, wear slightly looser jeans. My poor dick is going to have the imprint of my zipper on him for eternity after spending the last hour hard and pressed up against it.

I even tried thinking of Marx to get the fucker down, but then Chewy would do something adorable (yes, I just said adorable) and my cock would harden again. We finally pull up to the diner and I'm hoping that perhaps concentrating on good diner food and not looking poor old Rosie in the eye after Pops' rant will help the situation.

I help Chewy off the bike and hold the door open before following her in and resting my hand on her lower back, just an inch above that delectable ass of hers. I understand what people mean when they say they swallow their tongue. I felt that deep in my soul when I saw Chewy on the porch of her wee house in her deep red top and spray on jeans. Low cut enough to tease a little bit of cleavage, tight enough to highlight her gorgeous round tits I can tell will fit perfectly in my hands. She has on her platform Dr. Martin boots, giving her maybe another inch in height. Her hair is out and unruly and from what I can tell, she has very little makeup on, apart from red lipstick to match her top. I wonder if it's the type that would leave a ring of color around my cock?

I'm snapped out of my thoughts as I hear Rosie's raspy voice tell us to follow her to the booth I requested. Chewy slides into one side and I decide to slide in right next to her. I know she's not always comfortable maintaining eye contact, and this way we can chat and touch without her having to stress about it.

Once I settle in, I look down at her to see how she's doing. She smiles shyly up at me before her eyebrows crease and she bites her lip. I'm about to ask if she's OK, but she surprises me by moving her hand the small distance to mine, and sweetly curling her little finger over mine.

I look down at our hands. Hers so soft and tiny, tanned from her natural coloring. Mine so large and rough, scarred across my knuckles from old fights, tattoos across my fingers and the back of my hands. Yet, this beautiful creature wants to touch me. I look back at her and smile as I slide my hand so I can hook my pinky with hers. Her eyes light up and she leans into my body with a little sigh. It's fucking crazy, I'm almost thirty six years old and have had no shortage of pussy in my time, and yet here I am, in this diner, and the most profound thing I have ever felt was when a tiny woman hooked her pinky in mine.

"So, what can I get you kids?" Rosie's pack-a-day voice cuts through the moment as both Chewy and I jump apart, acting like kids caught with their hands in the cookie jar. I even see a blush over Chewy's cheeks. We place our orders and sit in silence for a moment. Before I can get the conversation started, Rosie is back with our drinks and as she bustles off, a shadow falls over our booth.

"Tuesday? I haven't seen you around for a while. How's

things?" I look up and see some gaunt beige suit type smiling down at Chewy. He's either an overconfident douchebag or a fucking idiot. Can't he see she's on a date, sharing a booth with the damn enforcer of DRMC? I'm 6'1" and over 250 pounds. This guy is around my height but a lot leaner. Looks like he plays video games all day.

"Hi, Logan. I'm on a date, so I am doing very well, thank you," Chewy replies in a monotone voice, avoiding eye contact the whole time. *Logan* finally looks my way, and I give him my best death stare. I can almost see his balls shriveling into his body.

"Oh, ah, well, OK, sorry about that. Um, you know where to find me if you want to see me, or ah, anything." With that, he taps the table and shuffles off, probably to go crying to his mama.

"Who the fuck is that guy? Please don't tell me he's an ex-boyfriend or something. You can do way better than that boring suit, Chewy."

She looks up at me through her lashes before replying very matter-of-factly, at the same time I take a pull of my beer, "I know him from the sex club."

I spray my mouthful all over myself and anything else in the near vicinity. Whatever I don't spray goes down the completely wrong way and I'm left beating my chest until the coughing subsides to a nice, manly wheeze.

"Come again Chewy? I'm almost sure I heard you say you know him from the sex club."

"I DO know him from the sex club." She averts her gaze and I see a blush climb her cheeks before she sighs. "I've never been on a real-life one-on-one date and I'm not good at flirting. I sometimes miss signals and misread romantic situations. But

I still have needs and I really like sex, so I joined the sex club. This way I can have transactional sex. The rules are already outlined, all parties know what they're getting, and it's a way for me to enjoy my body and others' bodies in what I deem to be a safe environment for me." She's tapping her fingers, so I let her complete a rotation before I place my large hand over her tiny one.

"I get it, Chewy, and it makes absolute sense. I'm sorry if I made you feel embarrassed. I was being a jealous asshole."

I give her hand a little squeeze and when I go to remove it, she grabs hold instead. Smiling to myself, I work through what she's just told me. "Um, can I ask you something?" She nods her head at me so I carry on. "If we, or when, we decide to take this to the next level, would you prefer if we had some type of rules or contract like you did with Logan?" Just saying that beige bastard's name makes my fists involuntarily clench, but I press on because I know this is probably something we should discuss. "Would that make you feel safe with me?"

I watch her face as she thinks about this. She has a little frown, and she chews her bottom lip, fingers tapping once again.

"I think that when we have sex, I would like to try it without rules. I want to experience it the way everyone else does. Would that be OK?" She looks me dead in the eye with those whiskey-gold eyes and I use my thumb to smooth the creases between her eyebrows.

"Yeah babe, that's perfectly OK with me. I got you Chewy. Remember that." And with that Rosie delivers our food and I tuck into what I know is the best burger in the state. Chewy looks at me with her fork in the air, a small frown between her brows and her bottom lip in her teeth. "Do you want to know any other details about my sexual background before we go any further?"

"No. Nope. Fuck no. I definitely do not want to hear about you with any other men," I reply through a mouthful of burger and fries.

She smirks at me before taking a bite of food and quietly asking, "What about me with any other women?"

I choke on my mouthful and she laughs. I fucking love it when she laughs. We spend the rest of our dinner talking shit and laughing. Chewy has a complete whack job sense of humor and I find myself laughing harder than I have in a long time. To anyone else watching in the diner, you'd pretty much be seeing two people who are into each other.

What they wouldn't notice, however, is that I am well aware three rough-looking guys are sitting in the diner who have been watching us with more than passing interest. I'm not sure if Chewy has clocked them at all, but they reek of trouble, and I bet they're here for me. I need to figure out a way to neutralize the threat whilst keeping Chewy safe.

As we finish up dinner, I excuse myself to use the restroom. With every step, my heart beats faster, knowing that those dickbags are probably still watching us. Taking a moment to splash cold water on my face, I take a deep breath, waiting to see how many of them have followed me in here. I hear the bathroom door swing open with force; the door bouncing off the wall.

I watch through the mirror as two of the three goons walk in behind me. One is a scrawny man with a faded tattoo on his neck, and the other is a beefy guy with a bald head that the fluorescent toilet lighting seems to bounce off of. Both are wearing big Carhartt jackets, which seems odd given the warm weather we are having, but I don't really give a fuck about their fashion choices.

I smirk at them in the mirror before donkey kicking the knee of the scrawny one causing him to crumple to the ground in pain, knocking himself out as he headbutts the bathroom floor tile. The bald one lunges at me, but I sidestep and deliver a swift punch to his gut. He doubles over and I grab his head, slamming it against the sink. He falls to the ground, unconscious.

Quickly exiting the bathroom I come to a halt when I see Chewy in the narrow dark hallway, dragging the third guy by the hair. He doesn't seem to struggle at all and when I take a closer look; I see he has an enormous egg on his head. I look up at Chewy with my eyebrows raised.

"I whacked him in the head with that massive pepper mill Rosie has on the counter. I grabbed it on my way back to check on you," she explains with a grin on her face. "Oh, I also called my brothers. I'm going to dump this guy out in the alley for pickup, then Jules is going to tag him with a tracker and some of this new surveillance tech we just got in. They'll dump him somewhere and keep tabs on him as he scurries back to the shit hole he came from, hopefully giving us a lead or something."

I stare at her in awe for a moment before I grab her head in both my hands and I crash my lips down onto hers.

She makes a small whimpering sound before I hear a thud and then feel her hands come up and tentatively rest on my shoulders. I angle her head, deepening the kiss, swiping my tongue along her bottom lip before she opens for me, sliding her tongue along mine, and then the little minx sucks my tongue into her mouth gently and I almost come in my pants. I hear a low groan and for a minute I'm unsure if it was Chewy who made that sound, or me, but then I remember the man lying at our feet and we break apart, panting and breathless.

"You're amazing," I say, pressing my forehead to hers.

"I know," she replies, and I can't help but chuckle. The goon makes another groaning sound, and I watch as Chewy looks down at him before pulling her foot back and kicking him in the face, knocking him out cold again. She bends and rummages in the pockets of his jacket while I take a peek into the restroom to check on the other two.

"Ah, Rhodie?"

"Yeah babe?"

"We've got a problem." I turn back to look at her and see that she's pushed open the flaps of his jacket to reveal a leather cut underneath.

"I'm no expert, but that is a cut and it most definitely isn't Devil's Rose. Do you recognize that patch?" She looks up at me, eyebrows raised in question. Without answering her, I drag hallway guy into the restroom and dump him next to the other two. Chewy follows me in and locks the main door before checking to see whether the other two men are also wearing cuts.

I dial my brother and pace a couple of steps back and forth, as much as I can in the now incredibly cramped restroom of Rosie's Diner.

"Marx, me and Chewy ran into a problem. Well, three problems. Three guys from Death Riders MC."

"Fuck! What the fuck are they doing in our territory?"

"Not sure, brother, but I'm pretty certain they're here for me. Two followed me into the restroom. I put them down, unconscious, not dead. Chewy took care of the other one."

I hear my brother chuckle through the line. "Of course she did. How do you want to play this?"

I think for a moment before answering. "Chewy has already called her brothers. They're coming to collect one of these fuck knuckles. They're going to get a tracker on him and some high-tech surveillance, then cut him loose."

"Shit, that's a good idea. Might answer some of the fucking questions we still got swirling around. OK, I'll contact Savage and see what lies he wants to tell when I ask him why the fuck he has three men in our territory, and I'll leave the rest up to the Tombs. I'll also call Rosie and ask her to shut down the men's restroom for the rest of the evening and I'll give her a big tip for the trouble." With that, he hangs up. Rude bastard.

Chewy comes to stand next to me, so close I can feel the heat of her body. She kicks the guy she took out one more time.

"We should probably get this guy outside for tagging. The other two can stay here and nap," she says, not taking her gaze off him.

I let out a long sigh. "Your wish is my command, Chewy." I grab him by the hair just as Chewy had earlier. I tug him through the door and down the hallway until we reach the backdoor. With an extra shove, I kick him out of the building and onto the steps below, where he rolls down to land in a heap at Tav's feet.

"Aw, for me? Why thank you, sweet man," Tav swoons up at me, batting his lashes and causing Chewy to chuckle from behind me while I roll my eyes at him.

"Whatever, man, do what you need to do. Me and Chewy are going to head out to finish our date." He gives me a chin tip and gets to work, not so gently shoving the asshole into the trunk of his car. I grab Chewy's hand.

"Come on, Chewy girl, let's go for a ride."

Tuesday

This has been the best first date ever! Earlier on, I had done some research into what is considered a successful first date. However, I instead fell into the black hole that is Reddit and the worst dates to happen to humanity. In the end, I figured that as long as we got some food and enjoyed each other's company, then that was all I needed. But add in a little violence? Well, hands down Best. Date. Ever.

I look down at the man lying in a heap on the ground as my three older brothers all mess about putting tech into places and the like. I had wondered earlier on if Rhodie had noticed the audience we had. None of the men were sitting together and yet they all somehow ended up in the same diner, drinking coffee and wearing Carhartt jackets.

When I saw the scrawny one and the bald one head to the restroom straight after Rhodie, I knew that the last one was on me. So, like the level-headed woman I am, I headed to the back of the diner, beelining to the ladies' room, grabbing Rosie's oversized pepper mill off the counter on my way. By the time I reached the entrance to the hallway the third guy, stocky and covered in tattoos, grabbed my left arm, spinning me towards him, the momentum allowing me to bring the largest pepper mill in Texas into direct contact with this guy's face. He hit the deck out cold before I called Tav for a pickup. Bumping into Rhodie and getting the hottest kiss I've ever had was just the icing on the cake. I feel Rhodie take my hand.

"Come on Chewy, let's go for a ride."

I follow him through the diner and watch as he pulls a wad of bills from his wallet, handing it all to Rosie before leaning in and giving her a kiss on the cheek "Sorry about the mess in the Men's, Rosie."

"Nonsense! I'll not have that type of trash in here. You did good," Rosie says while patting him on the shoulder. He gives her a little squeeze of the hand before we head out the doors.

He gets on his bike, standing her up and kicking away the kickstand. I place my foot on the foot peg and throw my other leg over, nestling in behind him, arms curved around his waist. He takes off and I lean my face against his shoulder, letting his spiced leather scent fill my lungs. Never in my life have I been this relaxed with someone who wasn't my family. He takes us through the outskirts of Rose Grove, building up speed, the wind blowing my hair around us, the thrill overtaking me.

I hold on tight as we make sharp turns, pressing myself closer to his back. I want to feel every part of him. We ride for what seems like hours, the problems we have with Kraykowski and now the Dark Riders MC are unable to take my mind off the man in front of me. All too soon we pull into the long drive of my house, slowly making our way towards my cute little cabin nestled between my brothers'.

He turns off the engine and I swing my leg off, both feet hitting the ground before I feel myself buckle. Rhodie is there, offering me a hand.

"Little shaky there, huh? Sorry, it was a long ride for a newbie. I just didn't want to stop feeling you on the back of my bike." He gives me a half smile and in my security lights I can see a slight blush above the stubble on his cheeks.

"I didn't want to stop either," I whisper up to him. I look toward my bright yellow door, unsure if I should invite him in or what we should do next. Does he want to come in for sex? Because my pussy would welcome him with arms wide open, if that's what he wants. Do I come right out and ask, or do I take his hand and lead him inside? Shit, shit, shit, I don't know. I tap my fingers in thought, and by the time I look back up at Rhodie, I see he is smirking down at me.

"Let me walk you to your door, yeah?" I let out a breath and nod my head at him. He takes my hand and presses a kiss to my knuckles before we walk hand in hand up my porch until we are standing in front of my door. My hand is still in his and yet again, I'm unsure what to do next.

Rhodie leans close to me and whispers, "Relax, beautiful." He pulls back and looks at me with his bright blue eyes, his pupils blown with what I'm pretty sure is lust. He leans in once again, his voice rough near my ear. I can feel his hot breath on my neck, sending a shiver through me.

"I'd love to come inside if that's what you want?"

"Oh, thank fuck!" I exclaim, and then swing the unlocked door wide open, pulling him inside. Once the door is shut, Rhodie presses me against it and drops his mouth to mine in a fiery kiss. His hands are on my cheeks, angling my head to where he wants it, allowing him deeper access. We break apart for air and I stand on my toes, getting my mouth on his neck, licking a stripe from the base of his throat up to his ear.

"My bedroom is down the hall on the right." I wrap my arms around his shoulders and his large hands grip my ass as he hoists me up, which I am well-impressed with as I'm not a small girl.

Wrapping my legs around his waist, I feel his hardness through his pants right at my core, and now it's my turn to plunder his mouth. We bump into a few walls, causing me to giggle and him to grunt, but we make it to our destination. Unwrapping my legs from his waist, I slowly slide down the front of his body, his hard cock rubbing through his jeans and my wet panties on my way down. I drop to my knees in front of him and look up, my hands resting on my thighs, hair a mess and, most likely, lipstick smeared all over my face. His eyes bore into me, his chest rising and falling in deep breaths. His shirt pulled tight across his chest, muscles heaving. He's brutal and beautiful and I want him. All of him.

"My god you're perfect, Tuesday, my perfect girl," he rasps out, his hand coming up to gently rest on my cheek. He runs his thumb over my lips and I suck the digit into my mouth.

"Mmm, my dirty girl. What are you planning on doing down there, beautiful?" I smile up at him. There are so many things I want to do with him, however usually when I'm in this position it's because it's been a request and I've agreed. But this isn't the same type of sex I've had before. I can do anything I want, and I'm sure Rhodie will be fine with that, but I want to get this right, so I will ask if this is what he wants. I swallow before looking back up at him.

"I want to worship your cock, feel it in my mouth, and my hands, and my pussy. I want to make you come and I want you to make me come. Can we do that?"

"Fuck, Chewy! Anything you want baby, it's yours," he growls out, hands fisted. He takes a deep breath.

"Take my cock out, babe. See what you do to me." I unbutton his jeans, take down the zipper, oh so slowly, and giggle to myself when I hear him growl at me. I pull the material down his legs, taking his boxers along with his jeans. His large cock freed, it bobs in front of my face. Leaning forward, I press my nose to the base of his cock and breathe him in. I know I'm weird when it comes to smells, but this is all Rhodie.

He smells of the soap he uses and his own unique mouthwatering scent. I pull back and run my hand up and down his length, wrapping my fingers around him. He's so thick. I can see the pre-cum leaking out of the dark pink tip, so I bring the head of his cock up to my mouth. Running it over both my lips, covering them in his pre-cum, like lip gloss. I hear his curse and growl at me as I look up at him and lick my top lip and then the bottom.

"Oh fuck, Chewy, you don't know how many times I've fucked my fist thinking of your lips wrapped around my cock."

I smile up at him, then lean forward and take his cock into my mouth, easing down the length as far as I can go and then pulling back a few times. I run my tongue up his length then suckling the underside of the bulbous head.

"What else have you thought about?" I ask before sucking him back into my mouth, listening to him groan.

"I've thought about how sweet your pussy will taste, what noises you'll make, and what your pretty pussy will look like painted with my cum." He hisses as I pop off the top of his cock, swirl my tongue and then dive back in.

Rhodie's hands come to either side of my head, running his fingers through the length of my hair, massaging my scalp, holding it back from my face as I work his cock with my mouth and hands. His hips thrust, shallow at first, but I'm not happy with that. I want all of him. Gliding my hands up his thighs and around to his firm ass, I grip his ass cheeks and pull him further into the back of my throat, saliva slicking his cock and dripping from my chin. I hear him let out a yelp and then a string of curses, but I'm unrelenting.

"Fuck babe, pull back, I'm going to come, if you don't want it in your- fuck fuck fuck FUUUUUCK!" Rhodie lets out a roar when I take him to the back of my throat again swallowing around his length and gently tug on his balls at the same time. I feel him as his flavor bursts into my mouth and down my throat. I swallow it all down before gently gliding his cock in and out a few times. He softens slightly, and Rhodie lets out a groan before angling his hips away from my greedy mouth.

I wipe the back of my forearm over my mouth while he gazes down at me with shining eyes, a look I've not seen before. Cupping my cheek, he falls to his knees in front of me, leaning forward and kissing me oh so gently on the lips before deepening the kiss and tasting himself.

Chapter 12

I plunder her mouth with my tongue, going deeper and tasting myself. Fuck me, I have never come that hard in my life. My girl is dirty, and I can't wait to dirty her up a little more. My hands drift down from her beautiful face and move towards her gorgeous tits. I give them a squeeze before breaking the kiss.

"Take off your clothes, baby. I want to see you." Chewy stands. I'm still on my knees in front of her, for her. She smirks down at me and unzips her jeans, rolling them slowly down her legs.

My eyes try to take everything in, watching as her black lace panties come into view, barely covering anything. I can see her fat pussy lips against the damp material and I lean forward, pressing my nose to her core to smell her sweet scent. Darting my tongue out for a quick taste, I hear her gasp. I lean back to smile at her, watching the rest of the show as she kicks her boots off, dropping an inch in height, making me smile up at her.

She wiggles her jeans off and then drags her top over her soft stomach, up over her tits, and the matching black lace bra containing them, before pulling it over her head and throwing it somewhere behind her. I look up at her again and she has her brows raised.

"Your turn, Rhodie. I want to see you too." I slowly stand until I'm towering over her, my pants still around my ankles, cock pointing straight at her. Quickly shucking off my boots, I kick them to the side, my pants and boxers joining them. I take off my cut and toss it over the chair in the corner and I've taken too long fucking about with my clothing so that by the time I get to my shirt, I just rip the thing off, buttons going everywhere, causing Chewy to throw her head back and laugh.

"Bit excited there, Big Guy?" Growling at her, I pick her up under the arms and toss her on the bed, loving the giggle that erupts. I crawl up over her body, gently pressing my weight against her, my hips between her splayed legs, resting on my forearms so as not to crush her.

Smoothing her hair out of her face, I look down, drinking her in. Her eyes shining brightly, looking directly into mine, holding my gaze, unwavering. I lean forward and lightly drag my tongue along her bottom lip. She leans up and sucks my tongue into her mouth and I groan, leaning forward to deepen the kiss. My hands drift down to play with her nipples, tweaking and pinching the tight buds while I kiss down her neck, gently grazing my teeth along the column of her throat until I'm settled lower, her peaked nipples in front of me. Undoing the front clasp of her bra, her perfect round tits break free, dark nipples begging for my mouth. I suck one in, using my teeth to gently nibble while my other hand pinches and rolls the nipple of her other breast. I bite her nipple once more, then give her a lick to soothe the sting. She moans against my tongue.

"More Rhodie, please."

"More what, baby? What do you need? Tell me exactly what you need." She looks down her body at me, both my hands holding her tits, ready for my fingers or mouth.

"I need you to suck my nipples, hard. I want you to pinch them, squeeze them, please Rhodie." Oh, fuck yes, I will. I squeeze her left breast in my hand, bringing her tight nipple to my mouth. I lick gently over the bud before drawing it into my mouth and sucking hard. My other hand works her other nipple, pinching, rolling, squeezing her tit in my palm. I move to the other and repeat the process again. She's moaning and writhing beneath me, her hips working against me where I'm lying between her legs. She's shameless as she works her pussy against me.

"Keep grinding that greedy pussy against me, baby. Are you aching for my cock?" She doesn't answer, just moans and keeps working her hips. I take my weight off her and sit back on my knees, looking down at this gorgeous nymph. She's still gently moving her hips in the air, pinching her own nipples and gazing up at me. I run a hand over my face, watching her. I trace both my hands up her legs, over her thighs, curling my fingers into the top of her panties before slowly peeling them off her. The wet fabric sticks to her pussy lips for a moment before I slide them down further, removing them completely.

I bring them to my nose and breath them in before tossing them behind me. I'll find them later and take them home as a keepsake. I return my gaze down to her soaking pussy. Running my thumb over her cunt, she bucks up into the air. I spread her juices a little before I grip both her ass cheeks in my hands and raise them up. I lean forward and run my tongue from her ass to her clit in one long lick. She squeals and bucks her hips again and I've had enough of teasing her. I lean in, spreading her open for me, and devouring her sweet pussy.

I'm a man starved and Chewy is the only thing that can sate my hunger. I suck her lips into my mouth gently before releasing them and licking from bottom to top again, dropping a wet kiss on her clit and reveling in her whimper. Drawing her pulsing clit into my mouth, I suck gently, then bat her little nub with my tongue. Gliding one rough hand up her silky soft body I find her nipple and tug while I slide the thick finger of my other hand into her tight little hole. All while keeping my mouth, lips, and tongue on her. She moves her hips, fucking herself on my finger, her moans like music to my ears. Adding a second digit, I stretch her out so she can take me. My dick may not be the longest at around seven inches, but he's fat, so she'll need to be ready for when I stuff her full. I pump my fingers in and out, her juices running down my hand. Feeling her grow more and more desperate, I curl my fingers, rubbing against the front wall of her pussy at the same time as I clamp my lips over her clit and suck gently. I feel her getting closer and closer to her peak, so I pull back completely.

"No baby, the first time you come will be on my cock." She whines as I line myself up with her core, rubbing the head of my leaking cock through her folds before tapping her clit once, twice, three times. She's still moaning and I can tell she's on the edge. Her hands are in her hair, her head thrown back, and she's the most beautiful fucking creature I've ever seen. Her hips raise up, trying to make contact with me again, and I line up, letting the fat head of my cock breach her tight hole. Gripping her hips I slam into her until my balls hit her ass. She screams and I feel her clench rhythmically around me as she orgasms, her hands gripping my forearms as I hold myself still. As soon as her orgasm starts to subside, I pull back almost to the tip before pushing in again. She feels so fucking good, and I can't hold back anymore. I pump in and out of her in earnest, gripping her hips hard, pulling her back onto my cock roughly, grinding the base onto her clit. My balls are slapping against her round ass and I worry that I'm being too rough, or hurting her, but judging by her sounds and her moans of "more" I know she's fine.

Sweat is dripping down my chest, slicking down my thighs, mixing with the sticky sweetness dripping out of her. I can feel the telltale tingle starting at the base of my spine as my balls draw up, at the same time Chewy throws her head back on a low moan. Her legs are shaking on either side of my hips as her pussy clamps down onto my cock, milking me as I let out a roar and shoot my load into her fluttering pussy. I collapse on top of her, my head nestled into her neck as I listen to her low, breathy moans, her pussy still rhythmically massaging my cock, her legs still tremoring now and then. I think I've found my home. Right here with Chewy.

Tuesday

Holy shit, what the hell was that? I have never in my life been fucked like that and I can't wait to do it again.

"Oh shit, babe, I'm crushing you," Rhodie whispers, his usually rough voice sounding hoarse as well as breathless after the magnitude 10 fuck we just had. I feel him slip out of me and slightly roll to the side. I'd look at him and smile if I could, but my eyes are fused shut and I'm still coming down.

"Oh shit! Fuck fuck fuck, Chewy. Oh shit." Rhodie's panicked voice meets my ears and I can feel him rummaging around on the bed, then he stops and I can feel him somewhere between my splayed legs. Cracking one eye I look down my body to see Rhodie frozen, staring at my core. He's still panicking and the look he's giving me isn't comforting.

"Rhodie," I slowly and gently say, kinda like when you approach an injured animal. "Why are you staring at my vagina like that?"

He's not saying anything, eyes wide. I look down at my body, digging my heels into the bed to raise my hips to try to see what he's looking at. Is it my vagina? Is there something wrong with her? Now I'm panicking because I want to use her again with Rhodie tonight and I can't if something is wrong with her.

"Is it my pussy? Is something wrong with her? What the fuck Rhodie what's WRONG WITH MY VAGINA!!???" I squeal out and then accidentally kick him in his nonverbal face as I try to get a good look at her, which is tricky because I'm a little on the chubby side and my thighs and slight belly seem to be getting in the way of the view.

Rhodie finally comes to and grabs my thrashing legs in his big hands before gritting out, "We forgot the condom, Chewy! I'm so so sorry! Fuck I was so excited I never even thought. You felt so good and everything that was happening was like all my wet dreams rolled into one and I just, I forgot. I'm so sorry. Say something!" His eyes are wild and his hair is sticking up from his head from running his hands through it.

"Oh, no worries, Rhodie. I'm on the shot. It's fine. I got tested six months ago and haven't been with anyone since."

He lets out a long breath, his whole body sagging in relief. "I'm clean, too. Haven't been with anyone in a while and I got tested the week after I met you just in case. I can show you the paperwork if you want?" He raises both his eyebrows and I sit up. He's so handsome and caring and, for some reason, he chose me to hang out with. I run my fingertip over his brows and down the side of his face, the scrape of his stubble rasping in the quiet room.

"I trust you, Rhodie. I know you'd never do anything to hurt me. Well, unless I asked, of course." I give him a wee smile and waggle my eyebrows. He bursts out laughing before grabbing me behind the neck and pulling me down until I'm draped over his thighs. One of his big hands comes down on my left ass cheek in a quick slap, before he rubs the sting out. I moan because I could feel that reverberate right down to my most sensitive parts.

"Oh, you like that dirty girl?" he murmurs at me, still palming my ass in his large hand, his fingers dipping between my clenched thighs, tracing up my pussy before pulling back. Before long, I'm humping his lap like a shameless hussy and I don't care. Rhodie doesn't either, because it doesn't take too much longer before he slaps my ass one more time, the heat of it blooming across my cheek.

"On your knees, baby, chest to the bed. I want to see what's mine." I assume the position and I can feel Rhodie moving behind me, then I feel his breath on my exposed core, his fingers spreading my lips.

"Fuck baby, our juices are still leaking out of you, and it's the prettiest thing I've ever seen."

God, I need him inside me again, and I'm not above begging for it if he doesn't get a move on. It feels like all my wishes are answered as I feel his thighs against mine, his coarse hairs tickling my softer skin, as he eases his thick cock into me. He's gentler this time, less frantic. Slowly rocking into me, he runs his large, rough hands up and down my back. He never speeds up or snaps his hips roughly. I think this is what people call making love. It's intimate and unhurried and I can feel the care he's taking with my body.

He runs his hand around my hip, up my chest, and wraps it gently around my throat. Using this hold, he pulls me back, my back pressed against his front, his arms wrapping around me, cradling me as our hips rock in unison. Tingles start to burst out of my core, running up and down my body like an electric current. Stars flash behind my eyes and my moans combine with Rhodie's as we find our completion. We sit with me in his lap, his cock lodged deep inside my pussy, my pussy wrapped around him, never wanting to let him go. He peppers kisses along my shoulders, up the side of my neck, to the sensitive spot just behind my ear.

"I've never had it like that before," he whispers in my ear. I turn in his lap, him slipping out of my body. He holds me close, and I nestle my head between his shoulder and jaw.

"Me neither. Do you think it's because it's you and me? Do you think that's why it felt like that?" I look up into his blue eyes, wanting to know if he feels what I feel, even though I'm not sure what you would call this feeling.

"Yeah, Chewy. I think it's because it's you and me. And we're special together." He gives me a big smile and then kisses me on the lips. We cuddle for a bit and then I get up to pee because no one wants a UTI. By the time I come back, I see Rhodie has found the linen cupboard and changed the sheet, which makes me want to celebrate because I was certain I was going to have to roll his huge ass into the wet spot.

He's lying on his back with one hand behind his head, staring at me. I don't usually like people looking at me too much, but Rhodie's different. I like him looking at me and smiling at my antics. Deciding to play up to him, I give a saucy (I think it is) walk around the bed before yelling "CANNONBALL!" and diving into the bed. He throws his head back in laughter and then wrestles me into position, his arm around me, my head on his shoulder, one leg thrown over his. He gives me a kiss on my head and then murmurs, "Good night, sweet girl. Thank you for the best first date ever." I give him a kiss on his chest before snuggling in and listening to the slow thump of his heart.

Chapter 13

Rhodie

I come awake with a start and look down at the woman beside me. Chewy is still sound asleep, but instead of being nestled into my side like she was when we fell asleep, she now has her head on her own pillow, hair all over the place, and her arm and leg thrown over my body, essentially pinning me down.

Somewhere in the shadows, I can feel eyes watching me, and as I slowly look around the room, letting my eyes adjust, I see three big fuckers standing there. The widest one, which I'm guessing is Jules, points to the doorway and then leaves the room, the other two following him without making a sound. I slide out from under Chewy, smiling when I hear her make a wee grunting noise, but then she rearranges herself and goes back to gently snoring. I throw on my jeans and tip-toe out of the room, gently closing the door so as not to wake her. I make my way through the open front door and out onto the porch to face down Chewy's brothers.

"So, fucker, what happened to treating our sister with

respect?" Jules starts off. I can feel myself getting irritated. What the fuck?

"I always treat her with respect!"

"Oh yeah, do you always fuck the women you respect on the first date?"

"I wouldn't know! I've never been on a date, you dick!"

Gus hits Jules in the gut with a backhand, essentially shutting him up. It's around this time I notice Tav is just sitting in one of Chewy's rocking chairs, rocking back and forth, looking troubled.

"What the hell is wrong with him?" I ask no one in particular. Tav finally looks my way, murder in his eyes as he walks to stand directly in front of me. His usual carefree demeanor changed to anger, something I'd never seen from the big man.

In a measured, quiet voice, he whispers, "Do you know how traumatizing it is to be on your evening walk, enjoying the quiet night sky, all to hear the pure terror in your baby sister's voice as she screams 'What the fuck Rhodie WHAT IS WRONG WITH MY VAGINA??!!!'" With this, he lets out a shudder "Are you a gynecologist? Because that is the only reason I can think of that you'd need to be anywhere near her lady garden tonight!" He rubs a hand down his face and I open my mouth, then close it again, before opening it, "I thought you guys were all cool with me seeing Chewy?"

"We are in theory, but as you can see, it's taking a bit of an adjustment to get used to this. This is a first for all of us, Tuesday seeing someone in this manner. Tuesday is, well, you know what she is. She doesn't have many people close to her that aren't us. If this is only short term, we would rather you quit it now before she's in too deep." I nod my head in understanding at Gus. They're overprotective as shit, but I'm glad to know that my Chewy comes from this type of family.

"Look, guys, I get it, I do, but this isn't a one-time thing for me. If I have my way, I'm going to be your neighbor in the very near future." I throw them all a smirk and a raised eyebrow. Tav lets out an anguished sound whilst Jule's mouth is opening and closing like a fish.

Gus, however, just gives me a grin and a head nod. "Come on brothers, get some sleep. We have a little rat to track in a few hours." With that he shoves both his brothers off the porch.

Not before Tav gets in my face once more. "You either need to stay away from her down belows or soundproof this place because I can't handle hearing anything more outta there." He jabs a finger at Chewy's house before stalking off.

I shake my head as I chuckle to myself and go back in. Locking the door to stop any unwanted brothers or Pops, I kick off my jeans and slide back into bed with my girl. I like the sound of that. I pull her into my arms and curl my body around her, and putting my nose in her hair, the scent of her shampoo filling my lungs.

I must have fallen asleep after my early morning chat with her brothers because when I roll over and crack my eye open, it's to see Tuesday's lush ass bent over as she grabs something off the floor.

"Where you off to, babe?" My voice comes out in a growl.

"The shower. I have to get all your jizz off me." She smirks at me over her shoulder.

"Hold up then, baby. I'm coming too. I'm sure I can help with that" She bolts upright before shaking her head, her curls bouncing from side to side.

"No way, big man, I don't do shower sex." I can feel my eyebrows creep toward my hairline.

"What do you mean you don't 'do' shower sex?"

"I mean I don't do it. It's never good. The water is either too hot or too cold. You," she jabs her finger in my direction, "are massive. Which means you'll block all the water. If I'm on my knees sucking you off, then it's pretty much waterboarding because all the water will be in my face AND I'll have a fat dick in there essentially cutting off any air. It's a bloody nightmare. I don't do shower sex or sauna sex."

I can feel the massive grin on my face. "OK, so no shower or sauna sex. What else?" her eyebrows draw together and her nose wrinkles while she thinks. This girl is fucking adorable and I wonder if I should be concerned because the way my thoughts are going I'll be crying over puppies on TikTok at this rate.

"I think that's it. I don't think I'll be a fan of fucking in the bath, but for the right person, I'm sure I can overlook the wet queefs that will probably happen afterward." She stares right at me before both our grins spread across our faces.

"Better run the tub then, babe."

"On it!" she yells over her shoulder. I watch as her shapely ass jiggles its way into the bathroom with a goofy as fuck grin on my face.

An hour and about a dozen towels later, we are both dressed and standing on her porch. I pull her into my arms and her stiff body relaxes against me.

"I wasn't sure if it was OK to hug you or not," she murmurs into my chest. I pull back to look at her.

"Of course you can. I'm yours, babe. You can do whatever you like with me." I see a sly smile play on her lips before she stands on her tiptoes and pulls my head down to meet her lips. We kiss gently before being interrupted by gagging sounds. I look around to see Tav on his porch leaning over the rail pretending to hurl. Chewy jabs a finger in his direction.

"You can shut it. Do you know how many times I've had to see bimbo MILFs leaving your house in hardly any clothes, smudged mascara, and crazy-ass hair?" Bimbo MILFs? I feel like there's a story there I need to know. She then turns to look at Jules on his porch. Before he can even open his mouth, she starts in on him.

"And don't you start. Do you know how many threesomes and foursomes and moresomes I've heard coming out of your place? Too fucking many!" Jules' eyes are wide and he backs into his cabin, shutting the door quietly behind him. Gus's voice drifts over from his porch.

"Dayz, it's just a new thing for us, OK? No hard feelings, we'll lay off." She squints her eyes at him. The only word she speaks is the word "Sir." He squints back and nods at her once before going back to drinking his coffee. Damn, I'm getting the feeling that the whole Tombs family is a lot kinkier than they look.

"I have to go to work today. Me and the guys are going to be tracking the Death Rider we caught last night. I'm sure we'll be reporting to Marx what we find."

"I've got church as soon as I get back. Marx has reached out to Savage, Pres of the Death Riders. Hopefully, we'll be able to get some answers. Kraykowski hanging over us is pissing me off." She bobs her head at me and I kiss her again before heading down her porch steps and straddling my bike. She watches me as I crank my baby, then sends me a broad smile and waves in the goofiest manner I've ever seen. I smile at her before I touch a hand to my chest and then point at her. Then I turn my bike around, riding out of her drive and heading back to the clubhouse.

Tuesday

I knock on Gus's office door and head on in. I've been research-ing as much as I could find on Katya, which was sweet FA, so I think we're gonna have to head to the dark web to find her. My brother knows I hate it. There's so much human garbage on there that it raises my blood pressure and makes me very stabby, so the best way to go about this is to get Socks involved as well and we can divide and conquer, meaning less time for me to add more and more names to my kill list.

"Yo, what's up, chicken butt?"

I smile at my brother's welcome. He's been saying that since I was little. "I'm at a dead end on all the legal ways to find a person, so if you could contact Socks, we can hopefully divide and conquer the dark web."

Gus nods his head at me. "So definitely nothing of any worth that you can find?"

I shake my head at him. "Nothing at all. Which is weird in and of itself. If I'm reading the patterns correctly, I'd say she's had someone very powerful help her disappear, or-"

"She's dead?" Gus asks. I'm hoping she's not because, from what I did find, she was a sweet, shy girl.

"Yeah."

He curses under his breath. "Right, I'll contact Socks now. You go get started and see what you find." I give him a salute, but before I can head back to my desk I hear Gus ask, "Dayz, does Rhodie make you happy?"

I think about this for a moment. I don't really know what he's asking. "How do you mean?"

He thinks for a moment. "Does he make your belly feel all swirly when you see him? Do you feel a little sweaty or maybe a bit nervous when he touches you? Maybe you see something funny and he's the person you want to show it to?"

I think about what he's asking, and it's like he's inside my brain. I have been feeling all of those things! Perhaps it's a universal thing, where people feel like this when they spend time with someone special. I've read the definition of limerence before, how initial attraction makes you feel and think, but other than the physiological effects, other things are going on inside me when I think of Rhodie. I want to know what he's doing and if he's having fun. I want to make him laugh. I have this weird need to make sure he is OK and protect him from bad things, like the MC members from the other night. I tell Gus all of this, and he smiles my favorite smile. It's soft or something; one he doesn't use very often, but I've had it pointed at me enough times to know I like it.

"Well, it sounds like you might be falling in love, baby sis."

I'm not too sure what to think of this. I feel like I should be panicked, but I'm not feeling that. I am feeling a bit confused, so I just nod at my big brother, who thankfully doesn't say anything. He gives me a small smirk as I turn around and hotfoot it back to my office, where I google 'Falling in love' for the next hour or so.

I'm deep in the hole looking for symptoms of love when Gus knocks on my door and wanders in, followed by Jules and Tav. I wave at them and try to refocus my thoughts. I'm feeling pretty relaxed about that wee bomb that Gus dropped on me. I'm fairly certain I'm ticking all the boxes of love, and I hope

Rhodie feels the same. But we have lots of time to investigate what's going on between us, so I'll just think about that at a later date.

"What's up, losers? Why are you all in here? Got some new info?" I swing around in my chair and eyeball all three of my brothers.

"Well, the MC douche ran back to his compound and has actually done little of interest since. Very minimal findings, but we'll go into what we have at the Clubhouse. We're meeting Marx in half an hour," Tav lets me know.

"Oooook. So why are you all here, then?"

They all three look at each other before Gus clears his throat. "How well do you know Socks?"

I raise my brow at this because as hackers, you only know as much as the other person lets you know. "Well, as you know, hackers aren't the most open people you come across. However, I get on well with Socks and we speak most weeks, offering tips or info here and there. We have a pretty good work relationship. We might be friends but I haven't asked that yet, so I'm not sure. Oh, we recommend romance novels to each other, then chat about them." I watch my brother's nod again. "Whyyyyy?"

Gus and Jules share a look. "Well, that would be because once I contacted Socks and gave them the name of the person we are looking for and why, Socks asked a series of interesting questions and then demanded we meet in person. Not here though."

"Well, where then?"

"At the MC."

I sit back in my chair and frown. This is weird. Black hat hackers like Socks don't come out for anything. It's one thing to be friendly online, but it's another to want to meet in person. I worked alongside Wire tracking those girls and finding safety for them, but even knowing that he was working for a good cause and in the same town as me, there was no need to ever cross paths again in real life.

Socks' request is highly unusual in our world. The only reason they would want to do this is because they know something or someone this affects, or they know something that could be dangerous to know.

I stroke my imaginary beard and mustache for a bit, letting all the things I know about Socks cross reference and merge with the things I know from the case we're working on. It's not long before I hit a dead end. Without knowing any personal details like age, sex, or location, I can't knit together all the clues. I have some tentative theories but nothing of note yet.

"Hmmm, I guess we better get to the MC and find out what the hell Socks knows then." I shrug my shoulders, put on my shoes that I kicked under my desk, and follow my brothers out the door.

We decide to all drive in the same vehicle to save the earth and all that jazz, but that's as far as we've gotten because, as per usual, all three of my brothers want to be the driver. All of them have control issues when it comes to driving.

I've already watched Gus win rock paper scissors against Tav, and now we're down to the last round out of three for Jules and Gus. After a heated debate about whether Gus threw too late, it's agreed that Jules is the victor and will do the driving. Thank god, otherwise, we'd still be standing on the side of the driveway going nowhere.

We share our theories, chat about how well the new tech we tagged the Dark Rider with works, and we most definitely avoid my burgeoning relationship with Rhodie, which I'm guessing is because no one wants to hear about how happy my vagina is. And she very much is.

I keep getting pussy flashbacks now and then, where a flutter will hit my down belows, and my brain will go straight to an R18 scene. I'm pulled out of another flashback when we drive through the front gates of Devil's Rose MC and park up in what I'm thinking is our regular car park. Marx meets us at the front doors and ushers us in. I look around the common room and my eyes land on Rhodie, who is walking right toward me, a big grin on his face. I bob a little in place, as I'm not entirely too sure if I should meet him in the middle or wait for him to get to me. By the time I decide to just go with my gut, he's already pulling me into his arms for a warm hug before he pulls back and kisses me gently on the lips.

"Hey babe, I missed you," he whispers against my lips.

I snort a little and shake my head at him. "It's only been four hours and about thirty two minutes," I roll my eyes at him and he kisses me on the forehead. Looking into the room I see Rider and Wire with big grins on their faces, and Marx gives me a smile and a nod before going back to his conversation with Gus.

Once done, he lets out a loud whistle and the room comes to order. "Right. For those of you who don't know, last night, while on their date, Rhodie and Chewy were approached by three Death Riders." A rumble of curses goes around the room. "Rhodie put down two, Chewy put down another and the Tombs brothers picked him up, tagged him with a tracker and hidden surveillance. Gus, can you tell us what you know?" Marx waves at Gus who steps up next.

"Target went straight back to their compound. Never mentioned a thing to his Pres. Pres never asked anything either. Went to bed then this morning texted who we can only guess are the other two that were with him, stating they needed to meet up outside of the compound. We're thinking whatever they were doing there has nothing to do with the wider MC."

Marx rubs his chin whilst nodding. "I spoke to their Pres, Savage. He said they knew this was our territory and should never have been here. He gave no order for surveillance of anyone in Rose Grove. However, he mentioned that there's been a growing underworld presence on their turf, wondering if he has members playing both MC and mafia. He doesn't want any beef with us, so he's going to dig a little and see what his men are up to."

"That makes sense," Jules adds. "From what we saw, these three are working independently. We'll monitor it."

"I'll reach out to some of my contacts," Wire speaks up. "My sister is on their turf. She's a nurse. If crime has been kicking up there, she'll know. Usually, people say all sorts of things when they're off their faces on the good drugs waiting for stitches and shit."

Marx gives him a chin raise in thanks and Wire walks out with his phone to his ear. Marx's phone goes off and he looks down at it before addressing the room again.

"Looks like our guest has arrived." We look toward the door; I'm trying to look around my big ass brothers. I can't wait to see if my theory of Socks being a girl is correct or not. I lean to my side and a small person, probably a couple of inches taller than me, steps into the room, hood pulled over their head, hiding their face slightly. Once in the room, I shove my brothers out of the way.

"Move back, you big bastards! Give Socks some space." I

get close enough to see wide blue eyes that look very familiar looking back at me through blonde hair. A gentle voice says, "Hi Tombstone."

Chapter 14

Rhodie

"Katya?" I hear Chewy say, and my head whips around. It can't be. 'Socks' removes their hood, long blonde hair falling to mid back. My eyes dart all over her face, taking in an older version of the girl I took to prom.

"Hi, Rhodes." There is silence in the room, but looking around, I can see the bewildered looks on all my brothers' faces. Wire has just walked back into the room and has come up short before blurting out,

"Holy shit, it's you! We've been looking all over for you. What the fuck is going on?"

Katya looks around the room, her eyes landing on one of the main tables.

"If we can have a seat, I'll explain all I know from my end." She gestures for us to sit. Chewy sits down right next to her. My brother and her brothers also sit, but I have too much nervous energy, so I remain standing with Wire and Rider and a few other brothers. Prospect is still manning the bar and I'm thinking I might need a shot before this kicks off, but before I can make an order, I remember that I'm meant to have a kid out there. I'm about to ask when Katya looks up at me. She tilts her head before giving me a small smile.

"She's not yours Rhodie. If that's what you're worried about."

"But we had sex. Twice." She smiles wider this time. "Ah, yeah, but we also used protection, both times."

"So why the fuck do I have guys on me wanting to know where this kid is?" Before I can say more, Marx jabs a finger at me. "Sit down, shut up, and maybe you'll find out." Grabbing a seat I sit my big ass down. I rub a hand down my face, my knee jiggling up and down, full of nervous energy. Then I feel a small hand on my shoulder. I look up to see Chewy coming around the side of my chair and then she plants her ass directly in my lap. She gives me an impish smile and I wrap my arms around her waist, holding her tight. Sinking my nose into her hair, I breathe in her citrusy scent. I'm already feeling much calmer than I was. Katya clears her throat before addressing the room.

"My name is Katya Voronov. My biological father is a man called Nikolai Ushakov. He made a lot of money privatizing oil mines in the late 80s, because of this he has a lot of powerful friends and a lot of political pull. He's also a cold-hearted bastard. As a child, my mother was forced to be his mistress. She was fourteen when she had me, and he abused her for years. When I was seven, she smuggled me out of Russia and gave me to her sister. Her husband, my uncle, has 'connections'. They gave us new identities, and we came to America."

"Kaz and Kaya Voronov are covers. No wonder we could never find much on you all," Chewy murmurs.

Katya grins at her, then continues. "We lived a relatively

normal American life, although we moved around quite a bit. Then in my last year of high school," she gives me a brief grin "we had heard word that Nikolai had some people looking for me. For whatever reason, after a decade, he decided he wanted me back. Rhodes, do you remember what I said to you on prom night?" She looks at me expectantly and I play back the evening. She was always pretty quiet, but I remember us making out.

"You said 'I want to choose my first'. That's right, isn't it?" She smiles at me and nods. "Got it in one."

"What did you mean by that?" Marx asks.

"The day before prom my aunt and uncle realized I would never be as safe as they would like. I was officially eighteen and my father had upped the ante with his search. To remain safe, they decided our best bet was for an arranged marriage to an old family friend of my uncle's. My virginity wasn't a bargaining chip, so the night with you Rhodes? That was me having a small amount of control over my life. Two weeks after we left Rose Grove, I was married to Roman Bartashev. He is Lexi's father and still my dear friend. We may not be married anymore, but he's a good man who has protected us. Well, as good as a man in the Bartashev Bratva could possibly be."

"How the hell did you get a divorce from the Bratva?" Tav asks what we are all thinking.

"We grew up together. Our families are friends. Many of my uncle's family members have married into the Bratva and Roman suggested the marriage. He needed an heir, and our families are compatible with arranged marriages. I was also a cover for who Roman was really in love with. Around four years into our marriage, Roman became the Pakhan and was free to be with his love. We divorced and have remained as close as we can be." She looks around at all of us. There are around a dozen brothers in the common room along with the Tombs family. She may still seem quiet, but this Katya has a steel backbone to her.

"What do you mean 'as close as you can be'?" Chewy asks.

Katya gives her a small smile. "My family was safe while I was married to Roman. We love each other like family, but I knew that giving up my marriage to Roman so he could be happy would leave me exposed to Nikolai again. Roman has given me the resources and protection to live my life the way I do. Yes, I am in hiding, but the dark web is where I can monitor everything. I can keep my family safe from there."

"Can you tell us why they're after you? I'm guessing you are the reason they came after Rhodie?" my brother asks. I can see there's a lot working behind his eyes. Her answer is going to determine how he handles the rest of the shit coming our way. Katya takes a deep breath and looks at the ceiling for a moment before rolling her shoulders back.

"After the dissolution of the Soviet Union, criminal groups rose up. My father is a Russian oil tycoon, but in Russia, businessmen, politicians and the mafia are all the same. There is no difference between them. Many government officials are on the payroll or are part of the Bratva. My father is not Bratva, but he is an evil man who's not above using his illegitimate daughter for his political or personal gain. I was meant to marry the son of a high-powered politician linking our two families. When I married into the Bratva instead, that caused a falling out between my father and his associate. This was bad for his business. Once he found out that I was divorced, he made a new deal. He sold me to a new suitor, a human trafficker with political aspirations. His inability to find me has led him to set his sights on my daughter. Hence, why he's come looking for you, Rhodie. Lexi was born prematurely, so to anyone on the outside, that timeline would fit with her belonging to you. I'm sorry you have been caught up in all this."

We all look around at each other. This story is fucking mental, and yet I can tell everything she is saying is true. She is in hiding, watching everyone's movements to keep her family safe and, for some reason, all our paths have collided.

"Has your father ever come close to getting you, Katya? Or Lexi?"

Katya shakes her head. "No. My father cannot leave Russia. He uses his Polish-American contacts. He thinks that by not using Russian manpower, it'll keep his public records clean, even though everyone is aware of his criminal activities. Kraykowski is in charge of the business here."

Chewy pipes up "We know who Kraykowski is. He's a piece of shit. So, are we assuming that his sights are actually on Lexi and not on you, Katya?"

Katya takes a breath and thinks for a moment before answering. "I don't know for sure. But of all my father's men, Kraykowski is the one most willing to take risks. He's been working for my father for a long time and is not above violence and threats. If he gets his hands on Lexi, then they undoubtedly have me, as I won't let them take her alone. My father gets to sell me, marry Lexi off, and Kraykowski gets whatever my father promised him. With me and Lexi out of the way, Roman will be significantly weakened. His family is his Achilles heel. It would be a win for my father and Kraykowski and leaves the Bartashev Bratva with an unstable Pakhan."

I hear Marx let out a curse and all of us are left sitting in silence. This shit is a lot bigger than some douche having eyes on me or even Alan mistakenly murdering Chewy's parents.

Kraykowski over the years has been slowly expanding his territory. Rose Grove has always remained untouched as its DRMC territory, but would we be able to hold it if he had more resources and power? We are a small MC, a dozen men at the most, and only two prospects. Would we be ready for a war if it came to it? I look over at my big brother and I can see the stress lines on his face. I'm sure he's asking himself the same thing.

"Speaking to my sister, there are a lot more violent injuries coming into the ER. From what's been mentioned, Kraykowski has taken over the territory next to the Death Riders MC, and he's expanding into their turf. It's not stupid to assume he may have an in with a few bikers wanting to work both sides," Wire pipes up. Depending on how strong Death Riders MC is and whether they want war, they too may end up being a new enemy of ours. This is turning into a clusterfuck.

Chewy has remained silent on my knee for a good few minutes, but I can see her fingers tapping so I know she is busy formulating a plan.

"OK, so, here's what I think we should do. First, we need to gather as much information on Kraykowski, his allies, and his plans as possible. Jules, that may involve you and your network of people on the streets. Katya and I will take the dark web. Second, we need to beef up our defenses. I know that we only recently upped the security here, but I think Marx, you may need to fortify the clubhouse more, maybe even train the prospects more extensively." She looks at Marx with raised eyebrows.

"As much as I don't want to, I agree with you, Chewy. Katya, how long will it take you to pack some things and get yourself and Lexi here to the clubhouse for protection?"

Katya shakes her head at him.

"Marx, I never came here looking for protection. I came here to tell you how and why you've found yourselves on Kraykowski and my father's radar. I'm not asking for anything-"

Marx cuts her off. "No can do, Katya. This has been brought to our doorstep and we're going to take care of it. You and yours became ours when my brother was dragged into this. We've been stalked and shot at and I've frankly had e-fucking-nough of it. So, I ask again, how long to get you and your daughter here?"

Katya shakes her head, huffing under her breath, then Chewy speaks up

"Think about it, Katya, this way we can pool our resources with Wire here and stay a step or two ahead of everyone. If we have any chance of getting rid of the problem, it needs to be done as a team."

Katya huffs again and takes a long look at Marx before agreeing, "OK. Gimme 12 hours to organize my daughter. Do you have enough room? Because I can guarantee you her father will not let her leave without joining her himself. I can share with Lexi, but Roman will need his own room."

Marx nods his head, then yells out to a couple of the club girls to get six rooms ready. I raise my eyebrows at him.

"We're going to bring everyone in, brother. Tombs family, are you against bedding down here on lockdown until we get this shit sorted?"

Gus looks at his siblings before shaking his head. "You sure you can handle Pops? He'll have to be here too, so we will need another room."

I wrap my arms around Chewy's waist. "No need. Chewy won't need a room. She'll be with me, right, babe?" I tilt my head to see her face and there's a wide smile covering it. She doesn't say a word, just gives two thumbs up. Chuckles go round the room and the tension lifts slightly.

"Right fuckers, sort yourselves out and we'll plan church with all our guests once they all arrive."

Tuesday

People are bustling about all over the place, club girls are getting all the rooms ready for lockdown, brothers I've never met before are all turning up and Rhodie has been busy introducing us.

So far I've met an enormous man named Squeak, which I found out was short for Pip Squeak, so one of those unfunny ironic names and his Ol Lady Tabby, who is the nicest lady I've ever met. I also met another couple of brothers who work with Rhodie at the garage, Fox and Nitro. I'll find out later how they got those names. Both are around six foot, lean, but where one is dark, the other is blonde. I've been told that they're best friends and share everything. They gave me a wink and before I could do anything, Rhodie growled "Mine" and told them to fuck off before laughing.

"Those cheeky fuckers! They know you belong to me. They just do that to wind me up," Rhodie says as he throws his arm over my shoulder, pulling me close.

"That's too bad. I bet those two would be hot to watch together," I say, smirking up at him. He looks at me for a moment before a slow smile covers his face.

"Do you enjoy watching?" I nod up at him. "Fuck, I'm lucky

you're such a dirty girl". He dips his head and slams his lips on mine, thrusting his tongue past my lips in a steamy, and yet far too brief kiss. Sheesh, if this is how he gets when I let slip a little detail like that, I really need to chat to him about some of the other ideas I've had.

I've had a varied sexual history, however, it was always with strangers through the club. Being with Rhodie means we can learn from each other and build our experiences as we go. There are things I want to do with him I've never done before.

I wonder if he's open to butt stuff? His butt specifically. I turn to ask him, but then notice Katya and her family walking into the common room. Her ex-husband Roman looks exactly like the photo I saw of him when Wire and I were doing background checks. He's tall, over 6 feet, with black hair and the darkest eyes I've ever seen on a guy so pale. He exudes danger, but also an odd air of elegance. With him are three guys and I'm guessing his and Katya's daughter. She has straight black hair down to her waist and dark eyes, just like her father. Like her father, she also exudes danger, which I find interesting. She looks me dead in the eye, squints a little, and then gives me a little nod. I'm not sure what passed between us, but I have a feeling she may not be as harmless as an 18-year-old should be. I see Marx come stomping out of his office in his big black boots before coming to a stop in front of the group.

"I'm Marx, the Pres here. I know this is a pain in the ass for you, but because of circumstances, I felt that this is the best call to keep our people safe. I hope you agree." He shakes Roman's hand and gives him a steely look, one I imagine he used on his team regularly when he was in the military. Roman gives it back before a grin spreads across his face, transforming his features dramatically.

"Roman. Thank you for the invitation. My home has been under surveillance and when Katya informed me of her history with your brother, your involvement in her issue, and your request, I agreed with her it would be best to move our daughter here. However, please don't take my willingness as a sign of weakness. Sometimes, where there is a mutual enemy, the intelligent thing to do would be to pool resources. So, consider us allies, and hopefully in the future, friends. The Bartashev Bratva is at your disposal."

Marx gives him a curt nod. "After you settle in, I'd like you to join us and we can go over what we know. This here" Marx turns to indicate to my brothers and me "is the Tombs family. They run a high-level security business and have been working with us from the beginning as they also have a hatred for Kraykowski."

Roman's brow raises at this knowledge. He then nods at us one at a time before indicating his people. "You know Katya already. This is our daughter, Lexi." The dark-haired girl moves forward. She looks around the room with a stoic face, making eye contact with everyone, not giving anything away until she reaches Rider, where she gives a small smirk. "This is my husband, Sasha". Roman indicates the tall, tanned blonde man behind him.

You can almost hear the record scratch. The MC brothers' eyes are wide and yet you can tell they're trying not to let their surprise show.

"Holy shit, that is unexpected," Pops' voice booms out. I roll my lips between my teeth so as not to laugh while Gus splutters and apologizes for Pops.

"Not to worry, this happens to us all the time." Roman waves his elegant hand through the air.

"He loves the reaction," Sasha adds whilst rolling his eyes at his husband.

After that, any tension that was in the room has subsided and Roman introduces his two men who will be with him for security, as it's what's expected of the Pakhan. I watch as their eyes scan the room, landing on me for a moment too long before moving on. They must have gotten eyes for Christmas.

Roman claps his hands. "Why don't we get down to business now, go over what we all know? Men, take our bags and get us settled in. Sasha, I'd like to join us."

Marx nods once and then indicates a seat at the largest table in the common room. Rhodie seats me next to him and then hooks his foot around my chair leg to drag me closer.

Roman's husband notices this from his seat beside me and gives me a small grin before whispering, "Ah, the alpha male in his natural habitat. My husband will be happy here."

He gives me a wink and a smile and we sit while the men all make their presentations. Marx and Gus tag team what they know, whilst Roman sits quietly listening, his eyes darting around the room, taking in everything so far. Lexi stands as sentinel beside her father and it's uncanny how alike they are. She seems to have inherited nothing of her mother that I can see thus far. Once Marx and Gus have finished, Katya and I share what we've found, which at this point is the deep dive stuff into his illegal dealings and his offshore accounts that are clearly being funded by Katya's birth father, Nikolai Ushakov.

As we finish speaking, Roman leans back in his chair and interlaces his fingers over his stomach. He looks around the room, taking in each person before finally resting his gaze on me. I stare hard at the top of his nose, refusing to back down.

"Interesting," he says, a small smile playing at the edge of his lips. "Very interesting indeed."

His words send a shiver down my spine. I can't tell if it's fear or excitement that's causing it. Roman is dangerous, in a different way to the men I've surrounded myself with. However, I don't get the feeling that he's going to be trouble for us.

"Is there something you would like to add, Roman?" Marx asks, his voice even but with an underlying tone that conveys you shouldn't mess with him.

Roman chuckles, the sound low and throaty. "I believe it's time Kraykowski is relieved of his duties."

There's a murmur of agreement throughout the room, and Marx thumps the table with his fist a couple of times.

"Alright, you fuckers. It's time to bring Kraykowski in and try to stop Ushakov from marrying Katya or Lexi off to some shithead for clout." Marx looks around at each of us while he's speaking, making sure that everyone knows what their role is in the mission. I can feel the excitement bubbling up and at some stage, I'm going to need my tools because once we find him, I'm sure I'll be able to use my skills in a little act of revenge. I won't kill him, though. There will be a long line of men after me wanting their piece.

"Roman, are you able to take care of the political side of things? From what I know about Russian politics, a lot of them are bent. I'm sure you must know someone who can generously offer some services." Roman smirks up at Marx from his seat before tipping his head at him. He turns and murmurs to Lexi and, for the first time since they arrived, a large smile spreads across her face.

"Gus, you and your team, including Katya, are intel. Forget about past dealings. We know he's after gaining territory.

Look into new associates, businesses, that sort of shit. See if we can clue into his next moves. Wire, tag in with those guys. Rhodie, you're in charge of everyone's safety, no funny business. I'm looking at you Pops." Thus far Pops has actually been suspiciously quiet, up at the bar. But at the mention of his name, his head whips around, fluffy eyebrows pulled low over his eyes.

"What the fuck you on about, boy?!"

I see Sasha's shoulders shake from the corner of my eye and across from me Roman smiles wide before standing and walking over to Pops to introduce himself. Pops looks him up and down before waving him away and storming over to Marx.

"Wanna say that again to my face, small dick?" I can hear chuckles around the room and Marx takes a deep breath, pulls his shoulders back, and looks Pops dead in the eye.

"You heard, Pops. We have enough going on at the moment, no shenanigans. Got me?" Pops gives him a very aggressive stink eye before shoulder-barging Marx and heading back to his seat at the bar. "Shit. OK, Sniper, Judge, Tank and Switch, I know you all struggle with staying in one place so you're in pairs on the streets looking for all the info you can find. You come across one of Kraykowskis, tell them to fuck off out of our town. Or take them out. Up to you."

Gus moves up next to Marx, giving him a look. Marx nods and steps back slightly.

"We all have something at stake here. Katya and Lexi's freedom, Rhodie's safety, Tuesday's revenge." At this I see Roman's eyebrows raise "So I suggest we make this quick and efficient. Let's get moving."

Chapter 15

Rhodie

"Yo, Rider, Imma need you on Lexi. Cool?"

Rider rolls his eyes before huffing out a breath. "Yeah, I'm cool. Why do I have to watch her, anyway? Can't her father's men watch her?"

I shake my head at him. "They're on Pakhan duty. Just suck it up man, we're all on lockdown apart from the brothers on fact-finding missions, so it's not going to be too hard."

"No, it'll be listening to her squealing 'OH MY GOD' over some Kardashian bullshit or making us all watch 'Say Yes to the Dress' where those brides, or their families, behave like utter bitches to the poor staff who are trying to fit them." I watch Fox and Nitro, along with Squeak, who were all in the room, slowly turn their heads toward Rider.

"How do you know that, brother? You been watching it?" Squeak booms out before laughing his ass off. Rider just shakes his head, grumbling, before sitting his big ass down on the couch to scowl at Lexi across the room. Who I have to give props to is scowling right back at him.

"What's up with Rider's face?" Chewy pops up under my arm and I wrap it around her shoulders. I've noticed that she's gotten a lot more comfortable with initiating touch, which I love. I look down at her and take in her "comfs" as she calls them. Given that we're all locked down, Chewy told me there is no reason to wear 'hard pants', so she may as well be comfy. She's in yoga pants that make her round ass look abso-fucking-lutely biteable and a t-shirt with Oscar the Grouch on the front. Her mass of curls is all piled on top of her head and she has thick-rimmed glasses on. I can feel my cock hardening in my jeans at the sight of her. I think I may have a geek girl kink.

Shaking my head, I kiss her on the nose before answering. "Rider is pissed because I've put him on Lexi duty."

Chewy screws up her face and asks, "Why's he pissed at that? He should be happy to hang with Lexi. She is super cool. She reminds me of myself when I was younger. Remind him to wear cologne when he's with her. Sometimes he smells like old onions." She beams across the room at Lexi and it takes a beat before her words settle in.

From what I've seen so far, Lexi is almost the antithesis of Chewy. Chewy is warm and funny and yeah, she can be kooky and dangerous, but Lexi is cool, calculating, and stoic. The only time I've seen her warm up some is when she's been spending time with Pops. Which seems to be an unusual friendship, to say the least, and now has me a little worried.

"Chewy, what do you mean she reminds you of yourself?"

"Oh, she's good at doing bad stuff for a good reason. Do you know she's trained in three different martial arts AND was also privately trained by a retired Spesnatz guy? That's the Russian secret services. How cool is that?" Chewy rabbits on and all I can think is fuck my life. I'm going to have to run interference between Lexi and Pops because who knows what type of fuckery those two could get into? Although maybe watching this shit unfold between Rider and Lexi could be funny. I bet she could take that fucker on and he doesn't even know it yet.

I look around the clubhouse and see it filled with people. Squeak's woman Tabby and my dad's girlfriend Lisa are in the kitchen, and I know that Chewy and Katya have been taking turns helping, along with the Prospects who take turns on kitchen duty. Thank god Tabby is in catering and is used to feeding this number of people.

It reminds me of my childhood and when my mother was alive, seeing the ol ladies cooking or looking after us kids. It's nice to see my dad fall in love again after all these years, and Lisa has fit in with the MC like she was always here. I miss my mom and always will, but I'm glad my dad has someone. I pull Chewy tighter into me and think about what our life could be like here. Chewy is like a sister to my closest brothers, and she fits in well with the ones she's just met.

Although those kinky fuckers, Fox and Nitro, had better stay away. I look over at them and see they are deep in conversation with Jules, who I've heard is a horny bastard like them, so that makes sense. Tav is so easygoing. He gets on with everyone. He's currently chatting with Roman and his husband. I have had a few conversations with Sasha and if I was that way inclined I'd snap that man up, too. Gus and Marx are both looking over paperwork, making sure everything is thorough and precise. Everyone is where they are meant to be, I think to myself. Even me.

I can imagine growing old here with Chewy, and that's when it hits me. I love her. I love her so much that I cannot imagine my life without her and her family in it. Looking up, I see Pops staring back at me, but instead of mean-mugging me like he usually does, he smiles at me and tips his head. I smile and tip my head back, and then the fucker flips me the bird and laughs his head off.

Pops

It's been a week of lockdown and I've about had it. After the first 24 hours, Marx banned me from the pool table for hustling. Not my fault his men are shit at playing. The same goes for darts and foosball, which I've also been banned from. This place is a prison. On planet bullshit.

I take a swig of my beer and look around the room. The clubhouse is full tonight. Marx has ordered them all back for a break as everyone has been working nonstop and we seem no closer to taking this fucker down. My boys look relaxed on the couches, shooting the shit with Rider and Wire and a few of the other MC brothers. Chewy is frowning at her computer, sitting next to Katya, who is also frowning at hers. That whipped Rhodie is hanging around, delivering drinks and food to my grandbaby and I smirk to myself whilst I watch. That is my special girl, and I thought no one would be good enough for her, but even though I bust his balls, Rhodie treats her like a princess, and that's all I could have hoped for.

Marx is scowling in the corner, so his usual setting, although I have noticed he seems almost pleasant when dealing with Chewy. It's interesting watching how he deals with her quirks. Speaking of interesting, the Bartashev guy took me by surprise when he turned up with his husband. Nice enough folk considering they're criminals and kill people for a living, but you can't really hold that against them. Especially Lexi. She may come across as aloof, but now I've gotten to know her, she's a wee sweetie and I've taken her under my wing. Or she has me under hers; it's hard to say sometimes.

"What are you thinking about so hard over here, Pops?" Lexi flops down next to me on the loveseat and rests her head on my shoulder.

"Nothing much, Lexi girl, just thinking how freaking bored I am. This Kraykowski shit is a real ball ache."

She snorts at me before speaking. "Well, I was dropping the eaves a little earlier and have since found out that Kraykowski is livid that his men keep either running or turning up dead. He's also pissed because he had a team of goons taken out by my dad's men when they tried to break into the apartment we stay in when we're in the city. Oh, and according to what I overheard Wire telling Marx," we look at each other and grin at that "he has men routinely driving past the clubhouse watching us. Dark sedan, comes by every half hour or so."

I stroke my chin and beard for a moment. "Hmmmmm, it sounds like he's getting sloppy and maybe a little impatient. Good work, Lexi girl. You keep the info coming and I'll keep making you that special hot chocolate you like so much."

She grins at me before stating her terms. "Or you can teach me some sweet moves. You know I've been trained by former Spesnatz and I'm good for most forms of bodily harm, but I need more subtle techniques. Like the ability to paralyze with the least amount of bodily damage," I look down at her and remember why I've taken a shine to this kid. She's Tuesday 2.0.

"OK. Keep bringing me info like that and we'll meet first

thing tomorrow morning for a quick lesson, yeah?" She smiles big and hops up off the couch with far more energy and finesse than I've ever had. While she flounces off to do some high-level lurking and listening, which I must say the kid is damn good at, I have a bit of a plan forming. I take another look around the room and everyone seems to be preoccupied. Heading up to my room, I grab everything I'll need and even some stuff I may not. I wander back toward the common room but slide out the side door and head to the gates. The prospect, Richie, is on and he's a nice kid and all, but if he was the sharpest tool in the shed, he'd be a hammer. Maybe I'll suggest that as his road name if he ever patches in.

"Hey Pops, you know you're not meant to be out here."

"I know, kid, but I had a bit of an idea, so I'm gonna go do that."

"Ah, you know I can't let you do that. I can't let anyone out or in. Prez's orders. Head on back inside, yeah? If you need anything, I can get James to pick it up when he does the next town run."

"Not gonna work for me, kid. This is something I have to do alone." The whole time he's been talking to me, I've been backing up to the fence on the far side of the guard shack, away from the front gate, and this dumbass has been following me the whole way. Once we are in the perfect spot, I handcuff him to the fence.

"Fuck, Pops! Let me out! This is bullshit! What the hell are you doing anyway?!" He yells after me as I hit the opener and leave through the front gate. I turn back to the poor kid, give him my best smile and wink.

"I'm going to get myself kidnapped, young buck. Catch you on the rebound!"

And with that, I whistle as I wander off down the road, waiting for the black sedan that's going to stop by and give a kindly old man a ride to town.

Chapter 16

Gus

We've been at this for a week now, and it feels like we are no closer to getting this shit done. Tuesday and Katya have been trawling the dark web non-stop looking for any mention of Kraykowski and what seem to be his never-ending business deals. From what we know so far, he has slowly been gaining territory, squeezing innocent, hard-working people for protection costs with the men that he's planted in their neighborhoods.

To begin with, we thought he was just a mid-level criminal until Tuesday and Katya found out that his business has many levels. Can't afford the protection costs this month? You're taken away from your business and used as free labor in one of his other territories. That way, his slaves can't access family and friends for help. Innocent men and women have been put to work in his drug operations or his brothels. Katya's father, Ushakov, may have provided the capital to get Kraykowski started and currently pays him well for other private work, however, it seems that Kraykowski may have plans to eliminate

Ushakov completely. Especially with the intel that the girls have discovered. From emails they've hacked, it seems that things may not all be happy between the two.

I rub my hand down my face and look around the room. Everyone seems to be having some downtime and yet I feel wired.

"Marx, I've gotta get outta here for a bit. I know we're on lockdown, but I need to take a break and think some shit through. Anything need doing in town?" Marx looks at me for a beat too long before nodding.

"Yeah, apparently Roman has an intel guy, Petrov. Old school, as in completely analog. He has a packet of information that we may need, dropped it at Roman's home office. Roman doesn't want anyone from his inner circle to deliver it to us, as he doesn't want them compromised or hurt." I raise an eyebrow at this. Surely working for the Bratva it's a common occurrence to be compromised or hurt, especially after the attack on his city apartment, but who am I to judge?

"You want me to pick it up?"

He looks at me before tipping his head. "Yeah, but be careful. We don't know what's in the package or what we're dealing with. Roman's secretary is there guarding the information. According to him, she's probably more dangerous than anyone that may want to get their hands on it."

I give him a nod and head towards the door. I get his apprehension. Unlike him and a lot of his men, I don't have a military background. What I have is a protective streak a mile wide. You don't come out of what happened to my family unscathed. Since my parents' deaths, it's been my sole mission to keep my family and others safe. I look around for Pops to let him know I'm heading out, but I can't see him in the common room, so perhaps he's headed for an afternoon nap or something.

I give Tuesday a chin lift and nod my head towards the door. She sends me her signature goofy wave as I grab my keys and head out to my SUV. I see the prospect kid has already opened the gate for me, so I settle in for the hour-long drive.

Turning onto the tree-lined streets of the gated community, I key in the code that Roman texted me and nod to the security guard before driving past him. A glance around reveals many of the houses back onto sections of woodland, the perfect spot for attackers to hide out and gain access.

As I pull up to the second guard shack stationed at the entrance to Roman's property, I keep my gaze on him while giving him my business. Marx told me that Roman had already informed his secretary of my arrival, so this should be smooth sailing, but something feels a little off with this guard. His gaze is darting around, and he seems jumpy. I can feel it creeping up the back of my neck and I need to keep an eye on my surroundings. He waves me through and I park in front of a sprawling mansion, admiring how much crime really does pay, before pressing the intercom and stating my name.

An older man opens the door almost immediately and ushers me through the foyer and into what I'm guessing is Roman's home office. Standing to the side of what I assume is Roman's desk is a short woman. She has big tits, thick thighs encased in black business pants, black hair pulled into a low ponytail at the back of her head, stunning green eyes, and a killer frown on her face. Fuck me, I think I just fell in love.

Tuesday

I stop working on my computer to take off my specs and give my eyes a rub. I try not to make it too obvious, otherwise Rhodie will be all over me to take a break, have a nap, or feed me a snack for the 100th time today. It's really sweet but I have a task I need to do and stopping for anything will ruin my flow.

Katya, Wire, and I have been at this for a week now and we seem to keep running into dead ends. We know a ton more about his business than we did before, but nothing is throwing up his location, just the location of his minions, and given that the brothers that are out trawling the streets have "dispatched" a few of these men and Kraykowski hasn't retaliated at all, shows me he doesn't care about the men lower down the totem pole. I glance around the room and note that Gus still isn't back from wherever he disappeared. I plop down on the couch next to Tav.

"Have you seen Gus? I saw him leave a few hours ago, but I haven't seen him come back."

Tav looks around the room. "Nah sorry, sis. I didn't even know he'd left. We're on lockdown, so whatever he is doing must be important. He'll be fine." I know he will be. He's a badass, but with everything going on, I'm feeling a little unsettled not having eyes on my people.

I watch Roman stand and head toward Marx. He moves fluidly across the room, much like a panther. I watch him lean in towards Marx. Whatever he has just said has Marx's head snap up, and he mouths the word "Fuck" before rubbing a hand down his face. I feel a large hand land on my shoulder, and I already know that it's Rhodie.

Somehow, it's like my body knows when he's near. I don't think I have any type of sixth sense. I think somehow, probably due to continued sexual relations, my body is sensitive to his pheromones, so I have this new awareness. I make a note to do some research into this once everything calms down. Before I can turn to Rhodie to share my thoughts, Marx bangs his fist on the table a couple of times.

"Right, listen up. Gus left to pick up a package from Roman's secretary at his country home office. They've been ambushed and took off into the woodland. They've only just now got word out to us. Chewy, can you pull up any security footage from Roman's?"

Rhodie plops my laptop on my lap so I don't have to move from Tav's side. I work as fast as I can; I need to know my brother is safe. Roman's security network throws up screens from numerous cameras around his house and holy shit, does this man have full coverage.

"The woodland that backs onto my home is part of the National Forest. You go far enough, you end up in Louisiana. They'll be fine in there until we can get to them. Your brother is ex-military, no?"

Tav lets out a snort. "Nope. We're townies. If Kraykowski's men don't kill him, a night in the woods might."

"That is not ideal. Thankfully Ana has outdoor knowledge, so they will be fine for a time. She knows where I have placed cameras in the woodland. If we're lucky, she'll lead them that way so we will have eyes on them at all times."

"Got them!" I pull the footage up on the common room big screen so we can all see what's happening.

"What the hell are they doing?" Wire asks, his head tipped sideways.

"Is that lady hitting him?" Jules squints at the footage on the screen. We watch as a short woman hits my brother with a switch and then watch as he turns to storm off but stumbles on a tree root. We then watch as the short woman places her hands on her hips and shakes her head at him, then gesticulates wildly. Obviously, they've shaken whoever was chasing them. Man, my brother is really shit in nature. We continue watching everything unfold and then Roman's phone goes off. He grins down at it and puts on the speaker function.

"We need extraction ASAP. We've lost the two tracking us, however, there were at least six others at the house, unsure how long it'll be before they venture into the woodland to draw us out."

Everyone within earshot shoots each other confused looks. That is not the accent any of us were expecting. Roman grins wider before raising a brow at Marx.

"I have four men riding in who will be with you in about 10 minutes. Think you can wait that long?" Marx rasps out.

"I can wait 10 minutes. I don't know if this big bastard can." We then hear whisper bickering in the background and we can't help but laugh. This must be killing Gus. I backhand my brother.

"Tav, go get Pops. He's going to love this shit. Gus's big ass is being handed to him by that little lady." I feel him move away from me, but I'm not looking away from this shit because it's comedy gold. Everyone in the clubhouse has eyes glued to the big screen.

"Who knew that Gus was completely useless in the wild?" Rhodie states as he takes Tav's place on the couch and throws his big arm around my shoulders.

"Ah, guys, has anyone seen Pops?" All heads swivel towards

the puzzled look on Tav's face and then to the murderous look on Marx's face.

He slowly lifts his phone to his ear and waits a beat before growling, "Wire! Check footage for any sign of Pops."

Within moments, he's running out of his room and out the door.

"Everyone stay here!" Marx barks before following with Rhodie and Rider.

I look back at the big screen and then notice from the corner of my eye Roman looking at me intently. He moves panther-like across the room until he is standing in front of me.

"Tuesday, would you mind if I sit?" I shake my head and he takes a seat a respectable distance from me. I wait for whatever he wants to say.

"I have admired your work ethic and your dedication to the cause."

"Um, OK."

"I have been thinking that you are the exact type of person that I need in my organization. How much would it cost me to secure your services?" He tilts his head and smiles a pleasant smile.

"Oh, you'll have to talk to Gus or Jules. They handle our accounts, so they'll let you know."

"I think you misunderstand. How much for you to perma-nently and exclusively join my organization?" I shake my head at him, slightly speechless. I could never leave my brothers to work for the Bratva. Would I lend them my services? Absolutely. But I could never work anywhere my brothers weren't, and I tell Roman this. My future comprises my Pops, my brothers, and now Rhodie and his brothers.

"I'll leave you to think about it. I think that between my

business and your skills, we could come to a very lucrative arrangement."

"No, it's OK." I smile up at him so he doesn't think I'm abrupt or rude. He gives me an odd look before the door slams open and Marx storms in with Rhodie, Rider, and a sheepish-looking prospect. I share a look with Tav and Jules and know this has Pops written all over it. The only other person who doesn't look overly pissed or concerned is Lexi. How interesting.

"So, it seems Pops has set off on his goddamned own on a mission to be kidnapped by the fucking car that has been doing drive-bys all damn week!" I'm trying really hard not to laugh as Marx runs his giant paw of a hand over his face and tries to control his breathing.

"So, I have a compound full of people; MC, security specialists, and Bratva all working together to bring down this motherfucker. All listening to instructions and fulfilling their roles, like Gus, who was given instructions to retrieve a package and has now found himself waiting for extraction - Roman, we're bringing your secretary in with him for safety," Roman gives a swift nod at this information. "- everyone working together while the oldest fucker in this clubhouse, has waltzed off into the sunset to lure a fucking criminal. Prospect! I need a drink." He stomps to the bar, throws back a shot, then taps for another. Once this one has gone down the hatch, he turns around to look at my brothers and me.

"We'll get him back. Trust me. We'll deal with Gus first, then Pops. Collect all the addresses that Kraykowsi frequents so we can make a start."

"You know, I'm sure Pops will be fine for a while. I wouldn't worry too much about him if I were you," Tav manages to get out around his smirk.

Marx and Roman both raise their eyebrows at our nonchalance over our grandfather's actions, but we seriously aren't worried. Rhodie seems to be more concerned than we are.

"You gonna be OK, baby? I know you and Pops are close." Rhodie pulls me into his warm embrace after kissing my temple. I snuggle in because it feels so nice, and then speak directly into his chest.

"He'll be fine, babe. Pops is tougher than a cheap steak."

He snorts beneath me. "Did you just call me babe?" I nod, with my face still in his chest. The name feels odd, but it's something I've seen and heard other couples say and I want to try it out.

"I'm trying something new."

"I like it, Chewy. Keep it up." I smile to myself and snuggle in. I hear a rumble of bikes and before too long Rhodie's brothers Sniper, Judge, Tank, and Switch walk in, with Gus and Roman's secretary in tow. I walk over to my brother and he puts his arm around me and pulls me to his side. He smells like pine and outside fresh air and I giggle to myself when I remember what he's been through.

"Everyone, this is my most trusted friend and secretary, Ana Adams." I smile and wave to her and I'm pretty certain I hear my brother mutter "pain in the ass" under his breath. Well, well, well. Isn't this an interesting turn of events? She smiles back at everyone, tips her head and says hello. She's incredibly pretty, with dark hair, and tanned skin, around the same height as me, and built similarly but much classier in her business attire, and weirdly enough, hiking boots. She acknowledges us and then Wire asks the million-dollar question,

"What accent is that?"

She smiles up at him and then whips her head in Gus's

direction when we all hear an audible growl from him. She scowls before turning back and smiling. "It's a New Zealand accent."

"Wait, like Lord of the Rings New Zealand? What's your house look like? Is yours built into the hills?" Rider asks, eyes as wide as saucers.

She looks him directly in the eye and answers. "Yes. We all live in tiny houses carved into the hills. I'm actually from Hobbiton myself. I'm the tallest person in my family." Rider's eyes get even bigger, and I see Lexi roll her eyes at him.

"Wait, really?"

"No. We have normal houses, dude. What is it with Americans asking me that?" She turns towards Roman, shaking her head as everyone gives Rider shit about his lack of international knowledge.

Ana untucks and pulls up her blouse, revealing a thick, plain manila envelope tucked into the top of her trousers and hands it over to Roman.

"This is what Petrov delivered. According to him, this is Kraykowski's shot at the big time and the best chance you have to find him."

Marx motions Roman into his office with the package while Gus places a gentle hand on Ana's lower back and motions for her to follow him to the bar. Wire plops down on the couch sandwiching me between him and Rhodie.

"So Rider, a big fan of the Hobbit, huh?"

Chapter 17

Rhodie

It's been half an hour since Marx and Roman went into his office. Gus finally joined them after settling Ana with a drink and giving all the men in the room the stink eye. I think he has designs on that woman and I think she thinks he's an idiot. I also think she's seriously cock blocking me. She's stolen Chewy away from me and they're sitting up at the bar with Katya and Roman's husband Sasha, drinking and having animated conversations.

I had plans to take my woman up to my room to decompress and have a bit of fun, seeing as there isn't much we can do right at this minute. Oddly, neither she nor her brothers seem to be panicked about the fact that Pops has gone and gotten himself kidnapped. If I'm being honest, I'm not either. I have a feeling that he's out there, causing all sorts of problems for Kraykowksi and his men.

Looking back over at my woman I hope that this little girls' night will wrap up soon. She's been in my space for a week now and I've learnt that after a lot of time spent either concentrating on her tasks, or with people, she gets really tired.

"You know, you making moony eyes over here is making you look pussy whipped." I scowl at Jules whilst Tav and my MC brothers snicker.

"Fuck you. Just because you don't have a good woman waiting for you. Go rain on some other poor bastard's parade."

Jules smirks before he slaps me on the shoulder. "Don't need a good woman. Fox and Nitro invited me to a sweet little party with some club girls. That, to me, sounds like a hell of a good time."

Tav looks over at Fox and Nitro and the three club girls they're standing with while we watch Jules make his way over. I raise my brows at him.

"Too young for me." He shrugs before heading over to the pool table. I swing my head to look at Rider and Wire. The youngest club girl we have is probably not much younger than him.

"I'd love to be that family's therapist," Wire states while tipping his beer back.

Stomping comes from the direction of Marx's office before our three fearless leaders emerge from the hall.

"Chewy, Katya, Wire, I need you all to look into these names." Marx hands them a piece of paper, each with a list of names. They all sit at the long table, laptops open. I have to admit, it looks impressive. Gus is over at the bar whispering to Ana and I see her scowl at him in full force.

"$50 says that tension is sexual," Rider pipes up.

"$100 says he's the next guy that's pussy whipped," I smirk back.

"OK. Most of the names on my list have all gone missing from their homes over the past few weeks. They're from Rose

Grove and the next two towns over," Chewy announces to the room.

"Mine is the same," Katya says in her quiet voice. Marx looks over at Wire, who nods in agreement with the others. Roman remains quiet, but I can see he's watching everything play out intently.

"Where did you get these lists and what do they have to do with Kraykowski?" Katya asks

"The names we gave you are women who feature in this book, including pictures, all their physical stats, and reserves," Gus informs us.

"How come we haven't found any of this through all the research we've done? There's no mention of any of these people on the darknet," Katya asks the room.

Roman nods his head. "My contact Petrov is old school, only deals in information not on the internet. Word of mouth, hard copy, old school spy. Could be why it's been so hard to pin Kraykowski down; he's keeping the big business offline."

"Wait, back up a minute. The delivery was a book. Are you saying Kraykowski has, like, a catalog of women for sale?" Ana scowls from the bar.

"But not all the women on the list have gone missing. According to this, some women are still safe and sound. Like this one, she clocked into work as per usual," Chewy states.

"How in the hell do you know that?" Roman asks. Chewy just smiles up at him and shrugs her shoulders.

"Tuesday, I'd really like you to rethink the offer of working for me." Everyone glares at him. Chewy is ours. She just shakes her head back at him and he lets out a long sigh. Marx's obnoxiously loud ringtone goes off and he, as per usual, yells into it, "Yeah?" Whoever it is causes Marx to stiffen up for a moment. "Wasn't us. We have no beef with you. What's her name? Yeah, let me look into it and I'll get back to you." Marx scrubs his face with both of his hands while we wait for whatever he needs to tell us.

"That was Savage, Death Riders' Pres. His woman has just been taken. You guys, any of you have Naomi Knight on your list?" Katya puts her hand up like she's at school. The room is quiet and I can see Chewy doing her thinking fingers. I head over, stand behind her with my big rough hands on her shoulders, and press down a little. I've found that she likes the feeling of pressure, it seems to not only help her think but also seems to stop any meltdowns.

"She was on the list but hadn't been taken until just now. That means the women on the list that haven't gone missing are about to." She looks up at me with worry in her eyes.

"It's a fucking shopping list. Are there more women on the list that we haven't checked on yet?" I ask my brother.

He shares a look with Gus and Roman before looking at me and nodding his head. I don't know why they're acting shady all of a sudden until Roman speaks up.

"Katya and Lexi are on the list." Katya drops her chin to her chest. There's an audible inhale and I can feel the tension in the room rising. "As is Ana. And Tuesday."

"What!?" Gus and Ana yell at the same time.

I pick up a glass from the table and launch it at the wall.

"I want to see this book," Katya says. Marx hands it over and she and Chewy look through it. Ana is so pissed she's been stomping around the room ranting and I'm not entirely too sure she's been speaking English the whole time, either.

"Why is my asking price so low?" Chewy asks. Like actually out loud asks the room.

"I'm guessing it's because you aren't a virgin," Katya answers back.

"But that doesn't make any sense. I have an extensive repertoire of sexual skills. I could even gather references. I feel like that should add to my value, not decrease from it."

"Hold up, you're pissed because they've put a low reserve on you, not because they are planning to sell you?" Ana looks confused as all hell while Chewy nods at her seriously.

I run my hand down my face. I have the only woman in the world who would get upset that her sexual skills have not been marketed properly. I take a few deep breaths to lower my blood pressure.

Then it completely skyrockets when I hear Chewy say, "Hey, they've advertised me as 'good for breeding.'" Oh, hell no!

"Nobody, and I mean NOBODY, is breeding you but me!" I growl out at her.

She turns her cute little face up to me before scrunching it up and asking the room, "Is that a "Thank You" type compliment?"

"Yes!" Every MC member answers at the same time Gus, Ana, and Tav growl out "NO!"

Marx has been pinching the bridge of his nose this whole time and thank god Wire brings us back to where we need to be.

"That son of a bitch. He's targeting the women of his enemies. All the women on the list are related to, or in relationships with, people who want him dead, or whose businesses he wants. Kidnap them, sell them, and everyone working against him will be too preoccupied getting their women back." It's pretty fucking genius if it wasn't so fucking evil.

"OK. Sniper, you, Judge, Tank, and Switch, I'm gonna have to send you boys back out. I need you on the women that are yet to be taken." Judge gives Pres a swift nod and motions for the others to mount up.

"I've just sent the info to your phones," Wire yells out to their backs whilst typing and not looking up from his laptop.

"The auction is taking place in three days. So Katya, Chewy, Ana, and Lexi, you four are going to have extra security on you. It's shitty, but I don't want you out on the grounds in case we have eyes on." They all nod at this. "We'll get to planning on how to take the auction and Kraykowsi down. Details to come." Marx then turns to look at Chewy, a regretful look on his face. "Tombs fam, I'm sorry, but we haven't heard any word on Pops and so far the usual Kraykowski haunts that we've had Rider's and Jules' street contacts watch over have come up with nothing. No one in or out."

"I wouldn't worry too much just yet if I were you," Tav interrupts Marx. We all look toward him. It seems weird that none of them seem overly concerned. Tav pulls out his phone and taps on the screen a couple of times. "According to this, he's fine."

"What do you mean, he's fine? How the hell do you know?" My brother growls out. Roman's eyes ping between the two, a smile playing on his lips.

"Pops has a biometric tracker implant," Chewy answers. All heads whip her way.

"A fucking what?" That was Squeak, I can tell by his voice.

Gus sighs before answering. "A biometric implant. It acts as a tracker, but along with location, it also sends back information on the overall health of the implantee. We all have them."

"Yup. Reading Pops' stats, he's not under any stress or duress. There was a bit of a heart rate spike, but that was more of a cardiovascular exercise-type event, so he may have been going upstairs or jogging or hand-to-hand combat. He's perfectly fine, and he's currently on the move, so he'll be good for a while yet."

Marx slowly turns around, shoulders slumped, head hung forward and I swear he mutters, "Mother fucking old man's gonna be the death of me."

"Look, I appreciate you want to bring back Pops for us, but I think all of us can confidently say that he will be fine in the meantime. And he would also be pissed if we put him before helping those women and bringing Kraykowski down. So, Tav, you keep tabs on Pops and let us know once the tracker stops or if he's in trouble, yeah?" Gus states.

"Sure thing, big bro. So far, he's still in the area. They made a few stops here and there but haven't really stopped for any period that would suggest they are holding him somewhere." Marx and Gus both nod at Tav's' recount.

"Remember, you also have my men at your disposal. Once you have a location, I'll send a car and a team for him," Roman speaks into the room. Gus dips his chin at this. No matter how confident he is in Pops, it'll still take a weight off his shoulders, knowing he has the Russian mafia as backup. Even though I have a feeling that sneaky bastard is doing it for his own gain, rather than what we are trying to do. I don't quite trust him yet.

"OK, Gus, can you and Roman join me in my office? Everyone else, call it a night. It's getting late and there isn't much more we can do. Everyone has their assignments, but you also need to rest. Nothing more doing tonight." I nod at my brother and

Gus before I gently close Chewy's laptop.

"Come on baby, let's get you up to bed, yeah? The sooner you sleep, the sooner you can make a start tomorrow." She looks up at me with her gorgeous eyes and nods, before standing and taking my hand. I lead her up to our room, and that's exactly what it is. OUR room. She has her things on my bathroom countertop, and her clothes are next to mine in the chest of drawers, where we made space for them. She has weird knick-knacks on her side table. I've even started finding her hair everywhere and I wouldn't want to change a thing. I didn't realize how empty my life was before I found her, but I damn sure am not gonna let her go now. I let her shower in our ensuite and I nip down to the communal shower on this floor. Luckily, my old man had the foresight to put in a lot more bathrooms than you would expect.

By the time she steps out of the bathroom, I'm already lying back on our bed with the sheet over my lap. My gorgeous girl is standing there as naked as the day she was born, and I can feel the sheet moving over my thickening cock.

"Baby, put your PJs on and get over here so we can get some shuteye." She tilts her head at me with a smirk, her wet hair dripping onto her shoulder. I watch as a water droplet glides down her breast, over her stomach, and down between her legs. Fuck, she isn't going to make this easy on me.

"Rhodie, do you trust me?" I look her directly in the eye and answer her.

"Baby, I trust you with my life. One of the few people I do trust." She grins and then moves to tug the sheet slowly off my lap, the caress of the sheets across my cock making me even harder. She places her knee on the end of the bed and crawls, fucking crawls, up between my legs.

I watch her perfect tits swaying and then she comes to a stop, sitting back on her knees as she reaches a hand out to rub my aching cock. She pumps it a few times before leaning forward, swirling her tongue over the angry-looking head, and then taking me into her hot, wet mouth. She works my length with her mouth and her fist whilst her other hand gently massages my heavy balls.

She is a master at this, teasing me, stroking me, coaxing me. Over the short time we have been together, she has become the master of my body. I tangle my hands in her hair, watching those pretty lips of hers wrapped around my length. She keeps sucking and licking my cock, gently tugging on my balls. Her hand slides lower, massaging my taint, which, along with her mouth and fist, is making me lose my mind. So much so that I almost miss the fact that she's rubbing along my back hole, gently pressing before moving back up to my taint and balls. She keeps doing this little dance, all whilst never losing the rhythm her mouth has set. After a few more moments her slicked-up finger breaches my hole at the same time she deep throats my cock, hums, and swallows and the feel of her throat constricting causes me to let out a shout and I blow down her throat whilst her finger rubs the inside of me.

Holy fuck, there are stars in my eyes and my chest is heaving. I think I may have almost blacked out one part there because when I raise my head to look down my torso, it's to see Chewy looking pretty fucking proud of herself.

"Fuck Tuesday, you dirty little thing. Payback is a bitch," I smirk before I jackknife up, grab her under her knees, and flip her onto her back.

"My turn to play."

Tuesday

"My turn to play," he growls at me. I thought he'd be pissed that I snuck into his back passage, but the fact that he just came and his cock is still hard enough to pound nails, I'd say he's less mad and more turned the fuck on. That was my first time playing with Rhodie like that and I really hope it's not the last time. The other night I had a great idea, and I placed an order to an adult toy store so fingers crossed he's open to more butt stuff.

I look up at him, and he's gazing down at me with a hungry look. That's the only way I can describe it. His hands are fisted on either side of my head, and I can see his jaw ticking. I smirk up at him and run my hands up over his hard chest, looping my arms around his neck. He slowly leans forward and his tongue slides against my bottom lip, then my top, before easing between them. He gently tastes himself on my tongue before pulling back and fluttering gentle kisses across my face, down my throat, licking across my collarbone.

His gentle barely there kisses all over my chest are driving me mad, and when I'm about to complain he captures my nipple between his lips, his tongue batting at it before he sucks so hard my back arches up off the bed. His rough fingers are gently playing with my pussy lips, spreading them and smearing my juices all over my clit. I can't stop the noises coming from my lips, there's a pulse between my legs and I arch up, trying to impale myself on Rhodie's thick finger to get some relief but he's content to keep teasing my body, bringing me to the edge. At this point, I'm trying to think of anything that will stop me from exploding, but nothing is helping as my thoughts are scrambled thanks to the way Rhodie is toying with my body.

"Rhodie, p–please, I need you," I pant out, my body writhing beneath his large frame. He stares down at my face, a devilish smirk spreading across his face.

"What do you need, baby?"

"I need to come, Rhodie, please!" I'm whining and begging now. I'm a few seconds away from exploding when the bastard pulls his hand away from my aching core, sitting back on his knees he brings his fingers up to his mouth and slowly licks my juices from them, one by one, moaning as he does this. I growl and kick out at him. He's left me on the edge and I'm seriously pissed off, so I take the matter into my own hands, my hand drifting down to my pussy, gently working myself. It won't take much with how on edge I am.

"Mmm that's right baby, fuck yourself with your fingers, show me how much you want my cock."

Rhodie's feral gaze is on my hand and I press my fingers inside, pumping a few times. I'm almost ready to go over the edge when he grips my wrist and brings my fingers to his mouth.

"Uh, uh, I want to feel you flooding my cock with your come." He surges forward, lines himself up, and thrusts into me all the way until his balls are nestled against my ass.

I gasp at the sudden intrusion. My body is wound so tightly and is so sensitive I'm sure I'm going to come immediately, but Rhodie holds still, his fat cock throbbing inside me. I let out a long moan. Rhodie's hands roam all over my body, hitting every erogenous zone before he settles a hand on my clit. He rubs in slow circles, the weight of his body on mine making me even wetter.

He begins to move, his hips rocking in shallow thrusts,

making me pant and moan, trying to get him to move deeper and faster. I'm aching to be fucked, but the big bastard is teasing me. I buck my body up into his in an effort to get him moving, but he just grins down at me when I growl in frustration.

"You'll come when I let you," he whispers through his smirk.

He thrusts two of his fingers inside me alongside his cock, filling me to the hilt before he slides them out and around to my ass. I feel them rubbing against my back hole and I know that he's going to do to me what I just did to him. A single slick finger presses against the tight ring there before easing its way inside me. It feels foreign and yet so good at the same time.

Suddenly, he pulls out, flips me onto all fours, and thrusts back in. We both groan at the change of position. I feel the weight of his body against mine as he leans over to open up the bedside drawer, where he pulls out a bottle of lube. I hear the snick of the cap and then feel the cool liquid drip down over my ass.

His fingers spread it over my pucker and I feel his fingers breach me back there, sawing in and out at the same time his fat cock powers into my pussy. My body is shaking, my legs clenching, and tremors rush through my body as my orgasm detonates. My arms collapse from under me and I find myself with my ass in the air, cheek pressed to the sheets of Rhodie's bed as he continues fucking me.

All of a sudden, I'm left empty. I turn to ask him what's happening, but my thoughts are fuzzy when I feel him spread my ass cheeks, the head of his cock pressing into my puckered hole. I take a breath and then push out while he presses the head of his cock past my tight ring of muscle. He pushes in slowly, his hands running up and down my back, over my ass.

"Good girl, taking my cock so well in your tight little ass. Fuck baby, I wish you could see what I'm seeing." His husky voice washes over me.

Once he's fully seated inside me, the foreign feeling makes way for absolute pleasure. Rhodie owns every part of me. I can feel the pulse of his cock in my ass and all I want is for him to fuck me. Rhodie makes me wait, taking his sweet time until I'm shaking and begging for it before he thrusts in and out, long slow strokes stoking the fire inside me higher and higher.

My orgasm is edging closer and I don't think I'm going to stop myself from coming all over the bed. I'm loud, I have no shame in the position I'm in, and I'm not embarrassed to be begging for my release. Rhodie's hand slips around my hip, cupping my pussy, his palm against my clit as he thrusts two fingers into me and I explode, wetness flooding out of me at the same time I feel Rhodie stiffen and his hips stutter, a long, low groan leaving him at the same time I feel him unload in my ass. We collapse on the bed, sweaty, sticky, and sated.

His cock softens, and he pulls out of me, scoops me up, and carries me to the bathroom, holding me tight against him as he turns on the shower, waiting for it to warm before washing my body oh so gently. Once he's satisfied I'm squeaky clean again, he dries me and carries me back to bed. He lies me on my back, then lays between my legs, holding himself up on his elbows. He kisses me gently, twice, before staring down at me.

"I love you, Chewy. I've never said that to another person other than my own blood. But you, I couldn't live without you in my world." He rubs his thumb across my cheek and I feel a tear leave my eye. No one has ever chosen me to be theirs.

I cup his bristled cheek with my hand and even though I never know quite how to react or what to say, I kinda know how I feel.

I feel heavy but light at the same time, I feel like Rhodie is the biggest thing in my world and yet not big enough. I feel like I want to crack open my chest and let him crawl inside of me so I can keep him safe and warm, but I know if I told him that I would sound like a Stage 10 Serial Killer. I think and feel so many things about him, but none of them have words. Maybe I love you is what you say when you don't have enough words big enough to describe things.

"I love all my people, like my brothers and Pops. But you?" I frown a little, to make sure I make the words important enough "You are my person." I look into his eyes and hopefully, he can see what I feel. He's clever and he can read my eyes. A smile splits his face, and then he settles down with his head between my tits. I run my fingers through his hair until we both fall into a deep sleep.

When I awake the next morning, it's to Rhodie, fast asleep with the bulk of the blankets on his side, the damn blanket hog. Checking my phone, I see that even though it's early, it's not too early to get up and get my day started. Dressing in my comfs, I stare down at Rhodie's handsome face for a moment. I feel this pressure in my chest when I look at him, and a flutter in my belly, knowing that this hot hunk of man meat is all mine. I lean forward and kiss him gently on the forehead before making sure he's all tucked in, and then quietly leave our room.

When I walk into the common room, it's to a few of the brothers eating the delicious-looking breakfast Tabby and Annie have served up. I've noticed that the longer I stay here, the less the clubhouse smells invade my senses. When I first arrived, every smell was new to me. Now it sits in the background and fresh smells like breakfast break through. I grab myself a plate of eggs and bacon and park up next to Ana and Sasha at one of the long tables.

"Ana, I wanted to thank you for keeping my brother safe. I owe you one." Ana looks at me for a moment, head tilted to the side, before a slow smile blooms on her face. She waves a hand at me.

"No need to owe me one. I would have saved that giant asshole, anyway." I snort and keep eating, although I really want to know how the hell a woman all the way from New Zealand ended up with the Bratva. I must have been staring at her whilst pondering this, because I see her put her cutlery down and turn to me.

"You can ask, you know. I know you want to." Aw shit, busted!

"Oh shit, sorry about that. I was just wondering how you ended up with the Bratva." Before she can answer, Sasha does.

"She saved me. I am forever in her debt." Ana shares a smile with Sasha before taking a deep breath.

"I grew up in care in New Zealand. It wasn't nearly as shitty as the foster system you have here, but it's not great either. The longest I ever stayed in a place was eight years, but they were the best eight years of my childhood. My foster father, who I called Dad, taught me everything I know about the bush, how to survive outdoors, that sort of stuff. He died when I was sixteen and child services wouldn't let my foster mum keep me, and that's when I got moved on. Anyway, his dream was to tour around the US, and somewhere along the line, it became my dream too. So when I turned eighteen, after aging out of the system, I got myself a job and worked my ass off to raise enough money to travel here. I was at a gas station in Louisiana when these shitty dudes came in throwing their weight around, acting all suss. I figured I needed to get out of Dodge, slipped out the back and on the way to my car I could hear weird noises coming out of their trunk. Popped it and found Sasha." She shrugs her shoulders and I think I might have a girl crush on her.

"It wasn't quite that clean cut. Another Pakhan with a hate on for Roman kidnapped me to blackmail my husband. Ana risked her life for me and has been Bartashev ever since." Sasha smiles indulgently at her.

"I may not be married to you freaks, but you're my family." She tosses her head back and laughs as Sasha throws a bit of pancake at her. I see Gus walk into the common room and glance at Ana. I watch her follow him with her eyes for a moment before she dips them back down to her food. Sasha catches my eye, and he has a big smile on his face. We've had a few chats here and there, and I really like the big man. His personality is the polar opposite of Romans; he's laid back, almost sunshiny, to Roman's grump.

"Do you mind if I ask you something about Roman? You can tell me no, if you like." He tilts his head before raising his eyebrows and smiling. I'm going to take that as a yes, even if he hasn't said it in so many words.

"Roman is the Pakhan, the big boss. Why is it he's at ease cooperating with Marx and Gus? Shouldn't they be having a big alpha pissing contest over who is the boss of our current enterprise?" I've been wondering about this for a while. Roman came with his family to lock down here when, in reality, he could have stayed at home with his men. I'm not silly enough to think that Roman doesn't have the means to take down Kraykowski on his own. Sure, it may have taken longer and yes, working together is more efficient in the long run. However, he doesn't really need any of us.

"What makes you think Roman is an alpha?" Sasha asks, breaking me out of my thoughts. My eyes shoot to his and I see a small smile play on his lips. I look at Ana, the same smile on hers. I'm interrupted by a kiss on my temple and Rhodie's big hand smooths over my hair.

"Hey baby, how's that fine ass of yours today?" I smile up at him through my eyelashes before pinching him in the ribs. He laughs as he wanders off to find breakfast, and I turn back to find two sets of eyes on me.

"Uh, what?"

"Nothing girl, just that's a fine man you have," Sasha answers. I follow his line of sight to Rhodie, ribbing his brothers in the kitchen. He must feel my eyes on him as he looks up at me and winks.

"Yup, he sure is, and I'm gonna own that ass one day." The table around me laughs and then we all jump when the door to the compound swings open and slams against the wall.

"What the fuck!?"

Chapter 18

Pops

I have just finished arranging my captors into a lovely little vignette, even if I do say so myself. It was pure luck that it was these idiots who picked me up on the side of the road yesterday morning. I mean, I did put a little more stoop into my posture and made my gait a little more pronounced to fool these guys into thinking I was the feeble old man I was portraying.

I thought it was going to take a little more acting on my part to convince these pussies to kidnap me, however; it turns out that Kraykowski is a little more organized than I would have thought. Tweedle Dee and Tweedle Dum had a whole ass folder on my Tuesday, so a quick ID check and they thought they'd hit the jackpot kidnapping the Tombs patriarch.

I could hear the excitement in their voices as they dumped me in the trunk. Then they walked me, unblindfolded, I might add, into their hideout, an old storefront on the main street of Rose Grove. Rookie mistakes, really. After that, they chained my ankle to a metal bed leg in the back room, giving me enough chain to wander about but not escape. I could see their pride shining plainly on their faces as they saw their plan coming to fruition. These fuckers thought for sure they were gonna level up in the villain stakes. I almost felt guilty when I picked the lock from around my ankle and then lured the first guy to his death. By the time I dispatched the second guy, I was more irritated at their lack of care. I mean, it was so easy; they were almost begging to be killed. Next time, they'll give me better captors.

I check my watch and the weapons that they never confiscated from me. Thanks to their loose lips, I know Kraykowski will be here in around half an hour to interrogate me, so I ready myself. I look at the bodies that I have artfully arranged, propped up in chairs around the small card table, facing each other, cigarettes smoldering in the ashtray.

For all intents and purposes, it looks like these guys are playing cards. I'm almost giddy at the reaction Kraykowski is going to give me. I wish I had some cameras set up in here. I don't have time to arrange anything, so I'll just have to download his expression directly through my eyeballs into my brain. I take up my position in the shadows of the storeroom. From here, I have an uninterrupted view of the entrance and my dead guys without them seeing me. It's also the perfect place to take out any security he may travel with.

I think back over the events of the past week. If I had my way, I would have bided my time a little, try to get some more information, but for the life of me, I just don't think I could have put up with those two any longer. Maybe you could blame it on the "woke" youth or the gays or something, but goons in my day were proper bad guys. These two were so fucking soft I bet they would cry to their mommies had I let them live.

Hearing a car pull up to the curb two doors slam. Kraykowski would be one, and I'm guessing he only has one guard with him. The odds are in my favor today.

The front door opens and I know this is more than likely to be the guard. He does a cursory look around the room before nodding back to Kraykowski, who enters and shuts the door behind him. They both walk over to the table and the guard grunts something before hitting Tweedle Dum on the shoulder. The body slumps sideways and the guard jumps to attention, but before he can move, I've come up behind him and shot him point blank in his head with the gun I stole from Tweedle Dee. Kraykowski is across the table, he goes to raise his gun however I shoot fucker out of his fist before I slide over the table, kicking Tweedle Dee in the face, causing him to hit the ground, before I pop up and pistol whip the hell out of Kraykowski, knocking him out cold.

Another pussy. I end all that with my arms up in the air like an Olympic gymnast and grumble once again that there are no cameras here. I would have loved to watch a replay of that display of athleticism from a geriatric like me, but I'll have to settle for a play-by-play description. My baby girl will love that.

I look at Kraykowski before squatting down next to him. He's starting to get a nice egg forming on his forehead and he has a trickle of blood running down his temple. He's middle-aged but still looks like he could fight me if he needs to, so I take my knife out of my boot and slide the blade through his suit jacket, and his shirt, into the soft flesh between his two lower ribs. I flick my eyes up to his face and see he's still out of it. I snort before stabbing between another two ribs. He's gonna feel that when he comes around. Taking out Tweedle Dum's phone, I punch in what I need. Time to bundle this fucker up and get back to the clubhouse for a little fun and games.

Rhodie

I look through the kitchen hatch into the dining room and I can't help but let my gaze search out my girl. She's laughing with Ana and that good-looking bastard Sasha. I'd be worried about him spending time with my girl if I didn't know that he was married to Roman. Taking a bite of my bacon, I choke a little when the main door swings open and slams against the wall with force. Obviously it's been kicked in. I vault through the kitchen hatch, gun in hand, making my way to Chewy to keep her safe when I look up.

"What the fuck?" Marx roars. With good reason. Standing just inside the door is Pops, with Kraykowski slumped at his feet. There also seems to be blood dripping from somewhere.

"Guys, tracker says Pops is on the move. According to this he's -" Tav's disembodied voice says from the hallway, growing louder before he enters the room, then stops walking abruptly when he glances up from his phone. "Oh, hey Pops."

"Ho, ho, ho, I bought you kids a present. Your way was taking too long, and no offense Marx, this place is nice and all, but I'm used to slightly higher class entertainment, if you know what I mean." He waggles his eyebrows and I hear Chewy, Tav, Gus, and Jules all groan. I am damn certain if Pops wasn't an old man, Marx would have punched him in the face by now. Instead, he takes a deep breath, releases it, and gestures to me and Rider to grab our guest. He doesn't need to tell us where we're going, our guest will be accommodated in the back shed, and I'm guessing Chewy will be in on the interrogation. Once Rider and I have secured Kraykowski, we head back to the common room where I can hear Marx barking out orders.

"Right, we have two goals. First goal is to get as much info out of Kraykowski as we can and get rid of him. The second goal is to bring down the auction and get those women to safety and back home. The plan for that will depend on what we find out from our guest. Pops and Chewy, I'm guessing you'll be in on the interrogation?" Chewy grins wide and nods like a bobblehead. She's bouncing in her seat and I just know that twisted mind of hers will come up with all sorts of violent ideas.

"Right, so we'll have Rhodie and myself, Chewy and Pops, Roman, do you want two people to represent Bratva in there?"

I look toward the Russian, who, even though it's still early morning, is sitting in his three-piece suit, hair immaculate. His dark eyes stare at the wall for a moment before he nods his head.

"Lexi and Sasha will represent us." Before Marx can comment, he holds his hand up to stop him. "Yes, I know that this may not be the ideal place for a young woman. However, she is learning the ropes from Sasha and I believe she will bring value to our endeavor." Marx flicks me a look and I shrug. I mean, yeah, it's probably not the best place for an 18-year-old, however looking at Chewy, she seems perfectly normal and who knows how long she's been at this. If Lexi's father isn't worried, I don't see why we should be. Whatever is on my face must convince Marx, because he gives Roman a chin lift before barking orders.

"OK, those chosen gather your shit and meet back here in five minutes."

Those in on the interrogation get busy, gathering our favorite methods of torture. Chewy is beside herself and I see her and Pops across the room having a serious conversation. There are a lot of hand movements and nodding. My shit is always in the shed, ready and waiting, so I just hang around waiting for the others.

"Wow, so you guys are like real bikers, huh?" Ana asks from her spot at the table. She's sittingwith Katya and Gus.

"Yup, pretty much. You have a problem with what's about to happen?" I raise my brow at her. If she has a problem, then I have a problem and we'll have to remedy that before we go any further. She waves her hand at me.

"Shit no. You do you. I just need that fucker sorted because I didn't come halfway around the world to be sold to some old rich dude. Fuck that!"

We all smile and I watch as Gus places his palm on her upper back, his thumb stroking the side of her neck. "It'd never happen. Trust me, we have your back."

She squints at him slightly before a small smile tugs at the corner of her lips. "I don't need you to protect me. But thanks anyway," she answers him. They do a stare-y eye fuck thing before she shakes his hand off and turns to look at me. "Oh, will we be able to watch the fun stuff?" she asks.

"Yeah, why the fuck not?"

Marx lets out an ear-piercing whistle. I grab Chewy's hand and we follow him out the back. We have the main guys, me and Marx, Chewy and her Pops with her tool bag, Sasha and Lexi with a sleek black case, Roman, Gus, Tav and Jules, Ana, Katya, Wire, and Rider. She's a tight fit, but we all cram in, champing at the bit to get going.

We circle around Kraykowski and I'm sure he's putting on a

front. We are one scary bunch of motherfuckers and he doesn't seem overly concerned. Nor has he said anything.

"Oh shit, I forgot I dislocated his jaw when I was cramming him into the Uber. Paid extra for the guy to look the other way, but in my rush, I accidentally dropped him face-first into the trunk." Pops shrugs like his sentence made any sense at all.

"Hold the fuck up, you took an Uber? Scrap that. How the fuck did you end up with Kraykowski, anyway?" Rider asks the room the question I've been dying to know, but no one seemed to ask.

"Oh, his henchmen sucked. I killed them and set them up in a sweet little scene. Security didn't realize they were dead and led Fuck Knuckle into the room. I shot the guard, shot Kraykowkski's gun from his hand," he flicks his head to the bleeding hand that Rider and I have cuffed to chains above his head. "THEN I vaulted across the table like goddamned Simone Biles and pistol-whipped him. Stabbed him a coupla times, then called an Uber for pickup, dropped him on his face, and voila! We're here. Lemme fix his face quick smart and we'll be able to get him singing like Aretha."

Without hesitation Pops grabs Kraykowski's head, his thumbs on either side of his mouth, his fingers digging into the underside of his jaw and with a quick movement, pushes Kraykowki's jaw back into place. He moans long and low whilst Pops slaps him a couple of times on the cheek and calls him a "Good boy." Chuckles and snorts are heard around the room before Marx's booming voice cuts through.

"Right. How do we want to run this? Chewy, you have a little payback you want to exact. Does this need to be done with him fully intact?"

Chewy uses the hand holding mine to guide my arm up over

her head, settling it across her shoulders and snuggling into my side.

"He stuck his dirty dick in my mouth when I was thirteen years old. So I'm going to teach his cock a lesson. But that can wait till just before the grand finale." She smirks up at me and I feel like I know where this is going.

"We are happy to attend where needed, so, after you," Sasha tips his head at Marx before settling in next to Lexi, who is leaning against the metal table. Marx nods at me and Rider and I get to work. We both have the knuckle dusters that Mad Dog gave us for Christmas when we were both eighteen, and we target Kraykowski's soft parts. He grunts here and there and even spits blood onto the floor. When we feel we have softened him up a little, I share a look with Sasha as Marx starts with his questioning.

"You know why you're here. We want to know the ins and outs of the pending auction. What does Ushakov stand to gain? Who will be the big players at the auction?" While Marx has been spitting out his questions, Sasha and Lexi have taken Kraykowski down from the pulleys and have placed him into a metal chair. Sasha has shown Lexi how to tie him down with some pointers from Chewy and Pops. This is some fucked up lesson they're teaching this poor girl and yet she seems happy to be given this instruction. She looks up at them once she's done and they all inspect her work before giving her smiles, thumbs up, and, in Chewy's case, an awkward pat on the shoulder.

Kraykowski is squirming a little in his seat and thus far has kept his mouth shut. I'd admire the man's dedication if we weren't trying to get shit outta him. Roman steps up and passes his husband a sleek black case. Sasha places it on the table and opens it to reveal some tools I recognize and some I don't. Lexi steps up and grabs a pair of heavy-looking pliers, whilst Sasha picks up something that looks like a mini blow torch. Lexi pulls her arm back and then hits Kraykowski across the face with the pliers, causing him to grunt and a long gash to open up along his swollen cheek. He slowly turns his head to look at her, opens his mouth, calls her a 'bitch', and then grins, blood smearing his teeth. Before I can step forward, Sasha is there and fires what looks to be freezing air directly onto the cut. This time Kraykowski screams in pain, chest heaving before Sasha takes his finger off the trigger button.

"What in the fuck was that!?" Pops explodes in excitement. Chewy is right there, bouncing on her toes, making grabby hands.

"Liquid nitrogen. So cold it freezes everything it touches." Before anyone can move, Pops has it in his hands and sprays it directly onto Kraykowski's pinky finger on his good hand. The way Lexi has restrained him, his hands are tied to the chair armrests, so no matter how much screaming and wriggling he does, he can't move his hand away. Pops holds it for so long that Kraykowski's finger has turned an unnatural shade of purple. He stops spraying and then pokes the purple finger, pulling his hand back quickly, making a hissing noise. "Fuck, that's cold!" Chewy leans forward and does the same thing because, of course, she does. I'm surprised she hasn't sniffed it yet. Oh no, no, she has now. Jesus. I look up and lock eyes with Marx, his eyebrows raised.

"Yup, that's my girl," I tell the room, shrugging my shoulders. I hear a whimper and turn back to see Kraykowski, eyes as big as saucers, and Chewy holding the purple finger.

"Whoops, I accidentally snapped it off."

Pops is giggling like a little girl, bouncing around. Chewy is grinning wide and Lexi and Sasha seem to be happy to watch the live Tombs Shit Show. It's gonna be a loooong night.

Chapter 19

Tuesday

So, it seems Kraykowski is a little more badass than we once thought. I just figured he was a middleman, working for Ushakov, which he is, but what I didn't know was that he is also one tough son of a bitch. So far, as a group, we have liquid Nitrogen-ed various cuts and gashes that Rhodie, Rider, and Lexi have given him.

Pops and I have also been allowed to wield the spray can and have systematically frozen and snapped off all of his fingers. Pops is currently ridding him of his shoes, and so far, he hasn't said a word other than calling me and Lexi bitches, which is totally uncalled for. I feel like he's reaching his threshold, though. He's making a little more noise now, and he keeps pleading with us, which is new for him.

I look down and see that he's scrunched his toes trying to move them away from Pops. We don't need him to have his legs for what I have planned for him, so I slice off his pants, starting at his crotch. I'm none too gentle because I really don't care about his pain levels, so I make sure I slice a little deeper down his legs. I need his sad manhood intact, which I can see lying limp against his thigh. I see it swell a little before his bladder empties, flowing down his legs onto the floor, directly onto Pops.

"Ew, you filthy mother fucker!" Pops jumps up from his place at Kraykowski's feet, tosses the liquid nitrogen can to the side, and picks up Rhodie's tomahawk, bringing it down on his toes in one fell swoop, making Kraykowski howl, snot dripping down his face.

"I'll ask you one more time," Marx barks out, "Where is the auction and who are the key players?" Kraykowski gags a little and shakes his head back and forth.

"Listen, I admire your ability to stay tight-lipped, but you know you aren't getting out of this alive. Tell us what we need to know and I'll make it quick. Keep your lips shut and I will make sure my people maim you a little more before I pack you up and send you back to Ushakov. He may want people to think he's just a Russian politician, but I've heard what he does to people who displease him. Do you think he'll be happy to find out that you've been cutting him out of the equation? I've heard that he's worse than the Bratva."

Kraykowski makes an odd wheezing noise, the sound getting louder as I realize he's laughing. "You think I'm afraid of that fat Russian fuck?! He used to be spoken about like he was the devil incarnate, but there's a bigger, worse wolf in town. Ushakov is dead."

He laughs once more, blood staining his teeth, one eye swollen shut, blood oozing out of the rib wounds Pops gave him, gashes across his face and down his torso given to him by Rhodie, Rider, and Lexi. Missing fingers and toes thanks to me and Pops. He's an absolute mess, and yet I kind of respect how tough this bastard is. I go back to carving up his legs whilst Marx asks him about the auction again.

"Look, you filthy fucking biker scum, I'll never tell you where or when. I'd rather die knowing that all those bitches I took will go to their new owners. My men will see to it." He gives us a smile before sticking out his tongue, then he slams his mouth shut, biting his own tongue off before spitting a chunk of it on the ground. He glares at me and smiles again. I hold his gaze and reach my hand back to Tav, who delivers me my Candiru fish. I'm going to slip this bad boy up his wang before the big finale Pops and I have planned. I thought all my Christmases had come at once when I realized there was a large pond on the MC land, complete with a small dock and a few small row boats that the guys like to use to mess about on the pond.

"I'm going to need him back up on the chains please, Babe" I turn to look at Rhodie. He knows what's coming and gives me a jerk of his head before he and Rider cut the cable ties from around Kraykowski's wrists, Rider taking the bulk of his weight whilst Rhodie secures him to the chains before cranking the pulley and raising him up to standing. Sasha removes the scraps of Kraykowski's trousers until he's naked from the waist down. His beady eyes watch me as I take the lid off my jar, his gaze following me as I stoop in front of his gross, shriveled appendage, bringing the jar up and over it, letting it dangle and bob around in the water. I watch the fish swim around it, not one of them taking the bait just yet.

"You know, I always wondered what your dick looked like after I bit it." I watch as his face pinches slightly and I know that my wee fishy has traveled up his urethra as intended. I remove his gross manhood from my jar, screw the lid back on, and hand my babies to Tav.

"Right, Marx, is it time for the big finale?"

He clenches his jaw before sighing. "Go ahead, Chewy, without his tongue he's not going to give us anymore. Do whatever freaky shit you and Pops have planned."

He waves his hand in our direction and, with a few directions to Rider and Rhodie, we get Kraykowski down from his chains and out next to the pond. The guys dump him into the rowboat and, at Pop's instruction, secure another rowboat over the top of him, leaving his head out. His biting his tongue off is going to do us a big favor, as the tube that I insert into his mouth meets no resistance. Tav helps pour a lovely mix of milk and honey into the tube, force-feeding Kraykowski the sweet mix. Once we've filled him to the brim, I cover any exposed skin in honey before dusting my hands off and high-fiving Pops.

"Ah, does anyone want to enlighten me about what you have planned?" Roman asks, looking around at everyone.

"Boat torture. Trap the fucker between two boats, force-feed him honey and milk, and wait for the bugs to eat him alive. The sweet mix in him will breed bacteria, the fish will infect his cock and he will beg for death. Pretty sweet really," Pops tells him before shuffling off and whistling.

"Remind me never to piss you people off," Roman states before following Pops inside, the rest of us trailing behind with Marx yelling "Church" over our shoulders.

Tuesday

The guys have been in church for a while now, leaving the rest of us stragglers to entertain ourselves. About half an hour into it, Roman and my brothers got called in, so obviously some serious shit is going down. Katya and I have been tracking the other two women that are yet to be taken. The MC guys are watching them and from what I've heard, they have foiled their kidnappings already. We have two days until the auction and we are no closer to finding out where it's happening or where they are holding the women they've taken so far. We are running out of options and the longer this goes on, the less safe the women are. I check my list again and note that the woman who was taken first has been gone for three weeks already. That's long enough for awful shit to happen to her, and for her to start losing hope.

The church doors swing open and Rhodie stomps toward me. He looks tense. I stand to greet him and his hands go directly to my ass where he lifts me into his arms, his nose going into the crook of my neck, breathing deeply. I hold him to me and gently pat his back to let him settle. After a few moments, he lets me down.

"Sorry, babe, I needed that. Church pissed me off, and I just needed to check that you're safe."

"Why wouldn't I be?"

He scrubs his hands through his hair. "Look, we are quickly running out of options. We have no idea where the women are being held, no idea when this shit is going down, so some ideas were tossed about and I didn't agree with one of them."

I raise my eyebrow at him. "And what was this idea?"

He won't look at me, so whatever idea it is, it involves me. I think I know what it is because I've been thinking along the same lines.

"They want to use me as bait?"

Rhodie flinches, and I let my gaze roam around the room. Some of the brothers are avoiding my eye contact. Marx and Gus both hold my gaze and Pops raises his brow at me. I feel Rhodie's big hand on my face, turning me toward him.

"I'll never let you put yourself in danger. We will find another way to get this fucker."

"I think it's a good idea. I mean, I'm tagged, you will know where I am at all times. If you think about it, I'm the only one who can do it. I can get in, get the intel and you guys can get us all out." I shrug my shoulders, unsure why he's fighting this. It makes perfect sense.

"No, if we have to send anyone in, it was decided that Lexi or Katya will go."

"What? No, I can't let them go alone. I'm the one who has a tracker. I know all the risks, Rhodie. I've done this type of work before. It'll be fine,"

"No Chewy, you don't get it. You'll be in there unprotected. With Kraykowski out, we don't know who's calling the shots. You won't have any weapons on you, you won't have any backup, we won't have eyes on you."

"I know all this, Rhodie. Why are you telling me?"

"He has Correctile Dysfunction. Plagues many a man. Because you know, you're a girl, and even though you know things, you don't REALLY know things." Ana pipes up in her Kiwi accent. I let out a snort and then notice that Rhodie is frowning at her, arms crossed over his chest and he doesn't look like he's backing down anytime soon.

"No. Your brothers and I have discussed this, and we don't think you should go. You know what you're like, you don't really have the skills to take this on Chewy. Trust us."

"Wait, what do you mean, you and my brothers decided?" I look at my big brothers. Gus holds my eye contact and I can see his jaw clenching. Tav and Jules look uncomfortable, avoiding my eye contact. I turn my eyes back to Rhodie and, in a measured voice, I ask him. "What am I like, Rhodie? What skills don't I have that Lexi and Ana have? What am I missing?"

He rubs his hand down his face and looks at me, letting out a long sigh, "You have limitations, Chewy. You can't read people the same way they can. Baby, you have sensory issues. What happens if you have a shutdown while you're in there? That could become dangerous for you because you have to be alert to everything happening. You won't be safe Chewy, you're just, you're just... different," He looks up at me, jaw clenching.

I look around the room. Everyone else is avoiding my gaze, and it feels weird. Wrong. Usually, it's me avoiding gazes, not the other way around. My chest feels weird and uncomfortable. My throat feels tight and I blink because my eyes are watery all of a sudden.

"I know I'm different. I just didn't think you all thought so, too."

I have to get out of here. Everything feels too much. My clothes are bugging me now and the lights are too bright. I can hear people talking to me and I feel someone's hands on me, but they're too heavy and too hard, so I shrug them off and dart into the hallway, gulping deep breaths until I get to Wire's room. He spins to look at me.

"Chewy?"

I ignore him and head straight for his closet. Sitting cross-legged on the floor, I pull the door closed behind me. I let the darkness wrap around me, feeling the cool, calm invade my arms and legs, working its way through my body. I rest my head against the wall and I swipe angrily at my cheeks to get rid of the wetness. All that's doing is illustrating what they all think. I get it. I know Rhodie wasn't wrong in his observations. I know they want what's best for me, but they're treating me like I don't know my own mind. Like I don't know what I can and can't do and that hurts. I've spent a lot of my life with people looking at me like I was incapable, but here, they see me differently. At least, I thought they did. Now I'm not so sure. I hear a soft tapping at the door. I don't know how long I've wallowed in here, but I'm feeling more myself now. I don't answer, but it's OK because I hear Lexi's voice whispering to me.

"I think you're capable Tuesday. In fact, I think you're a badass. Fuck them. I'm with you on this. If you want to do this, then we do it together. I'm ready to leave when you are. With or without their help." I hear some rustling, and I know she's moved away from the door. I can sit in here and wallow about how everyone has underestimated me, or I can go get those women home to their families. Fuck it. I've got this.

Chapter 20

Rhodie

"Are you just going to sit here and wallow?" I turn to look at Pops, whose menacing face isn't bothering me as per usual. Looking around, I see Chewy's brothers looking how I feel, like utter shit. I rub my chest, not liking the feeling and down the rest of my whiskey, enjoying the burn it's giving me. After Chewy took off, her brothers told me to leave her for a bit, let her settle down. She headed straight for Wire's closet, so I knew she'd be safe there. That's all I want, her safe and sound with me.

"Look son, I know you were trying to do the right thing, but our Tuesday, she's not like other women. She knows what she can and can't do. Do you think she got this far in life pandering to all the fears me and her brothers had? No way, not my grandbaby. She's a fighter, whether you like it or not. If you can't trust that she's got this, you need to move the fuck outta the way and let a real man step up and take a chance." He slaps his hand on my shoulder a little harder than he needs to before shaking me and wandering off. Before I can order another drink, Marx slips onto the stool beside me.

"You know, we would never put Chewy or any of the girls in danger willingly."

I nod in agreement. "It just, fuck, I don't know what I'd do without her. She came sneaking into the compound and since that night, I've not been the same."

My brother looks at me for a moment. "You love her?"

"Yeah."

"Making her your ol lady?"

I nod at my brother. "If she'll have me after what I said to her."

He slaps his hand on my shoulder. "Proud of you, baby brother. We'll keep her safe. Finish up here and go get your woman. It's been long enough."

I wave goodnight to everyone and make my way to Wire's room. Tapping gently on the closet door I slowly open it, expecting to find my Chewy, but instead, it's empty, only the faint smell of her fresh scent lingering. Shutting the door behind me, I head up to our room, hoping she's in there getting some rest. The bed is still made and no sign of her. I check her brother's rooms, and outside, not finding my ol lady. I feel sick, my stomach dropping further and further until I burst back into the common room, chest heaving.

"Chewy! Has anyone seen her? I can't find her!" Everyone's heads spin towards me, men jumping up, chairs clanging to the floor.

Tav pulls out his phone and taps a few times. "Fuck! She's off compound!"

"Fuck!" I yell into the room, gripping my hair in my hands. I feel my dad's arms wrap around me. "Settle down boy, we have eyes on her whereabouts, she's got this." I take a couple of deep breaths and stand tall, looking toward my brother and pres for guidance.

"Right, it looks like Chewy has decided our next steps. Rider, organize the Tombs SUVs, we'll load up, stick close. I'll let Savage from Death Riders know that we may have one of our own tracking the women. Roman, any news on Ushakov? With Kraykowski out of the picture, it would help to know who's pulling the strings and who we have to take down."

Roman looks up from his intense conversation with Katya, her frowning at him, Sasha shaking his head, looking none too happy with whatever is going on.

"It's been confirmed. Ushakov is dead. My associate says he's been dead for a week. His business dealings are left up in the air with no leader. I'll be loading up and taking Lexi with me as soon as I can arrange it. She is the heir since Katya denounced him." He straightens his lapels and looks directly at Marx. "I can trust you'll take care of business here for me? I would hate for anything to impede Lexi's birthright, and that includes whatever Kraykowski has going on."

"You never needed protection, did you? You were here simply to make sure Ushakov and Kraykowski were taken out, one way or another. Am I right?"

"Now, now, that's not the only reason I was here. I needed to know that I could work with you. I'll need contacts here that I can trust with some of the, shall we say, darker parts of my business whilst I help Lexi settle in Russia. She's been training for this moment all of her life. Sasha, can you tell our daughter to pack her things? We'll be wheels up as soon as it can be arranged." Sasha shakes his head at Roman, clearly disagreeing with this turn of events, and leaves to find his stepdaughter.

Every one of my brothers and Chewy's brothers are looking at Roman a little differently. Did we trust him? Not fully knowing he had something up his sleeve, but we didn't think he was going to infiltrate us purely so he could use us as his minions.

"She's not here. Phone and ID are in her room, but her knives are gone."

"Roman, I'll deal with your bullshit later. Looks like we have two women who don't know how to listen. Load up whatever you can, DRMC on bikes, Tombs and Pops will be in the SUVs sending out coordinates. Mount up!"

Marx circles his finger in the air, and we all head out as a unified team. Even Roman and his men get into their sedan, waiting for further instruction. As much as I want to be in the SUV with Chewy's brothers, I mount my bike and rev the engine, the rumble below me doing wonders to calm my nerves. I need to hold it together, get rid of all emotion until this shit is done. I hear Marx's voice over the Bluetooth in my helmet and lead my brothers through the club gates tucked close behind the SUVs. Hold on, I'm coming, baby.

Tuesday

"Lex, black sedan coming up. Been past three times now," I throw my head back and laugh, Lexi following my lead. After Pops went out and got himself kidnapped, Lexi and I figured Kraykowski's men surely aren't dumb enough to fall for the kidnapping ruse a second time. Instead, we hijacked one of my brother's cars and decided to get coffee, sitting at one of the outside tables at a cafe on Main Street. To anyone else, we just look like two girlfriends catching up, having a gossip. Little do they know we are both tooled up, knives in our boots and at our backs, blades hidden in our bras, and both of us are wearing defender rings. Lexi and I keep our eyes open, surveilling our surroundings and chatting about nothing for a few more minutes before Lexi spots them.

"Yup, two headed our way. By the looks of it, both have guns. Neither looks wary of us." Lexi's wide grin doesn't quite match her words and I fake laugh once again. A shadow casts over us as both men box us in, one on each side of our table. The one closest to me places his hand on the table and leans over me.

"Get up. You bitches are coming with us. We've been looking for you for a long time." I feel the barrel of his gun press against my soft stomach. I have to use all my strength to keep my hands in my lap, and not grab the knife on the table and jab it into his fat hand.

"No, please, what do you want with us?" I look up at him with wide eyes. I can hear Lexi quietly crying across from me. The man on her side already has his hand wrapped around her bicep and is pulling her out of her chair. My goon jabs me with his gun and I get up, pretending to be the scared girl they're expecting.

We get manhandled to the car we spotted earlier, and we both get slammed up against the side whilst Bad Guy No. 1 walks around and opens the trunk. Yeah, that's not gonna work for us. Lexi and I had already decided we would take these guys out fast, and then I can hack their phones to find out where they're taking us. I look at my partner in crime and quick as lightning, her leg kicks out, taking out the knee of the guy holding us at gunpoint. She lunges forward, grabbing the wrist holding the gun, angling it away from her as she slams it down on her knee, breaking his arm. He yells out to his friend, but I've already gotten my dagger from my boot and brought it up into the soft part under his chin. He's gurgling and scratching as I pull it out and slice across his throat. I turn to find that Lexi has also just dispatched her bad guy with a knife to the eyeball.

We look at each other, slightly winded, and laugh as we high-five. Thankfully Bad Guys No. 1 and two parked in an alley, so we search their pockets for their phones, then dump their bodies behind a dumpster and cover them with alley crap. It's what they deserve, really.

We pile into their car and before Lexi can hand me the cell phones; I turn the key to light up the SatNav.

"Keep the phone, Lex. Looks like these guys are dumber than we thought." SatNav shows us exactly where they've been the past three weeks, the prime location being a set of warehouses the next town over. I look at Lex, who puts on her seatbelt, the sunglasses of one of the dead guys, and turns the stereo right up. Looks like we're set.

We drive by the warehouses to get the lay of the land. Lexi and I agree to park up a few streets over and then go in on foot. We had time to call my brothers but decided against it because who am I kidding? We all know that once Rhodie figured out I was no longer on the premises, he and my brothers would have been tracking me. The way I figure it, they're probably only half an hour or so behind us, giving us plenty of time for recon.

"Right, so by the looks of it, the trunk is full of goodies for us. Two guns each, complete with Kevlar vests, so I say we suit up." I nod in agreement with Lexi.

She's an awesome kid, way more advanced than I was at her age, so I'm happy that she has my back and I have hers. We slip on vests that are way too big on our bodies, but they'll do the trick in the meantime. I tuck two of the guns in the back of my pants, my knife situated in the middle of my back, guns on either side. Lexi has at least a dozen blades on her. It turns out she's a talented knife thrower. I am so going to get her to train me up when we get back.

Once we're set, we look at each other, grins spreading over both of our faces. We fist bump and then make our way closer to the warehouses. From what I can see, there is one that seems to have a couple of guys loitering outside it. I'm guessing this is our target, as it also has lights on the inside.

"Where the fuck are they? They said they had the girls and would be back."

"How the hell should I know? We've been waiting on Kraykowski for further instruction and nothing. Kovalev will be here soon and he's going to lose his shit if we don't have everything ready." Lexi and I look at each other, wide-eyed. Well, well, well, looks like we're about to hit the motherlode. Who the hell is Kovalev?

The guys resume bitching about being left in the dark and what the hell they're going to do as Lexi and I stick to the shadows and creep ever closer. I slide my knife from my boot, ready to do what's needed to get into the building when the cigarette butt of one guy goes sailing past my face.

"Fuck it. I need a beer. Those bitches are all secure. They're not getting outta there without us. Let's head to that titty bar around the corner. I'm sick of lookout duty. 10 minutes off-site won't matter, we'll go in and check the product when we get back." I watch as he storms off, then flick my gaze to see what his partner is going to do. He looks back at the warehouse, then shrugs his shoulders and follows his buddy. Jeez, Kraykowski needs a better vetting program. The guys he recruits are shit. My head jerks up when I hear the door creak open and I watch as Lexi makes sure the path is clear. She gives me a thumbs up and I follow her in.

The smell hits me before anything else: excrement, rotting food, and body odor. I can hear someone quietly crying and another person consoling them. I look around and see cages on either side of the room we're in, the dim lighting allowing me to see at least fifteen women altogether.

"Who the fuck are you?" A raspy voice grits out to my left. I turn to look that way and see a beautiful woman standing with her head held high and hands fisted at her sides. She's in better condition than some of the others, so I'm guessing she's one of the latest women taken.

"Are you Natalie? Savage's ol lady?"

She tilts her head before gritting out, "Who's asking?"

I clear my throat, "I'm Tuesday, Rhodie from Devil's Rose MC is my, um, well, I'm not sure. But we're here to get you outta here."

She looks us up and down before I hear her suck air through her teeth. "Why should we trust you?"

This is a fair enough question. I mean, I know what Lexi and I together look like. We look like we couldn't fight our way out of a paper bag.

"Because we have Kraykowski rotting at the DRMC compound. Because we are both on his bullshit auction list, and I don't know about you, but I don't think I'm cut out for being the sex slave of an old, fat dude." I shrug my shoulders at her.

I watch as a smile breaks out across her face. "Alright, then Rhodie's Whatever. Get us outta here."

Chapter 21

Rhodie

I've been white-knuckling this ride the entire way since I heard Marx's voice over Bluetooth telling me she was in Roxwell, the next town over. I'm definitely going to tan that ass of hers once I get her home, but first I have to grovel at her tiny feet for her to give me another chance. I've taken on board the advice everyone gave me, which was basically "Stop being a dumb fuck" and I get it, I really do. Chewy has been living her life, this life, since well before I met her. She can handle herself in ways that I'll never understand and my overbearing ass has convinced her I think less of her than Lexi and Katya, which is just not true, but that's something I'm going to have to prove to her.

"She's at the warehouses on Sixth. She went on foot, and Tav tracked the sedan two blocks over on Hale. We're going to pull in and Savage and his SAA will meet us there. Over,"

I point my bike in that direction and let the rumble of the engine lull me into the state I need to be in.

My MC brothers and I all pull in, backing our bikes into a line behind the Tombs Security SUV. We hear the rumble of more bikes and within moments Savage and his Sergeant Dex pull in and park, Savage heading over to talk tactics with Marx.

"Gather round, fuckers. We're about an hour behind the girls, so we don't know what we're walking into yet. I want small teams going in. Rider, Rhodie, and Gus, you're with me. Dex with your Pres. Tav and Jules, you're with the vehicles and any surveillance you can hack. The two prospects are bringing the vans to transport the women. Ana and Katya will be with them to help settle the women. They'll be untrusting of men, and rightly so. Mad Dog and Wire are on compound watch and Roman will be doing whatever the fuck shady deals the Bratva does. The rest of you brothers, fan out and watch our backs." Marx checks his guns, as do the rest of us, then hands out the earpieces we'll need to communicate. Once we're suited up, we walk the short distance to the warehouses, my brothers fanning out around the perimeter on watch.

Our two teams get closer to the building and a quick survey we did shows there is no one on the main door, which is weird, but fuck it, if they're too dumb to tighten up security, that's their problem. Marx uses hand signals to point Savage to the rear door as our team heads straight to the main door. We plaster ourselves along the front wall and I check to see if the door is locked. The handle moves freely, so I turn it, using the barrel of my gun to push the door gently forward. It's silent inside with very little light.

Turning back to my brothers, I flick my head toward the door and crouch lower. Rider comes up behind, his gun over my head, ready to fire if needed. We move slowly forward, my gun out in front, then me following carefully in behind until I feel something press against my temple. I stop dead in my tracks,

Rider pausing as well.

"Freeze motherfucker" I hear a feminine voice whisper in my ear before the lights go up, blinding me momentarily.

"What the hell, Rhodie?! We could have killed you!" I blink the light spots out of my eyes and see Chewy standing in the middle of the room, hands on her hips.

"Lexi, what the fuck!?" Rider growls out. I spin my head and see Lexi was the voice behind the gun, positioned right beside the door, ready to shoot anyone who dared enter. She smirks up at Rider before shrugging her shoulders, dropping her arm holding the gun, moving to stand beside Chewy, and walking past a cage that looks like it's holding two unconscious or maybe even dead men.

I've stood here staring at my girl long enough. I eat up the space between us until I pull her into my arms. She stiffens slightly, but I'm not letting her go just yet. Marx comes storming in but stops abruptly as we hear gentle shushing noises. Looking behind Chewy, I can see women huddled together in a bunch, with another woman standing with her head held high, jaw clenched tight in the middle of the group.

"NAT!" She spins to her right and I watch her face crumble as Savage runs towards her and scoops her up before she hits the ground, her head tucked under his chin.

He looks toward our group before giving us a nod. "I owe you a marker, Marx."

Natalie lifts her head, scoffing, "They did nothing. Tuesday and Lexi are the ones that came in, got us out of those cages, and took out those two guards. If anything, you owe these two a marker."

Chewy steps out of my arms to bump knuckles with Natalie. I watch Savage look over my woman and growl at the attention he's giving her when I hear Natalie laugh.

"So you're Rhodie, huh? You better make her your Ol Lady. She's one hell of a woman." She gives me a wink and then seals her mouth to Savage's.

Marx grunts behind me, hand on his earpiece. "Fuck. Eyes on says we have three SUVs heading this way at speed. We need to get the women to safety."

Chewy whirls around. "I know this is going to be scary as hell, but we gotta move. Are you all healthy enough to at the very least walk outta here?" All the women stare at Chewy. Natalie pats Savage's chest and indicates he put her down. She stands in front of the women, looking to be the leader of the group.

"We can do this, ladies. Get your shoes on or whatever other shit you wanna take and we'll hustle outta here."

I can hear Marx murmuring away behind me for a moment before he barks out more orders.

"Savage, you lead the women out the back, Gus, you take their rear. My men are in place to cover you. Vans waiting for you back at the rendezvous point. Rhodie, Rider, and I will stand our ground, take out whoever the fuck is running this now Kraykowski is out."

"We heard the guards mention a Kovalev if that helps," Nat says to the room, earning a nod from Marx, who has his finger in his ear.

"ETA around 1 minute. Get gone. Chewy and Lexi, you go with the women."

Chewy is already shaking her head from side to side "Nope, I'm staying. Screw that noise. I'm making sure this Kovalev is put down and out of the skin trade for good."

Marx gives me a look and I step up toward Chewy. I watch

her hug Lexi before she watches her race out the door with the other women, gun drawn.

"Babe, I love you and I know you are more than capable of standing your ground. I was so fucking wrong when I said there were things you couldn't do. I'm a fucking idiot. You are brave and clever and such a fucking little badass. I was scared and I said some fucked up shit. I should have had your back. I'm sorry, baby, and I will make it up to you, but I need you to go with them. I can't settle, knowing that you might be in danger." I look at her big whiskey-colored eyes, holding her gaze, pleading with her to go. She clenches her jaw and breaks contact, stepping back from me. She looks toward the door and watches as Gus gets the last of the women out before he looks back at her, gives her a wink, and runs out behind them.

"Time's up. They're here. Fan out, stay alert."

Tuesday

I'm really glad that Rhodie apologized, but I'm still hurt and if we're honest, now is not really the time for a heart-to-heart. We have shit to do. I melt into the background, going into stalker mode, so I can watch and gauge everything. Rhodie's eyes following me the whole time.

Marx is standing in the middle of the warehouse, Rhodie on one side, Rider on the other, when the warehouse door opens and a guy, I'm guessing is Kovalev comes strolling into the room. He stops abruptly when he sees them.

"Who the fuck are you?" his accented voice booms out. His men, of which I count seven, stand behind him, hands on their guns.

"We're the people you pissed off."

"I piss off many people. You're going to have to narrow that down a little."

"OK, well, how about you just know us as the MC that is going to put a stop to your little business here."

Kovalev chuckles for a moment before looking around and noticing the empty cages. "Who the fuck do you think you are, motorcycle scum? I've been running these auctions all over the world for years, bringing in bitches and selling them to men with all kinds of, shall we say, unique tastes. I will not stop just because you seem to have taken my girls for yourself."

"Unlike you, you sick bastard, we don't trade in women. We've sent them home to their families. Kind of like what we're going to do to you, but you'll be going home in a box." Marx smirks at Kovalev, and I'm getting worried that Kovalev is looking unnaturally angry, before his face blanks completely and he smiles.

"So you don't sell girls? Maybe you want to join me in this lucrative trade? You bring the girls I need and I'll pay you handsomely," he smiles again, but that's short-lived as I watch a knife whir past my head and embed itself in Kovalev's thigh, causing him to scream and his men to pull their guns. They shout in Russian, waving their weapons around, yelling instructions at Marx, who is yelling right back.

I can hear clapping, which is really freaking weird given that this has turned into a bi-lingual yelling match.

"Bravo, what a show you both are putting on. Allow me to introduce myself if you don't already know me. I'm Roman Bartashev, Pakhan of the Bartashev Bratva." Roman wanders in like he owns the place, going so far as to push one of

Kovalev's men's guns out of the way as he moves through the room, Sasha at his back, coming to a stop in the middle of the two arguing sides. It's weird to see him like this. The Roman I've gotten to know over the past week is admittedly stuffy, but amenable nonetheless. This Roman reeks of danger.

"So Kovalev, I have had an interest in your work for a while now. However, I became very interested in you in recent times."

Kovalev puffs his chest out. "Is that right, Pakhan? And what were you interested in the most?"

Roman looks down at his hands, picking at his fingernails a little like he has all the time in the world and that he hasn't just stepped in the middle of what could easily spiral into a gunfight.

"Well, let's just say I'm sure you can imagine my surprise when I saw my daughter's name on your list. Oh, and she's not just my daughter, she's Ushakov's heir. I'm sure she will be very interested in meeting with you. She would like assurances to, you know, make sure this egregious error doesn't happen again?" He shrugs and Kovalev's face is completely blank. However, the look in his eye is downright evil.

"That cannot be right. Kraykowski surely had his information wrong. What would I want with Ushakov's heir?" A slow smirk forms over his face then disappears.

Roman eyes him for a moment, before grinning widely again. "Well, we'll never know. Kraykowski is painfully engaged elsewhere. So, my daughter and I have a flight to Russia in a few days to meet with Anton Sorokin. Are you acquainted with him?"

Kovalev pales slightly before composing himself. "Why yes, we are, how would you say, old business associates? How is his health?"

"Thriving, from what I hear." Watching these two men is like watching sharks circling each other. All the while, Marx has remained sentinel, watching, waiting.

Roman raises his brow, eyes hard and voice cold, looking every bit the powerful Pakhan. "When I told him of the trouble that my daughter had been having, he was most displeased. I, on the other hand, assured him it was most likely a harmless mix-up of some sort. Why don't you accompany me -"

"What the fuck Roman!?" Marx barks out. Lightning quick, Roman is in front of him, staring him down. Marx grits his teeth and whatever unspoken conversation they have, Marx nods his head once, then steps back.

"After a quick consultation, my MC friends have agreed to let you walk out of here. Accompany me for a drink. As you can see, there is nothing for you here or in any Devil's Rose territory." I watch Roman stare Kovalev down, his jaw clenching, before his eyes dart down Kovalev's body, then back up.

"You might want to remove that knife in your leg as well." Kovalev squints his eyes at Roman before shaking his outstretched hand. I don't think any of us really know what game Roman is currently playing, whoever this Anton Sorokin is, or what business Roman may want with Kovalev, but it's something I will definitely keep my eye on.

Roman slaps his hand on Kovalev's shoulder and guides him towards the door, not before Kovalev leans in to say something to one of his men, looking back over his shoulder and smirking at us as he exits with Roman, Sasha at their backs. Kovalev's men close ranks and the man he spoke to opens fire on Marx, Rhodie, and Rider. I watch my new family dive for cover as I come out from my hiding place just in time to shoot one guy who has his gun aimed directly at Marx's back. Marx spins around wide-eyed, then gives me a nod and goes back to dodging bullets. I take out two of Kovalev's men in quick succession and turn to take another shot when a large body flies in front of me.

I watch in horror as Rhodie jerks and then lands at my feet. I'm frozen as I look down at him. The burnt acrid smell of guns firing burns my nostrils. The metallic scent of blood mixed in with the leftover smells of women who had been kept against their will surround me like a cloak. I can hear grunting and yelling, bangs from guns, metal clanging from bullets that are ricocheting off the cages. The whirring of knives being thrown, dull thuds where I can hear Rider hitting someone, and the rushing of blood in my ears. All the distractions disappear when I see dark red blooming across Rhodie's chest. I drop to my knees covering the wound, putting pressure on it while I stare at the soft rise and very slow fall of his breathing.

"Rhodie, open your eyes, babe. Let me see you." His eyes are closed, eyelashes fanned across his pale cheeks. Marx comes up and covers my hands with his much larger ones, pressing even harder on his brother.

"I need a vehicle NOW! Someone call the ambulance, single gunshot wound to the chest, HURRY!" he roars so loud my ears ring but I don't cover them with my hands. My hands are needed to keep Rhodie alive. I concentrate on my counting, first in twos, then threes, then prime numbers. I really want to tap my fingers but my hands are busy at the moment, counting will have to do.

I'm not sure how long it is before I hear the wailing of sirens and I feel my body relax a little. How the hell we're going to explain multiple fatalities is beyond me, but I feel like that's a problem for tomorrow. The door bangs open once again and I watch as they bring in a gurney and a bag of stuff.

"OK, step back please, ma'am. Let me look at what we're dealing with," I hear the voice say a couple of times and I growl at them. Can't they see I can't let go? I feel someone's large, warm hand on my shoulder, pulling me toward them.

"It's OK Chewy, it's me. Let the paramedics look at Rhodie, yeah?" I turn and see Rider's bright blue eyes looking down at me, full of worry, I move back, my hands shaking, warm and slippery with Rhodie's blood, I can't stop staring at them when I feel large arms wrap around me.

"Come on, Chewy, let's mount up, we'll meet them at the hospital." I nod and hope like hell I get to tell Rhodie I love him.

Chapter 22

Rhodie

Shit, that alarm beeping is really pissing me off. Where the hell is Chewy, and why the hell has she set an alarm? I turn my head and find that my eyes won't open. Fuck! How much did I drink last night? I flail my arm out to hit the alarm and a blinding pain shoots through my chest, stealing my breath.

"Hey babe, don't move. Stop thrashing. You'll hurt yourself!" Chewy's voice cuts through the pain and I feel the weight of her small hands against my chest. I shake my head and will my eyes to open, only to slam them shut immediately as I'm blinded by the brightest fucking light I've ever seen.

"Shit! Marx, dim the lights, please!" I can see the lights dim a little through the tiny slits I'm looking through now, and it all comes rushing back to me. Seeing Kovalev's man point his gun at Chewy, hearing the gun go off, and knowing that I had to protect her. I open my eyes fully, to stare directly into her whiskey-colored eyes.

"Baby," I choke out, I gingerly raise my arms, placing one

hand on her back, the other in her hair as I slowly guide her to me, placing my nose in the crook of her neck, smelling her, getting my fill.

"I love you so much, baby. So so much. I'm a fucking idiot and I'm so sorry and I want you to know that I will never underestimate you again, as long as you give me another chance to love you. Please baby, I need you." If I could get out of this bed and on my knees to grovel at her feet, I would. She pulls back from me, looking down at me with a small frown on her gorgeous face.

"Of course, you have another chance. You will have all the chances in the world because I know that you'll make more mistakes. Just like I'll make more mistakes."

"So you forgive me?" I place my hand on her cheek and watch as she leans into it.

"Only if you forgive me,"

"Huh? What the hell for?" I rack my brain, trying to figure out what she needs forgiveness for.

"For not leaving when you asked me to. For not using the words I love you."

"You've never said the words, but I'm your person, so I figured it out."

She smiles down at me. "You're so much cleverer than me at this stuff." She perks up a little, smiling before saying, "Do you know how I know I love you?" I give a head shake so she carries on, "When you got shot, I covered the wound to stop the bleeding. I felt your heart beating in time with mine. When your heart stopped, my heart stopped. It felt like your insides were my insides. Not physically, of course, but that's kinda what it felt like, and that's how I knew it was love. We keep each other's insides safe."

"Weird way to say you have each other's hearts," I hear Marx's low mumble but I choose to ignore him as I bring her face close enough to breathe her in, kissing her gently on the lips.

"You have my heart, Tuesday Tombs."

"And you have mine, Rhodes Paxon."

Epilogue

Tuesday

"Put a little more honey on him. He looks like he's drying out." I watch as Lexi dips the paintbrush into the bucket of honey that Jules somehow procured, from whom I have no idea, and I'm not asking either. There will be a kinky reason for it. Lex slaps the honey-covered paintbrush onto Kraykowski's face and neck, painting all available skin to encourage even more insect-feeding.

"Christ, he stinks. Are we sure he's still alive?"

I peer down at him and see a slow thud of a pulse in his neck, and he's also still reasonably healthy-colored despite all the goings on.

"Yup, he definitely is. Although judging by how bloated he looks, I'd say it's not too much longer to go before he blows." Lexi snorts and goes back to painting.

"You'll be leaving soon, won't you?"

"Yeah. In about an hour. I just wanted to see everyone first. I really need to see Pops. He wants to exchange emails so he can teach me things via the interweb, as he calls it." She rolls her eyes and giggles a little.

"He's inside tearing your dad a new one for not letting us kill Kovalev. You think there was any reason behind that?" I watch as the younger woman drops the paintbrush into the bucket and lets out a long breath.

"The DRMC are good men that do bad things to help others. My Dad is a bad man who does things to aid himself. Don't get me wrong, I love him, and he wouldn't hurt the people he cares for, but the only reason I can see him keeping Kovalev alive is because he needs him. I don't know why, I just hope keeping him alive doesn't come back to bite us on the ass."

"Yeah. So what are you going to do now that you're the heir to the Ushakov fortune?"

"I'm to take over all his business, both legal and illegal. Not sure of all his dealings yet, but you can guarantee that there will be no skin trade on my watch." I give her a big grin and she smiles back. I'm going to miss my friend. Katya and Ana are an absolute riot, both strong independent women in their own way, but Lexi and I understand and live in a much darker place.

"Can I ask you something?" She nods her head, giving me the go-ahead. "Why did you come back? I saw your knife land in Kovalev's thigh, remember?"

She smirks up at me for a moment. "I wanted to make sure my friends were safe. Why did you refuse to leave when Rhodie asked you to?"

"Same reason you were there, to make sure my friends were safe" She holds her fist out to me and we bump gently, grinning until a long, low keening noise escaping from Kraykowski's lips interrupts our moment. Lexi hums a song over the top of his noises and secures the lid on the honey bucket before dusting off her hands. We walk side-by-side back to the clubhouse.

"That stuff always makes me feel hungry, dunno why."

Rhodie

We're all sitting around the table in church and Marx is going over the last of the details from our auction bust.

"So, the last of the women have been returned home thanks to Katya and the Tombs family doing all the legwork on that one. I imagine they'll need some type of counseling to get over their ordeal. Savage has reached out to me, wanting to become allies. I've had Wire look through all their dealings and besides running drugs now and then they're on the up and up. Savage has really cleaned up their act since he became Pres, nowhere near being the 1% club they once were. If nobody opposes the idea, I suggest we get together for a cookout to meet the Death Riders and their members, then reconvene and decide. All in favor?" Ayes chorus around the table. Savage seems like a solid Pres and his sergeant served in the military, so I'm sure they're probably more like us than we realize.

"Katya is going to be staying in town for a bit, settling into a life of not having to hide anymore. Ana's running point on Roman's business while he's away. Roman, Sasha, and Lexi will leave for Russia in the next hour or so. That slimy bastard is hiding something. I know he is, however, I'm unsure if it's going to affect us. I just want to be done with that Russian fucker."

I rub my scruff and decide I'll monitor the Bartashev goings on through Chewy. I know she and Lexi are friends and if worse comes to worst, I'll ask Pops. He has plans to email her fun ways to kill a man, so I'm sure he'll do me a solid if I need it. He's been a lot better with me since I claimed his 'grandbaby'. He's only called me Shit Stain a couple of times. She wears my property patch with her name 'Chewy' on the front and I couldn't be happier or more whipped.

As soon as the doctor cleared me for strenuous activities, I have been making up for my dick move. I've been letting her act out her kinky little fantasies on me, well, most of them. There are still a couple I'm not totally on board with.

"The Tombs will look into Kovalev and Anton Sorokin for me, so you'll still see them around the compound. Right, I think that's about it. Get outta here, fuckers."

Marx slams the gavel, and we all file out of church. I make a beeline for Chewy before I'm interrupted by Mad Dog.

"Chewy girl, this package was delivered for you." He places it on the table before heading back to the kitchen, probably to smooch up his girlfriend.

"Ohhhh, it's here!" I see Chewy rush towards the box and, of course, she hits the side of a chair on her way past, but as usual, she just bounces off and carries on.

"What's in the box?" Rider asks her. She doesn't answer straight away because I can see she's trying to use her finger-nail to slice through the tape on the box, to no avail. Marx steps up to it, flicks his knife out, and slices it for her, all while she's dancing around flapping.

"This, my friends, is a special gift for Rhodie. I've been waiting for aaaaaages,"

I wander closer to her to peek into the box once my brother gets the tape cut through.

"I don't need any gifts, baby."

"Welllll, it's kinda a gift for both of us," she mutters as she rummages in the box and pulls out a silicone dildo with a triumphant look on her face. The whole of the common area falls silent.

"Um, is that a dildo?" Wire asks her carefully.

Chewy spins to look at him. "This isn't any old dildo Wire. This here is a perfect replica of my man's equipment." She spins back to face me. "Remember when I made you use that mold so I could make an exact replica of your junk for when I'm alone?" I nod in silence because this is way too much info for my brothers to be hearing and I thank god my father is somewhere other than here.

"Well, I sent it away and had the professionals make it AND I also got it with a special attachment so I can wear it on a strap and peg you with it! Cos you know, you have the most perfect dick and only the best for the man I love." With every word out of her mouth, her volume and pitch rise until she's hit full-on excitement. I can feel the blood draining from my face at around the same time I can see my brothers shocked into silence. I look at Marx. His lips are between his teeth and his color is not looking healthy. He looks like he's going to explode at any moment now.

"Chewy! We spoke about this and I told you there is no fucking WAY you are getting near my ass!" I whisper yell at her, hoping to put her in her place.

"That's ridiculous! Your prostate is in there Rhodie, that's where your G spot is for god's sake, don't you want to know what it feels like for you to have a g-spot orgasm? I promise I'll warm you up properly, with lots of lube, and I'll do that finger move thing you do on me." She holds her hand up and mimes the scissor-type action that I do actually use when I'm trying to get her ready for me. She's on a roll and there's nothing I can say because I'm standing here speechless with horror.

"Chewy, most guys are perfectly happy for that not to happen," Wire tells her in a gentle voice even though he, like Marx, is bright red from trying not to laugh.

"Well, that's just stupid," she spits out. "And super unfair! So ya'll out here trying to get your dicks in our balloon knots EVEN THOUGH we don't have a g-spot up there and then you clam up when we want to go near yours? Ugh, I have no respect for any of you," she growls whilst gesticulating wildly with my anatomically correct and erect penis in her hands. Then she thrusts it aggressively in my direction, making me jump.

"That's it! My ass is closed." With that, she throws my penis into the box, slams the flaps shut, hefts it up into her arms, and storms out of the room, the completely silent room even though there have to be around a dozen brothers in here. We sit in silence staring at each other before Marx lets out a snort, and then leans forward, letting out a huge belly laugh, setting all the brothers off. I drop my head and follow the love of my life down the hall. I finally find her face down on our bed.

"Baby, look at me" She rolls her head slightly until I can see one of her eyes. Her nose is smooshed into the comforter.

"You know I love you, right?" She nods her head. "And I'd do anything for you, yeah?" She rolls her head more so I can see both her eyes now. "How about we start off small? I don't think I'll be able to take that whole dildo, but what about a small prostate massager? We can find one online together if you like?" She athletically pops up and jumps into my lap, her pussy snug against my cock, kissing me all over my cheeks, nose, mouth.

"You won't regret this, baby! Trust me!"

I kiss her hard on the mouth, then rest my forehead on hers, peering at her.

"You have my heart, Tuesday." She gives me a happy sigh.

"And you have mine, Rhodes."

Thank you for reading!

Want to know more about me or what I'm reading? Well, I'm easy to find
Follow me on Facebook
Friend me on Facebook
Join my group Cleo Browne's Babes
Follow me on Instagram

Keep your eyes peeled for upcoming books in the Devil's Rose MC Series, The Tombs Security Series, and a new series, because I can't just write two concurrently, The Davies Family Series - Small Town Romance set in Rose Grove. There may even be cameos from some of your fave characters.

Cleo Browne Books

Rhodie – Devil's Rose MC Book One

August – A Tombs Security + Devil's Rose MC Crossover

Wire – Devil's Rose MC Book Two
Coming Soon

Tav Devil's Rose MC Book Three
In progress

About the Author

Cleo Browne is the pen name of a neurospicy geeky girl from Aotearoa New Zealand. As a child, she realized very early on that she wasn't a people person, so she would spend all her time reading and writing her own stories. These stories usually ended with the line "and then they died". As an adult, she has gotten slightly more people-y (not much) and better at not killing all her characters off when she writes.

Cleo loves to write about women who don't need a man to do their dirty work and the hot alpha men who turn to mush when they watch their women handling business.

When she's not writing romance novels about strong, curvy women and the men who adore them, she hangs out at home with her hubby, her boys, and her ancient greyhound who likes to creepily watch her write.

Acknowledgments

First off, I'd like to thank my writing partner Shaye Torrel. Thank you so much for putting up with my incessant chatting about whether or not writing this book was a terrible idea. Also, thanks for reading an almost complete manuscript of another book before I dumped it to start over again.

Thanks to my partner PN. Without his constant words of encouragement, "Just finish it already!" and "I'm sure it's fine." I would never have finished this book. Thanks also go to my boys. Ronnie, for being completely disinterested, and Louis for helping get my social media sorted out and making your lady friends read and review my book. Love you guys.